TYLER WHITESIDES

JANITORS

SECRETS OF NEW FOREST ACADEMY

Tyler Whitesides

Janitors

Secrets of New Forest Academy

Illustrated by

Brandon Dorman

Visit us at ShadowMountain.com

First printing in hardbound 2012.
First printing in paperbound 2013.

Library of Congress Cataloging-in-Publication Data
Whitesides, Tyler, author.
Secrets of New Forest Academy / Tyler Whitesides.
pages cm. — (Janitors, book 2)
Summary: The Bureau of Educational Maintenance (BEM) is after Spencer, and the only place he is safe is within the walls of the New Forest Academy—or so he thinks.
ISBN 978-1-60907-014-4 (hardbound : alk. paper)
ISBN 978-1-60907-546-0 (strippable paperbound)
[1. Students—Fiction. 2. School custodians—Fiction. 3. Elementary schools—Fiction. 4. Magic—Fiction. 5. Fantasy.] I. Title. II. Series: Whitesides, Tyler. Janitors ; bk 2.
PZ7.W58793Sec 2012
[Fic]—dc23 2012010795

Printed in the United States of America
R. R. Donnelley, Crawfordsville, IN

10 9 8 7 6 5 4

For teachers and librarians,
who fight for education.

And for Mikey B. and Porter—
I've told our tales many times.

CONTENTS

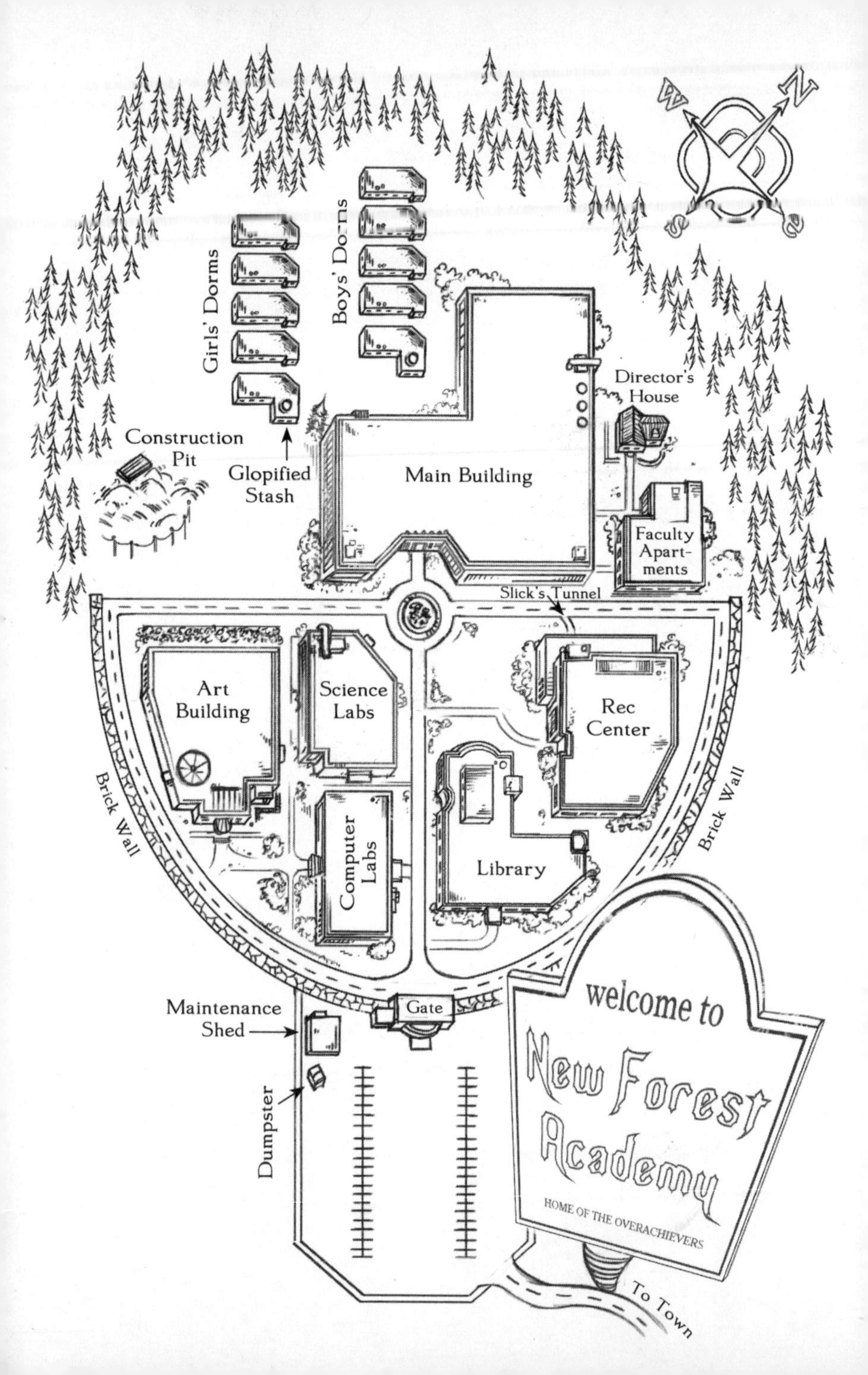

W
N
S
E
Girls' Dorms
Boys' Dorms
Director's House
Construction Pit
Glopified Stash
Main Building
Faculty Apartments
Slick's Tunnel
Art Building
Science Labs
Rec Center
Brick Wall
Library
Computer Labs
Brick Wall
Maintenance Shed
Gate
welcome to
New Forest Academy
HOME OF THE OVERACHIEVERS
Dumpster
To Town

CHAPTER 1

"WE'VE GOT TROUBLE!"

Dez Rylie belched. It wasn't a long belch by his standards, but it was certainly enough to get him in trouble again. It would have been nothing new in Mrs. Natcher's classroom. But this was the library, a sanctuary of research and silence.

Well, usually. Today was different, and not just because it was a Friday.

"That's enough!"

Spencer blinked the sleepiness out of his eyes and shook his head. Had the librarian just shouted?

"It's over!" Sure enough, Mr. Fields, the balding librarian, was losing his cool. And rightfully so.

Spencer's sixth-grade classmates were behaving ridiculously. Several students were slouched hopelessly at the study tables, books abandoned and research topics forgotten. They stared at the librarian, lazily chewing gum like they didn't care a thing about consequences. Other kids wandered between bookshelves, laughing and smiling, happily distracted from their work. A few students were sound asleep, drooling on expensive library books.

"I'm not going to deal with this behavior anymore. Your teacher's coming to fetch you! Gather your things." He shooed the students with the backs of his hands.

Spencer used his knuckles to rub the sleepiness from his eyes. When he opened them again, he noticed that the seat next to him was empty. Where was Daisy? Spencer glanced around the library and spotted the girl a few bookshelves away. Daisy was on her hands and knees in front of the picture books—laughing.

Oh, no. Something was very wrong.

Spencer had fallen asleep during research and Daisy was hopelessly distracted. That could only mean one thing . . .

Spencer stood up, anxiously scanning the library for movement. Instinctively, his hand reached into his backpack to grip a small Ziploc bag of vacuum dust. Spencer turned a slow circle, eyes flicking from bookshelf to bookshelf. The students were showing all the signs—so where were the Toxites?

The library door opened, and the air seemed to grow old and stuffy with Mrs. Natcher's arrival. One look at her unruly class sent a new streak of gray through her tightly pinned hair bun.

"Class!" she called in her usual manner. "Class! You will be silent in three, two, one." Mrs. Natcher clapped her hands, but this usual method did little against the potent breath of the Toxites that pervaded the library.

Spencer yawned big enough to make his eyes water. Then, with blurry vision, he saw a flash of movement. Spencer blinked away the tears to see a pale, slimy creature leap from the History section and land on a nearby table. Half a dozen kids were staring in that direction, but the monster scuttled invisibly across their notebooks.

Spencer snapped the seal on his Ziploc bag and pinched out a bit of vacuum dust. If the creature turned toward him, Spencer would have to stop it, no matter how crazy he might look throwing vac dust at invisible monsters.

Across the table, Dez stood up, his backpack gaping open like a dirty mouth. Before Spencer could move, the yellow, lizard-like creature leapt into the backpack's dark opening. Dez casually picked up his notebook, the pages discolored and crinkly from an old apple juice spill, and dropped it into his pack. With another belch, he zipped his backpack and turned.

Of all the kids in the class, Dez was probably the least affected by Toxite breath. The rich brain waves that the Toxites enjoyed didn't often come wafting out of Dez's head. The creatures mostly left him alone, saving their potent anti-learning breath for other, more sincere students. But, affected or not, Dez was about to unknowingly transport a Grime back to the classroom.

Dez was wandering halfheartedly toward the doorway where Mrs. Natcher stood with her nose turned up at her class. Spencer gritted his teeth and stepped into Dez's path, eyes locked on the big kid's backpack.

"What are you staring at, Doofus?" Dez asked. "Never seen a backpack before?"

Spencer glanced sideways at Daisy, but she was too far away and much too distracted to help. The slimy Grimes were toughest on Daisy. Their distracting breath didn't bother Spencer much at all, but seeing Daisy like that reminded him why he couldn't let Dez get past. If the backpack made it into Mrs. Natcher's classroom, then the Toxite would emerge. Spencer and Daisy had worked too hard to keep their classroom Toxite-free. And Dez was about to spoil it by giving this creature a free ride.

"Listen, Dez," Spencer said, "you've got to leave your backpack here."

"Huh?" Dez pulled a face. Then he narrowed his eyes. "You trying to steal from me? I'll break your fingers if you touch my Empty 3 Player."

"Your what?"

"My Empty 3 Player. Don't you ever listen to music?"

Spencer rolled his eyes. "This isn't about your *mp3*, Dez. Just leave your backpack here."

"Why don't you make me?" Dez smirked.

Spencer took a deep breath and gripped his vac dust even harder. He was losing time. Mrs. Natcher and the librarian were rounding up the students one by one. It wouldn't be long before they got to Dez.

Spencer stepped away, letting the bully think he'd won another fight. Dez threw back his head and started laughing.

It was an obnoxious, fake laugh, and Dez dragged it out so long that it lost any intimidation effect he might have been hoping for.

Just as Dez stepped forward, Spencer flicked his right hand, releasing the pinch of vacuum dust. With a sound like a suctioning vacuum, the backpack jerked out of Dez's hands and hit the floor.

"Hey!" Dez swung a fist, but Spencer jumped back and retreated across the library, fighting waves of Toxite fatigue along the way.

Dez stooped to retrieve his backpack. He pulled on the shoulder straps, but the backpack was suctioned tightly to the floor, rattling slightly.

"Huh?" Dez grunted and pulled harder.

A few bookshelves away, Spencer grabbed Daisy by the shoulders and yanked the girl to her feet. "We've got trouble, Daisy."

"Hi, Spencer!" Daisy said, like she was meeting him for the first time. "There's a really funny piece of carpet right here, did you see it?" She chuckled. "Oh, it makes me laugh."

"Snap out of it, Daisy! There are Toxites in here. Lots of them! I can't seem to find them, but they're affecting everyone."

Spencer glanced back at Dez. The bully had managed to get the backpack off the floor for a moment, but the suction pulled it down again.

"Dez has one in his backpack," Spencer said. "If we don't stop him, he'll take it back to the classroom!"

Daisy squinted. Spencer could tell she was fighting against the distracting Toxite breath. She glanced over at Dez. The sight of the bully with the backpack managed to break through her distractions.

"The suction won't last," Daisy said. "Maybe we could . . . Hey! What's that over there?"

Spencer's shoulders slumped as Daisy trudged away to inspect another patch of carpet. But there was no time to go after her. Mrs. Natcher was making a beeline right for the spot where Dez was thrashing with the backpack.

"Dezmond Rylie! What on earth are you doing to that poor backpack?" the teacher called.

Spencer backed against the wall, a sudden yawn overtaking him. Why not give up? He was out of options anyway. Why not lie down and take a rest? After all, he *was* exhausted.

Spencer leaned heavily against the wall. He was just sliding down to the comfort of the carpet when a gray lump fell from a bookshelf and landed in a quivering heap at his feet.

It was another Toxite: a Filth this time. This was the most dangerous type of Toxite for Spencer. Being close to the spiky dust gophers always made him sluggish and tired. But this particular Filth was suctioned to the floor, gopher teeth chattering and sharp quills clicking.

The Filth's breath was instantly stolen away by the puff of vacuum dust holding it down. But who had thrown the blast? The sleepiness vanished, and, with renewed energy,

Spencer looked up. Daisy stood a few feet away, a sandwich bag of vac dust in her hand.

"Get up, sleepyhead," Daisy said. Somehow she had managed to stave off the distracting Grime breath—at least momentarily. "We've got to stop Dez."

Spencer jumped up. Dez and Mrs. Natcher were conversing. At their feet, the backpack lay still. Spencer could tell that the suction had worn off. Any minute now, Dez would pick it up and take it back to infest the classroom.

How could Spencer possibly get Dez to leave his backpack in the library? Spencer leaned against the wall and felt the answer right at his fingertips.

"Careful," Daisy said. "That's the fire alarm."

Spencer nodded grimly. Then, with sweaty hands, he pulled down on the red handle.

CHAPTER 2

"WE HAVE TO BE EXTREME!"

It worked.

That was the only thing Spencer cared about. Consequences would come later, but at least he had stopped Dez from taking his infested backpack to the classroom. Dez didn't have a chance to grab it as Mrs. Natcher steered him toward the emergency exit, gathering other kids along the way.

"Go with them," Spencer told Daisy as he ducked behind a bookshelf.

"What? Where are *you* going?" Daisy asked.

"Got to get some supplies from the stash. Then I'm coming back here to kill that Grime before Dez gets back."

Daisy covered her ears against the blaring fire alarm. "Don't you think this is a little extreme just to keep *one* Toxite out of the classroom?"

Spencer ducked lower as Mr. Fields scanned the library for any lingering students. "We've kept our classroom Toxite-free for almost two months on our own. I'm not going to let Dez ruin that! We have to be extreme, Daisy! It's just us now. No Marv. No Walter."

"We've got Meredith," said Daisy.

Spencer rolled his eyes. Meredith List, the new lunch lady. Although she was a friend to Walter Jamison, she was definitely not the Toxite-fighting type. She'd never even been trained with Glopified equipment. Most of the time Meredith had her nose stuck in a paperback romance novel.

Meredith helped where she could, but her involvement with Spencer and Daisy had to be subtle. She passed notes to alert the kids of Toxite-infested areas and gave them occasional updates on Walter's travels.

Meredith's best help had come in a chicken patty more than a month ago. Meredith had served Spencer the chicken sandwich with a wink. When he bit into it, he nearly lost a tooth. Discarding the top bun, Spencer found a key. The key opened a door to the kitchen where they discovered a small utility closet stocked with Glopified janitor equipment: "the stash."

"Daisy Gates!" Mr. Fields shouted over the alarm. Spencer retreated farther out of sight. "That loud noise you're hearing? That means *evacuate!* Come on!"

Daisy glanced down at Spencer, a somber look on her face. "Don't get caught." Then she jogged across the library, through the emergency exit, and into the chill November morning.

Spencer navigated on hands and knees toward the opposite door. Rising slowly, he inched it open, stepped out, and raced down the hallway. The alarm echoed obnoxiously, and Spencer couldn't help but cover his ears.

Two months ago, he would have run to the janitor's office to get help from Marv or Walter. He wouldn't have done anything rash without consulting them. But there was no help now. Only Mr. Joe.

The man that the BEM had hired to take Walter's place was just a custodian. Until recently, Spencer had thought that *janitor* and *custodian* were different words for the same job. But after Mr. Joe was hired, Walter called Spencer to explain the difference.

Janitors were highly trained and qualified. They could see Toxites, and they used magically charged cleaning supplies to fight them. A custodian, on the other hand, was a person who went about cleaning and maintaining schools, all the while perfectly unaware of the existence of Toxites.

Spencer and Daisy had feared Mr. Joe at first. But it didn't take long to discover that he was just a custodian. Mr. Joe didn't know a thing about Toxites. He couldn't even see them, let alone fight them.

And right now, Mr. Joe wasn't aware of the sudden Toxite population surge in the library. He was probably wandering the school, trying to figure out how in the world to turn off the fire alarm.

It could have been worse. At least Mr. Joe wasn't plotting with the Bureau of Educational Maintenance. For hundreds of years, the BEM had protected students from the harmful breath of Toxites. But in the last year or so, everything had changed. The BEM had withdrawn its support for no apparent reason. They were letting the creatures overrun schools. Kids were getting dumber every day.

That was why Spencer couldn't let a single Toxite invade Mrs. Natcher's classroom. He was part of the Rebel Underground, an organization of janitors led by the warlock Walter Jamison. They had to fight the creatures—to save education. To protect the future.

Once inside the vacant cafeteria, Spencer pulled a key from his pocket. With a nervous glance over his shoulder, he disappeared into the kitchen. He reached the utility closet and, after fumbling with another lock, jerked open the door. Spencer pulled on an overhead string, and a bare lightbulb flickered to life.

It was a small closet, highly stocked with magical brooms, mops, and vacuums. Walter had only sent supplies that Spencer and Daisy already knew how to use. Janitorial equipment was risky in the hands of a novice. Two months ago, Spencer had learned that lesson the hard way when, against Walter's warnings, he'd used an overcharged vacuum bag. The result had been devastating: An entire classroom had imploded, the substitute teacher had been hospitalized, and half a dozen people had been sucked into the vacuum bag. Including Marv . . .

Spencer clicked off the light and locked the closet door. He had a 7T pushbroom in his hand. Anything struck by the pushbroom would be sent floating upward. It would be enough to get the job done.

The fire alarm finally went silent as Spencer reentered the library. He didn't have much time to destroy the Grime in Dez's backpack. Once the teachers got the "all clear" sign, the school would be flooded with people again.

Spencer approached the backpack quietly. If the Toxite sensed him coming, the creature would bolt. And Spencer didn't have time for a wild Grime chase.

He leveled the bristly end of the pushbroom toward the backpack. The zippers jingled slightly, and Spencer saw the backpack pulse like a heartbeat. Looked like the Grime had found something tasty inside.

Spencer shuddered. Wilted, black banana peels? Melted gobs of leftover Halloween candy? He didn't want to imagine what kind of nasty messes might be lurking in the folds of Dez's backpack. How could anyone live with such a filthy backpack? Spencer's was always tidy and clean, just like his bedroom, his closet, and nearly everything else that belonged to him.

Finally close enough, Spencer slammed the bristles of the pushbroom into Dez's backpack. The creature squealed as the backpack shot into the air. Halfway to the ceiling, the zipper parted and the Grime leapt out.

Injured from the first strike, the slimy creature landed ungracefully on the floor and scurried toward the bookshelves. Spencer thrust with the pushbroom but missed by an inch.

The Grime leapt onto the tall Biographies shelf and scrambled out of reach. Spencer wished that he'd grabbed an ordinary broom. A single tap would have sent him rising in pursuit. If he wanted to catch the Grime now, he would have to climb the old-fashioned way—shelf by shelf.

Gripping the pushbroom in his left hand, Spencer leapt onto the bookshelf. He was halfway up the Biographies when a crowd of voices drifted through the hallway. Time was up. Any moment now, the librarian, Mrs. Natcher, and his classmates might return to the library to look for him.

Spencer hoisted himself higher, reaching the top of the bookcase in time to see the Grime scamper forward, leaving footprints in the thick dust. Spencer swung the pushbroom, but the angle wasn't right and he missed again.

His best chance was to climb on top of the bookshelf. Spencer cringed. That wasn't going to happen. No one had dusted up there for months—maybe years! Anything could be hidden in that dust. Just at a glance, Spencer saw an old paper airplane, a Snickers wrapper, and a wad of fuzzy gray gum. It was like a breeding ground for germs. And there was nothing that Spencer hated more than germs.

Farther down, he noticed that a white plastic bucket had cut a trail through the dust. It was shiny and new, as if someone had recently slid it into place. But why would there be a bucket on top of the bookshelf?

The escaping Grime leapt, cutting through Spencer's thoughts. Its bulbous fingertips suctioned onto the side of the white bucket. With a twist and a slither, it disappeared over the rim to hide.

Spencer inched sideways along the bookshelf, finding toeholds between books as he worked his way toward the bucket. He set the pushbroom in the thick dust. Reaching forward, he could barely grip the rim of the white bucket. He dragged it toward him, ready to snatch the pushbroom if the Grime tried to dart away.

The library's emergency exit squeaked open. Mrs. Natcher was the first to enter. She gave a little shriek when she spotted her student standing halfway up the Biographies bookshelf.

Whether it was Spencer's utter terror at what he saw when he peered into the bucket or the powerful draft of drowsiness that struck him, something caused the boy's foot to slip from the bookshelf.

Spencer's arms pinwheeled as he fell. He struck the ground and rolled onto his back. Ten feet up, on top of the dusty bookshelf, the white bucket wobbled and teetered, threatening to spill its deadly contents.

"Please, no," Spencer whispered. Under Spencer's pleading gaze, the bucket righted itself and came to a standstill, overhanging the top of the bookcase by an inch or two.

Spencer closed his eyes and breathed a sigh of relief. When he opened them, he was staring into the powdery-white face of Mrs. Natcher. The teacher's lips were pursed tightly enough to crack a nutshell.

Spencer's escapade was the last straw. Students had been misbehaving in the library all morning. And how could Mrs. Natcher know that Spencer had just discovered the reason?

A bucket load of squirming, angry Toxites.

CHAPTER 3

"THAT'S ALL?"

Spencer sat on the bench in the front office, staring into the dull, lifeless eyes of Mrs. Natcher's infamous hall pass, Baybee. It was a plastic baby doll wearing nothing but a diaper. The shame of carrying it usually discouraged kids from making unnecessary trips out of the classroom. But Mrs. Natcher deemed this trip to the principal's office very necessary.

Spencer rubbed a finger over the scratches in Baybee's head. A couple of months ago, Daisy had used Baybee to fight off Dez, scuffing the hall pass violently on the bathroom tile.

At least Daisy was innocent this time. Spencer didn't even have a chance to tell her what he'd seen before Mrs. Natcher punted him down the hallway with the Doll of Shame.

A nasal, whiny voice suddenly drifted out of the open doorway of the principal's office. "Spencer Zumbro!" He said the name like a game-show host announcing a winner.

But Spencer did not feel like a winner. He rose from the bench, resolved to face his punishment. With Baybee dangling limp from one hand, Spencer passed through the open doorway. He glanced around the big man's office. A picture of George Washington hanging on the wall, an open can of peanuts on the desk. Everything looked the same as the last time Spencer was here. Even the reprimanding speech started out exactly the same way, with Principal Poach slamming his hand onto the desk, fat fingers jiggling on impact.

"Twenty-four years I have been principal of Welcher Elementary, and I have never—*never*—heard of such behavior."

His thick, pink fingers traced down the back of the telephone on his desk. "I just had a very informative conversation with the librarian." He offered a false smile. "Why don't you tell me your side of the story?"

Spencer remembered Daisy's last words to him: *"Don't get caught."* But Spencer had known all along that someone would catch him. Somehow, knowing that he would get in trouble gave him courage. He knew he was doing the right thing, even if nobody else could see it. There was no point in trying to weasel out of this.

"It's all true," Spencer said. "I pulled the fire alarm and climbed onto one of the bookshelves."

Such a quick confession really threw Principal Poach out of his groove. "No. I don't think you understand me."

He interlaced his hot-dog fingers. "I'm going to ask you one more time. Did you, or did you not, pull the fire alarm?"

"I already said," Spencer muttered. "Yes. I pulled it. And I climbed up the bookshelf—the Biographies section, I think."

Principal Poach leaned back with a *humph*. "What to do? What to do?" the principal muttered to himself. "Pulling the fire alarm is one thing . . . I might have let that slide. But this blatant disregard for library books must not go unpunished!"

He sat forward, and Spencer heard his poor chair groan under the man's weight. Spencer was imagining all the terrible judgments that could possibly escape Poach's mouth: detention, suspension, execution . . .

"Tell me . . ." The principal squinted. "Do you like to read?"

Spencer shifted Baybee from one hand to another. Was this a trick question? "Yes," he finally admitted.

"Then I'm afraid this is going to be hard for you to accept." Principal Poach cleared his throat like a judge pronouncing a verdict. "From this point on—for the rest of the school year—you are absolutely forbidden from reading any book from the library's Biographies section!"

Poach sat back, allowing his punishment to sink in. Spencer felt the corners of his mouth tugging into a smile. He wanted to pull Baybee into a victory embrace. That was it? That was the whole punishment? Spencer didn't even *like* reading biographies. Who did? In fact, Spencer knew a couple of his classmates who would love a punishment like this.

"That's all?" It came out with a relieved laugh before Spencer could choke it back.

Principal Poach suddenly floundered, seeing that the punishment had not carried the profound impact that he'd expected. "Oh, no! You think that's all? I'm just getting started! That was only the appetizer."

Spencer's smile faded as he realized that he had just provoked the principal into further punishment. "You will also . . ." Poach was stalling, probably trying to decide which of his usual punishments would be best. "You will also fill out a behavior form and turn it in to Mrs. Natcher."

Spencer inwardly breathed a sigh of relief but tried to look upset on the outside. Filling out a behavior form wasn't bad either.

"Now, let's see . . ." Principal Poach muttered. "Where are those forms?" Then he spotted them across the desk.

The large man leaned forward, stretching for the stack of behavior forms pinned under an elephant-shaped paper-weight. His round middle interfered, hitting the desk and preventing his short arms from reaching the papers. After squirming for a moment, Poach sat back and glanced at Spencer sheepishly.

"Why don't you just grab a form on your way out? Make sure you fill in all the lines."

Spencer stepped up to the principal's desk. He reached down and picked up the heavy elephant paperweight.

A harsh whiteness suddenly clawed at Spencer's vision, like a flurry of snow and fog had consumed him. He shut his eyes tightly, and when he opened them again he was seated behind the steering wheel of a vehicle.

A fuzzy radio station was playing music from the eighties. He glanced over at the passenger's seat. A young woman with red hair was slouched in the seat, fast asleep. Her seat belt had cinched too tight, leaving a mark across her neck.

Spencer suddenly started whistling along with the song. But that couldn't be possible, since he'd never heard the song before and the whistle definitely wasn't his. And the hands on the wheel were old and strong . . .

Why? Why was this happening again?

More whiteness, and for a moment, Spencer thought he would crash the vehicle. But the mysterious hands guided the steering wheel until a complete fogginess overtook Spencer's vision. He blinked hard.

"Now look what you've done!" Principal Poach squealed.

Spencer was slumped forward on the principal's desk, Baybee pinned under him. The elephant paperweight had rolled out of his hand, and the behavior forms were scattered on the floor. Spencer stood up abruptly, blinking a few times.

"Cheyenne, Wyoming," Spencer muttered.

"What was that?"

Spencer shook his head. "Never mind." He grabbed a sheet of paper and scooped Baybee off the desk. Spencer hurried out of the principal's office, glancing over his shoulder as the large man struggled to restack the fallen forms.

Spencer had been in the office the whole time, hadn't he? So who was driving on the highway west of Cheyenne, Wyoming?

CHAPTER 4

"THAT'S TONIGHT?"

Spencer arrived at the lunchroom rattled from his strange incident in Principal Poach's office. It wasn't the first time he'd experienced something like this in the past month or so. The handful of instances seemed random. They struck without warning. But each time, he'd gone somewhere and known exactly where it was.

This time it was Cheyenne, seen through the eyes of an old man in a vehicle. Last time it was a warehouse in Philadelphia, with men in hard hats driving humming fork-lifts. Each time, the experience was so short that Spencer was left wondering if it had really happened. He kept the incidents to himself, trying to make enough sense of them to be able to share them with Daisy or his mom. But there wasn't even enough to form a decent explanation.

Without thinking, Spencer fell into the dwindling

lunch line, tucking Baybee under one arm. When he got to the counter, he wasn't surprised to see Meredith getting his food together.

Meredith was middle-aged and pear-shaped, wearing the unflattering uniform of a lunch lady. Her formless shirt was pink, blue, and white with a few dots of yellow that might as well have been mustard stains. Her brown hair was held together in a hairnet, which made her forehead look rather large. She always wore plastic food gloves, but her fake nails usually poked through, defeating the whole sanitary purpose.

"Hi, bud." She slid a fruit cup onto Spencer's tray next to the mashed potatoes. Today her gloves were intact, so Spencer knew he could eat lunch with the reassurance of proper kitchen sanitation. "Heard you had some trouble in the library this morning."

"Great," Spencer said. "Does the whole school know about that?"

Meredith shook her head. "Your friend told me. What's her name?" She wrinkled her large forehead. "Daisy, that's it."

Spencer nodded. Meredith was pretty good at pretending like she didn't know the kids. Her acting usually convinced Daisy, who had in turn almost blown their cover a dozen times.

"Have a good lunch," Meredith said as Spencer walked away. "Make sure to eat your mashed potatoes."

Spencer found Daisy alone, finishing her lunch at a table in the corner.

"You're alive!" she grinned when she saw him.

Spencer sat down across from her and propped Baybee on the table next to their trays. "Fill out a behavior form and I'm off the hook," he announced.

"That's it?"

"Oh, yeah," he added, "and I can't read any more biographies from the library." He grinned. "Bummer."

"Just biographies?"

Spencer nodded. "That's the shelf I was climbing."

Daisy slid her tray aside and leaned forward. "Why were you climbing the bookshelf? I mean, I figure it's got to have something to do with Toxites. But Dez was suspicious so I told him you were trying to get away from the fire."

"But there was no fire," Spencer said.

"Well, the alarm went off." Daisy was notorious for believing anything, so this was a typical comment from Gullible Gates.

Spencer slurped a peach out of his fruit cup. "The alarm went off because I pulled it, remember?"

"Of course I remember. But I had to tell Dez *something*." She sat back and scratched her head. "So why *were* you climbing the bookshelf?"

"We've got a huge problem in the library. I've never seen anything like it." He picked up his fork and skewered a limp green bean. "There's a bucket on top of the bookshelf. Full of Toxites."

"What?" Daisy gasped.

"It was weird. There were probably like fifty of them, crammed in on top of each other. They seemed angry, like the ones I met in that apartment back in September. They were all thrashing around in there."

"Why didn't they climb out?"

"I don't think they could. It looked like they were trapped. The Toxite I was chasing crawled in there to hide. It probably didn't even know it was walking into a one-way trap." He shoveled a big forkful of mashed potatoes into his mouth.

"We need to get them out of there before someone else finds that bucket," Daisy said. "If only we could get into the school when nobody else was around."

"Ugh!" Spencer suddenly gagged. His mashed potatoes slid out of his mouth and back onto his plate.

"Eww!" Daisy turned away. "That's disgusting."

"You're telling me," said Spencer. "There's something in my mashed potatoes. I almost barfed!"

Spencer prodded the white mess with his fork. Sure enough, a piece of rolled-up paper was hidden in the soggy potatoes. "I'm never eating school lunch again." Spencer made a face and pushed the tray away.

"Wait a minute," Daisy said. "Maybe it's a message from Meredith. Like that time we found the key for the stash in your chicken patty."

The two kids stared at the prechewed mashed potatoes for a moment. "Go ahead." Daisy pointed. "See what it says."

Spencer held up his hands. "I'm not touching it."

"Oh, come on. It's *your* spit."

"Not anymore. I gave it to the potatoes."

Daisy rolled her eyes. "You're such a germ freak." She snatched up Baybee and used the doll's plastic hand to scoot the little scroll of paper from the mashed potatoes. Then Daisy dropped the hall pass and carefully unrolled the note.

Orchestra concert. Tonight at 7. I'll be here with a key to the library.

"Oh, no," Daisy said. "That's tonight?"

"It's perfect." Spencer glanced toward the kitchen to see if he could catch a glimpse of Meredith. Then he looked back at Daisy. "What's the matter?"

"I haven't learned my part yet."

"For what?" Spencer asked.

"For the concert."

"Umm . . ." Spencer tried to hold back a grin. "You're not in the orchestra."

"I'm not? Phew!" Daisy wiped her forehead. "I thought it was something everyone had to do."

CHAPTER 5

"VIOLINS."

A red Ford truck pulled out of the Gates' driveway, leaving a big black dog barking savagely in the yard. Despite all the times that Spencer had been to Daisy's house, the guard dog never seemed to grow accustomed to him.

"Orchestra concert, huh?" Mr. Gates said to his young passengers. He had insisted on dropping Spencer and Daisy at the school, even though it was only a few blocks from the Gates home, easily within walking distance. "I played in the sixth-grade orchestra once." Mr. Gates's country drawl gave the words a twang.

"You did?" Daisy gave her dad a surprised look.

"Yup. Played the triangle. But they kicked me out. Said I was too *obtuse*."

Spencer couldn't decide if Mr. Gates was telling the

truth or sharing one of the corny jokes he was known for. The truck rolled to a stop, and Spencer popped open the door. Daisy scooted across the seat, assuring her dad that they would be fine walking home after the concert. He waved out the window as he pulled away.

Spencer smiled. "Your dad's funny."

"Yeah," Daisy said, working through a snag as she tried to zip up her jacket. "He's good to have around."

The comment might have bothered Spencer a couple of months ago. Dad had been a sore subject for a long time. But back in September, Spencer had finally learned the truth. His dad had not deserted the family. Alan Zumbro was a Toxite scientist who had gone missing on a research project about two years ago. Walter was out there right now, investigating his dad's disappearance.

The news of Alan's true identity had brought hope to Spencer and his mother. Hope *and* fear. Alan Zumbro could be long dead, stung to death by vicious relocated Toxites. But maybe Dad was alive. And if that were the case, then maybe—just maybe—Dad would return.

The concert was happening in the cafeteria. The lunch tables were stacked out of the way and someone had set out rows of chairs, hopeful for a large crowd. The orchestra was already tuning when Spencer and Daisy entered. It was a dreadful sound, like a hive of overgrown hornets swooping in for an attack.

"There's Meredith." Spencer pointed to the back of the cafeteria. The lunch lady was still wearing her shapeless uniform. Spencer wondered if she'd had a chance to go home since school had let out.

Spencer whispered to Daisy, "You get the library key from Meredith while I get some Glopified supplies from the stash."

As he maneuvered himself toward the kitchen door, Spencer watched Daisy navigate the crowd of supportive orchestra parents and greet Meredith with an awkward gesture.

Meredith glanced down at Daisy and smiled halfheartedly. The crowd quieted as the orchestra finished tuning and the conductor lifted her baton. Something slipped from the lunch lady's pocket and landed on the hard floor.

Spencer watched Daisy pick up a ring of keys and innocently attempt to hand them back to Meredith. The lunch lady ignored the girl and continued staring straight ahead at the orchestra.

Spencer paused at the entrance to the kitchen. Sometimes Daisy couldn't take a hint. The girl jingled the keys in her hand, still striving for Meredith's attention. Spencer was about to go back for her when Daisy gave a sudden nod of understanding. A smile spread across her face and she slipped the keys into her jacket pocket.

Spencer sighed with relief and ducked into the dark kitchen. A moment later, he was rendezvousing with Daisy in the hallway, arms full of Glopified supplies. The fifth-grade version of *Ode to Joy* grew quieter as the two kids headed away from the cafeteria.

Daisy used Meredith's keys to open the security doors

at the end of the hall next to the janitor's stairwell. They slipped into the dark hallway beyond, but before the door could shut, a familiar face shoved through.

"Wait for me!"

"Dez?" Spencer and Daisy said together. Why was he always showing up at the worst of times?

Daisy glared. "What are you doing here?"

"Somebody said there was going to be violence in the orchestra tonight." He bumped his beefy fists together.

"Well, I think they meant *violins*," Spencer said. "So you're out of luck."

"I don't need the stupid dorkestra." Dez cracked his knuckles. "Maybe I can find violence somewhere else."

"Don't mess with us, Dez." Spencer tried to make his voice sound threatening.

"Just a punch in the nose," said Dez. "Then we'll be even."

"Even?"

"For messing with my backpack today," Dez said. "You made me look like an idiot."

Spencer shrugged. "That's really not hard to do . . ."

Dez lunged forward, his fist cocked back. Spencer flinched and tried to turn. Mop strings suddenly whipped past Spencer and coiled around Dez's whole body, pinning back his arm. The bully flopped to the floor, his screams muffled.

Spencer looked over his shoulder at Daisy. She was still holding the mop handle, her eyes wide.

"Daisy!" Spencer's mouth was agape. "Do you realize what you just did?"

Dez was thrashing on the floor, completely tied up in mop strings. Daisy swallowed. "He was going to hit you!"

"Shh!" Spencer said. "What's that?" There was a noise behind the security doors.

"Someone's coming!" Daisy hissed. "We've got to hide!"

"What about him?" Spencer pointed desperately at Dez.

"Got him." Daisy, still holding the mop handle, slammed her broom against the floor. She jetted toward the ceiling, Dez's wriggling form in tow. Spencer leveled his own broom and launched after them.

As soon as they hit the ceiling, the security door jerked opened. Mr. Joe was silhouetted from the light beyond. And even if they hadn't recognized his figure, they would have known his voice.

"Hey! Who's there? This part of the school is off-limits!"

Don't look up, Spencer silently pleaded. He and Daisy were gripping their brooms, bodies pressed weightlessly against the ceiling. Dez dangled from Daisy's mop. All wrapped in white mop strings, the bully looked like a giant cocoon.

"Hello?" Mr. Joe called again. Then he shrugged. Testing the security door to make sure it was locked, the custodian stepped out of sight and pulled the door closed behind him.

Daisy drifted down first, Dez hitting the floor with a thud. The mop strings were starting to retract, but the bully was dazed.

"Great," Spencer said, floating down from the ceiling. "What're we going to do with him now?"

"Tie him up again?" Daisy shrugged. "We can come back and get him in a few minutes."

"What if he gets free?"

"Let's bonk him on the head. Like they do in movies."

"Daisy!"

"What? He's the one that wanted violence."

"Violins."

"Whatever."

CHAPTER 6

"HOW ABOUT A TRADE?"

Spencer and Daisy stood shoulder to shoulder in front of the library entrance. Daisy had just inserted the key, and the door clicked open.

"It's bad in there, Daisy. The Toxite breath is strong. We're going to have to focus like never before."

Daisy slowly pushed open the door. "We'll watch out for each other."

Spencer nodded. "In and out. Fast as we can." He checked his pockets for vacuum dust, then hefted a mop in one hand and a broom in the other. "We've got to get back to Dez before he gets free. That mop won't hold him forever, and the vac dust we threw will only buy us an extra minute or two."

"I still think we should have bonked him," Daisy said.

They rushed side by side into the dark library.

Spencer yawned as he reached the Biographies bookshelf. In the dim glow of the exit signs, he could vaguely see the white bucket. It was balancing on the top of the bookcase, untouched from when he had fallen.

"You doing okay?" Spencer asked.

Daisy gritted her teeth in concentration. "I'm trying really hard not to get distracted by that table leg over there. It looks shiny."

"No! Focus!" But even as he reprimanded her, Spencer felt the awful temptation to lie down and rest for a moment.

Spencer shook aside his fatigue and took the broom in both hands. "I'm going to fly up there and grab the bucket. When I bring it down, you need to have your vac dust ready. A palm blast should take their breath away for a minute so we can decide what to do."

He tapped his broom on the library floor and drifted up alongside the bookshelf. Reaching out, he seized the rim of the white bucket in one hand. It was hard to hold on. He felt weak from lack of sleep.

His eyelids drooped, and Spencer thought he was going to drop the bucket. He wasn't even aware that his broom was descending until his feet brushed the carpet. A puff of vacuum dust revved past him and into the bucket. All fatigue vanished and Spencer set the bucket on the floor. Daisy tossed a second shot of vac dust into the mass of trapped Toxites.

The effects from the Toxites were momentarily subdued, and Daisy glanced back over her shoulder. "Oh, wow," she said. "That table leg is so *not* cool. What was I thinking?"

"At least they're all in one place," Spencer said about the Toxites, staring into the swarming bucket. "If my broom will fit in the bucket, I can just start smashing."

As Spencer pulled his broom around to test, the library door slammed open. Dez staggered through the doorway. He wasn't completely untied. The mop strings still bound his arms.

Spencer grunted, "Stay back, Dez!" He turned again to the Toxite bucket.

The answer that came from the doorway was unexpected and chilling. "Dez will stay right where I want him!"

Spencer and Daisy squinted through the darkness. There was a stranger standing behind Dez, holding the wooden mop handle like Dez was on a leash. He ushered the bully into the library and closed the door behind him.

"Who are you?" Spencer asked.

"No one you'll ever see again," the man said.

"Are you part of the BEM?" Daisy asked, gripping her pushbroom like a rifle.

"I'm not a janitor, if that's what you mean. But the BEM's reach extends to all kinds of maintenance. I'm simply an electrician. The Bureau hired me to come in this morning and fix a light above the bookshelf." He gestured toward the ceiling. "I see you found the bucket I left behind." The stranger smirked. "And it looks like I found something *you* left behind."

The man tugged on the mop handle, and Dez fell to the floor. He was whimpering, scared. Spencer had never seen the bully like this.

"How about a trade?" the stranger said. "My bucket for your friend."

Dez was anything but a friend. Yet, like it or not, Spencer knew he had to accept the trade. It wasn't worth someone getting hurt.

Spencer stepped away from the bucket. "All right," he said. "Come and get it."

The stranger strode forward, forcing Dez ahead of him. When he finally reached the bucket, the man let go of Dez. The bully took a step and crumpled to the floor.

The electrician lifted the bucket by the handle and peered inside. "Safe and sound," he whispered. "There're more than a hundred in here. Amazing how so many creatures can fit into such a small space."

Daisy had migrated to Spencer's side, and the two kids watched the stranger retreat toward the library's emergency exit. "Where are you taking them?" Spencer asked.

"Who says they're coming with me?" the electrician said. "The BEM is calling this an Agitation Bucket. The Toxites are trapped as long as the bucket stays upright. But they're getting angry in there. They feel like they're being relocated. Have you ever seen a relocated Toxite?" The stranger clucked his tongue. "Ferocious little beasts."

He glanced at the bucket again. "These have been stewing for a while. Once they're released, they'll be bloodthirsty for about a week. Very dangerous for those who can see them." He was at the exit now, leaning back against the door. "Very effective for ridding schools of Rebel Janitors."

With that, the electrician tipped over the Agitation Bucket. Toxites spewed out in a seething mass of wings, tails, teeth, and quills. Vicious eyes glimmered in the darkness as the Toxites came for the kids like a cloud of death.

CHAPTER 7

"THERE'S TOO MANY!"

Their only hope was to get outside. Spencer knew the angry Toxites wouldn't leave the school. But getting to the exit was another matter altogether. They would have to blaze a path through the oncoming creatures.

Spencer met the first wave of Toxites with a fistful of vac dust. Daisy swung her pushbroom and several creatures exploded. Adrenaline battled the sluggish effects of the Toxite breath as both kids struggled to maintain focus.

The Toxites were enraged from their time in the Agitation Bucket. One slip could be fatal. The creatures would pick apart the kids like ants on a cookie.

"Look out!" A Rubbish was swooping in on Daisy's blind side, hooked beak parted, sharp talons flexed.

Spencer lunged sideways, hurling his final puff of vacuum dust. The creature lost control as the suction force buckled its wings. It collided with a bookshelf and toppled to the floor.

Something heavy and much larger than a Toxite struck Spencer from behind and knocked him to the floor. His broom tapped down and shot out of his hand. Someone grabbed his wrists and flipped him onto his side.

"I always knew you were a freak!" Dez said, pinning Spencer under his bulky weight. Clearly, the big kid couldn't see the dangerous swarm of oncoming Toxites. "I want some answers from you. Like, how did you tie me up with a mop? And who was that jerk guy that dragged me in here?"

Spencer tried to twist away. Toxites were swarming over Dez's body, clawing and biting. But the bully felt and saw nothing. Unsatisfied with Dez's untouchable flesh, the Toxites turned to fresh meat: someone who could see them and feel the sting of their attacks. It took less than a second for the creatures to find Spencer, pinned and defenseless.

Each Toxite brought a new pain to Spencer's trapped body. A sharp cut on his leg from a Rubbish talon, a blistering welt on his hand from a poisonous Grime. A Filth scuttled past Spencer's head and climbed onto his shoulder, sharp quills raking scratches across his neck.

Dez was still shouting, but the breath of the Filth, so close to Spencer's face, overcame him. Despite the pain and fear, Spencer started slipping into forced sleep.

He vaguely saw Dez pull back a fist. The punch was meant for Spencer's face—and by the size of Dez's fist, it would probably break his nose. But the punch never came

down. It went up—high up—as Daisy slammed her pushbroom into the back of Dez's head.

The bully soared over a low bookshelf and landed with a crash, out of sight. Spencer was the next to get hit, with a much gentler tap from Daisy's pushbroom. He jerked off the ground, Toxites falling away as he rose toward the ceiling. A few Rubbishes kept pace, their leathery wings flapping. Spencer, weaponless in the air, batted them away with bloodied knuckles.

"Spencer!" Daisy slammed a broom against a bookshelf and sent it jetting across the library. As it shot past, Spencer snatched the handle, and the momentum pulled him away from an incoming flock of Rubbishes. He crashed into the Fiction bookshelf. Novels fell around him as Spencer stumbled to his feet.

Daisy screamed as a nearby Filth charged her, ramming its spiky head into her leg. She crumpled onto one knee, barely managing to immobilize the Filth with a bit of vac dust.

It was hopeless. This was the worst thing they'd been through on their own. The Toxites were thick and impenetrable. They would never make it to the door in one piece. Spencer turned his eyes to the emergency exit, wishing he could find a way to reach it safely.

Then, unbelievably, as Spencer's eyes were trained on the exit, the door flew open. A thin figure entered first: a young woman wearing a high school letter jacket and hood. She had a short-handled mop in each hand and wielded them like deadly ball-and-chain flails.

A second person shot through the open door, dangling one-handed from a speeding broom. In his free hand he clutched something small and black. He wore a baseball cap, but as the broom bore him into a flock of angry Rubbishes, the hat was stripped away. In the dim light, Spencer saw a shiny bald head.

"Walter!" Was it really him? The warlock janitor had appeared in the nick of time.

"There's too many!" Walter shouted to his hooded companion. "Switch to Plan B!"

The hooded lady somersaulted across the library like an acrobatic ninja and slammed her mops into a pack of Filths. She reached Daisy, and the two of them rushed for the exit. Walter cocked back his arm and hurled the black object in his hand. It struck the wall and exploded into a cloud of white dust. The billowing explosion grew like a mushroom cloud, engulfing half the library.

Spencer reached for his broom, only to jerk away. The wooden handle was crawling with Grimes. The monsters leapt toward him, and Spencer fell sideways onto one of the study tables. Walter was at his side in no time, swatting away the angry Toxites with his broom.

"Come on!" The old warlock grabbed Spencer by the sleeve and pulled him off the table.

They were almost to the exit when Walter reached into his coat and withdrew another black object. Spencer saw it clearly this time.

It was a chalkboard eraser.

"Go!" Walter said, shoving Spencer out the door. Then

he hurled the eraser across the library and it exploded in a white dust ball.

Walter stepped out of the library, pulling the door shut behind him to contain the explosion. Spencer glanced at Daisy, standing in the parking lot. But her expression was not victorious. It was horrified. Then Spencer remembered why.

"Dez!" he whispered. He had to act fast. The chalk bombs were filling the whole library!

"Wait!" Walter cried, but Spencer leapt past him, bursting through the door before the lock clicked shut. He heard the warlock shout something—a warning. But there was no time to discuss it.

The library was a dim mess of cloudy dust. Spencer coughed into his shoulder and drew in the deepest breath he could manage. He ran forward blindly, stumbling painfully into chairs and tables. Through the ethereal whiteness, an occasional Toxite would suddenly appear, only to vanish again like a ghostly figure in a sea of fog. They seemed to move in painful slow motion.

Then, as if that painful motion were contagious, Spencer's feet suddenly gave out under him. He caught himself on a low bookshelf and paused, trying to think about how to walk. It seemed like the message was taking forever to get from his brain to his feet.

A few steps later, he fell again. But this time, his legs wouldn't respond to his efforts to stand up. Dragging himself forward with his hands, Spencer came at last to the spot where Dez had crash-landed. The bully was covered in chalk dust, his face frighteningly white. But Dez was still breathing. Spencer could see the soft rise and fall of his chest.

Spencer coughed out his stale old breath and took another. The dust was thick, and he felt his fingertips start to tingle. Spencer grabbed Dez by the shirt, but there was no way he could lift the bully. Especially since Spencer's legs had stopped working.

He needed a broom to fly them out. Spencer cast his fingers around in the bleakness. His hand gripped something long and wooden. A handle. He dragged it closer . . .

A mop!

What good was a mop in a desperate situation like this? Spencer instinctively flicked the strings around Dez's ankles. A broom would have been so much better, but there was no time to be picky. Air was running short.

Turning away from Dez, Spencer began the painstaking task of dragging himself across the library floor. He gripped the mop handle, flicking out more length on the strings behind him as he crawled. At last, with his lungs almost bursting, Spencer pulled himself out the door and into the November night.

Walter was waiting. He grabbed Spencer and lifted him away from the billowing chalk cloud. "What's this?" The warlock janitor looked down at the long wooden handle in Spencer's grip.

"Hang on . . ." Spencer managed between fits of coughs. Walter grabbed the handle as Daisy and the hooded lady approached. The mop's head stretched back into the library, the strings disappearing in the white fog.

Then the mop strings began to reel in, followed by a tremendous crashing sound from inside the library. It was like something heavy was being dragged across the library floor. Not something—*someone*.

Spencer waited, hopeful. He had regained the use of his legs, but he still leaned heavily on Walter. At last, a figure tumbled through the threshold and the library door clicked shut.

"It worked," Spencer managed to say, still gasping for breath. At their feet lay the still, white form of Dez Rylie, the last of the mop strings unwinding from his ankles.

CHAPTER 8

"I DON'T MIND HIM LIKE THIS."

"What's the matter with him?" Spencer asked, leaning on Daisy for support. Walter carried Dez's limp form across the parking lot to where the janitor's van idled, the hooded lady in the driver's seat.

"He'll be fine," Walter said. "Those chalkboard eraser bombs are something the BEM invented. I picked up the Glop formula and made a few of my own. They cause temporary paralysis in Toxites . . . *and* people."

"Is that what was happening to my legs?" Spencer said.

"Exactly." Walter loaded Dez into the back of the van. "If you had stayed in there any longer, you'd be just like him. What were you thinking, rushing in like that?"

Spencer looked down. Why was Walter reprimanding him? He'd saved Dez from the chalk bomb, hadn't he?

"You had no idea what you were up against," Walter

said. "That chalk cloud could have been fatal, for all you knew."

Spencer hadn't considered the consequences. He'd simply seen a problem and rushed in to fix it. He was used to acting on his own. But now that Walter was back, shouldn't Spencer have turned to him for help?

"So Dez is okay?" Daisy asked. "He'll get better?"

"Of course," Walter said. "He should be back to normal in an hour or so."

Daisy peered at Dez's dusty form. "Actually, I don't mind him like this," she said. "He's not so bad when he can't move. Can't we make it last a little longer?"

"It would have lasted a lot longer if Spencer hadn't rescued him," Walter said. "I had no idea there was another person in the library. I threw two erasers in there. That could have paralyzed this kid for more than a day." The bald warlock looked at Dez's still form. "The erasers were our last resort, but there were just too many Toxites to fight."

"I thought we were doomed for sure," Daisy said. "You showed up just in time."

"Thanks to Meredith," Walter answered. "This morning, she phoned me about a suspicious BEM electrician. When the same electrician came to the orchestra concert, Meredith called me again. By that time, I was already in Welcher, grabbing a bite to eat. I came immediately to the library when Meredith said you might be in danger."

"You were already in Welcher?" Spencer repeated. His first thought was about his father. What if Walter had come to tell him more information about his dad?

"I've come to warn you." Walter lowered his voice. "The BEM is sending a dozen men to Welcher. They'll be here by Monday."

"What?" Daisy said. "Why?"

The warlock janitor took a deep breath. "They're coming for you, Spencer."

The boy took an unsteady step backward. "Me?" he muttered. He wanted Walter to keep talking, but the hooded young lady in the driver's seat interrupted them.

"We've got to roll," she said, "before anyone finds out we were here."

Walter gestured for Spencer and Daisy to climb into the back of the van next to Dez. "But wait," Spencer said. "What's happening? What do you mean, the BEM is coming for me?"

Walter silenced him, glancing nervously around the dark parking lot. "Whoever dumped that Agitation Bucket could still be around, listening. It will be best if we discuss things in the privacy of your home." The warlock motioned to the van again. The kids climbed in, careful not to step on Dez's prone form.

It was exciting to see the old warlock again. But Spencer and Daisy both knew this wasn't a social call. The BEM was up to something. That was clear from the Agitation Bucket in the school library. Spencer couldn't help but feel that Walter's arrival meant the beginning of new dangers.

Daisy extended a finger and slowly poked Dez's ample stomach. "Do you think he can feel that?" she asked.

But Spencer was caught up in his own thoughts. He

tried again to coax more information out of Walter, but the warlock was busy giving the driver directions. Then, pulling out a cell phone, Walter got in touch with Meredith and asked her to gather the Glopified equipment from the library once the chalk cloud settled.

The janitorial van pulled into the lavish driveway of Aunt Avril's Hillside Estates home. The Zumbros were house-sitting for a year, which meant that Aunt Avril and Uncle Wyatt would probably need to remodel when they returned. The rambunctious Zumbro children had already done irreversible damage to the hardwood floor and the walls. Not to mention the toenail polish spilled on the carpet and the burn marks on the banister.

Walter opened the back door of the van, allowing Spencer and Daisy to climb out.

"Let's get him inside," Walter said, taking Dez under the arms. Spencer grabbed the bully's ankles, careful not to touch his grungy sneakers. Moving around the van, they waddled up the driveway.

Alice met them at the door, her face a mixture of shock at seeing Walter and worry at seeing Dez. The warlock greeted Mrs. Zumbro professionally, his voice aimed to calm her nerves.

"So . . ." Alice raised her eyebrows at Spencer. "Looks like the orchestra concert was interesting." Then she retreated into the house, herding Spencer's siblings downstairs to watch TV.

Spencer and Walter laid Dez on the leather couch, a puff of chalk powder rising from his motionless form.

Alice entered from the kitchen, and, a few moments later, Walter's assistant appeared with a box of equipment.

"About time for an introduction, I think." Walter gestured to the young woman in the letter jacket. "This is my niece, Penny."

Penny smiled and pulled back her hood. She had a smattering of ruddy freckles across her thin face. Her eyes were a startling green and seemed to show a glint of adventure. Short, fiery red hair framed her face nicely. Spencer took an involuntary step back.

It was her! The young woman he had seen asleep in the passenger seat of a vehicle. Spencer recalled the vision with startling clarity. He had been driving, with the hands of an old man. Spencer looked back at Walter, glancing at the warlock's hands. Was it possible? Had he been looking through Walter Jamison's eyes?

"Spencer?" Walter said. "Is something wrong?"

Spencer looked back at Penny. "It's just . . . I thought . . ." He swallowed hard. "Have we met before?"

Penny shook her head. "I would remember meeting the famous Spencer Zumbro. Walter has told me everything about you." Penny's smile faded under Spencer's shocked gaze. Finally, she turned away and sat down on the sofa.

"Penny has worked as a part-time janitor since she was a senior in high school," Walter said. "That was, what, two years ago?"

Daisy was looking at Penny's letter jacket. "Did you play football or something?"

Penny smiled. "Gymnastics," she said. "I did a bit of that in high school."

"Don't be humble," Walter said. "My niece was the state champion in tumbling, vault, and balance beam."

"Wow," Daisy said. "You should try out for the Olympics! Can you do a backflip?"

"She's been backflipping since she was eight," Walter answered.

Penny shrugged. "Gymnastics is fun . . . but karate is more my thing."

"Cool!" Daisy didn't bother to hide her admiration. "Can you break boards with your forehead?"

Penny pretended to scoff. "I break boards with my pinkie." She lifted her little finger. Daisy totally fell for it.

"Anyway," Walter cut in, "Penny's an expert Toxite fighter. She's been a big help to me over the past month with all my travels. We've been a lot of places, seen a lot of things . . ."

"What have you learned about Alan?" It was Alice who asked the question. Spencer had wanted to, but he was worried that the answer might be . . .

"Nothing yet, I'm afraid," Walter said. "We haven't had much time to investigate. I've been too busy Glopifying new tools and supplying gear to the Rebel Janitors. The BEM is on the move. They're hitting all the Rebel schools. But I got word that they're on their way to Welcher for another reason." Walter looked at Spencer. "They think you have something. They're coming to get it from you."

"What?" Spencer asked. "What could I have that the BEM might want? Do they think I still have Ninfa?"

Walter shook his head. He reached into his cargo pocket and withdrew a bronze hammer. It was the hammer that had made Walter Jamison a warlock. There were three magic hammers, created by the Founding Witches and handed down since colonial times. Walter had a bronze nail, too, pounded into his van. His vehicle was the only place where he could experiment with raw magic, creating new formulas to Glopify more janitorial supplies.

Last September, Spencer had used the hammer to pound the nail into the School Board. He had become a warlock for a short time before giving the hammer back to Walter. Did the BEM think he had kept it?

"It's not Ninfa." Walter slipped the hammer back into his pocket.

"What, then?" Spencer asked. "What do I have?"

"The BEM doesn't know exactly what it is. But they think *you* know."

"Wait a minute," Daisy said to Walter. "If you don't know what it is, and the BEM doesn't know what it is, and Spencer doesn't know what it is . . . then *who* knows?"

"Alan Zumbro," the warlock said. Spencer's heart gave an extra beat and Alice put a hand on his arm, giving an anxious squeeze. "This has something to do with your father, Spencer. But that's all anyone can explain."

Spencer swallowed hard and looked at his mom. "And now the BEM's coming for me?"

"They'll be here by Monday," Penny said. "Come next

week, Welcher isn't going to be the friendly place you know and love. You'll have BEM workers in disguise around town and bloodthirsty Toxites inside your school."

"So what do we do?" Daisy asked.

"Leave," Walter said. "You must leave Welcher until we get things sorted out. A week should do it. The Toxites from the Bucket will have calmed down by then."

"What about the BEM workers?" Alice said.

"We're calling in Rebel reinforcements already," Penny said. "We'll show the BEM that they aren't welcome in this town."

"But where can we go for a week?" asked Spencer.

"I have a grandma in Nevada," Daisy said.

Walter shook his head. "I can't send you to stay with relatives. If the BEM tracked you down, you'd have no protection. You need to go someplace secure."

"A bank!" Daisy said.

Spencer shot her a glance. "We can't live in a bank for a week."

"What about the White House?" she said.

"Are you serious?" Spencer rolled his eyes.

"Hey, I'm just trying to brainstorm some secure places."

Walter held up his hands. "We've already done the brainstorming," he said. "And we have a plan, if you'd let us tell it."

He rubbed his hands together. "There's a private school called New Forest Academy. Located in Colorado. They run a recruitment program where students experience a week on campus to see if they would be good candidates to attend the Academy."

"It may not be as exciting as living in the White House," Penny said. "But it's listed as one of the safest schools in the country. You'll never be alone. You'll be surrounded by other students and Academy faculty. You'll even sleep in dormitories on site."

"Won't there be Toxites there?" Spencer asked. "Since it's a school?"

"Toxites at New Forest Academy don't last long. We've got a Rebel Janitor in there. He does a remarkable job keeping the school Toxite-free. It's the best learning environment you'll find in the country. When you get there, contact the janitor. Guy by the name of Roger Munroe. He's a good friend of mine and you can trust him with anything."

"But I don't want to go to a different school." Daisy's eyes showed that she was on the verge of panic at the thought of leaving Welcher.

"It won't be permanent," Penny said. "It's just for the week. Even if you fit the Academy's criteria and they want you to study there, you can still turn down the invitation."

"Exactly," Walter agreed. "We don't expect you to move to Colorado. We're just going to pretend that you're interested in attending the Academy so you can have a safe week in their facilities." Walter glanced at Alice. "Of course, we'll need your support in this."

Spencer turned to his mom. His hair was still white with chalk dust, his face and hands welted and scratched from the Toxite attack. He was afraid. Afraid of sitting around and letting the BEM come for him. And evidently the hint of fear in Spencer's eyes convinced Alice.

"I'll drive them," she said.

"It's a long way," Walter said.

Alice shrugged indifferently. "I'm no stranger to long road trips," she said. "I can get work off on Monday and I'll take them to the Academy."

Of course. It wasn't enough to simply agree. Alice had to take her support to the next level by personally driving them.

Walter nodded gratefully to Mrs. Zumbro, then turned intently upon Spencer and Daisy. "Everything I've read about New Forest Academy says it has a large campus, college style. There should be plenty to see and explore. But I want you to follow one simple rule." He held up a finger. "Don't go anywhere alone. Stay with the groups. There's safety in numbers."

The intensity in Spencer and Daisy's eyes caused Walter to lighten up. "And try to relax." Walter ruffled Spencer's dusty hair. "New Forest Academy will be safe. Roger will take care of you. I have his word."

Penny pulled an envelope from her back pocket. "Here's the paperwork you'll need to get into the program." She handed it to Alice. "We printed the forms on the Academy's website. Getting the necessary signatures was a bit trickier. Normally, students send their applications weeks in advance. A committee reviews the paperwork, and if the student is approved, then a bunch of important people sign it. Well, we didn't have that kind of time, so we took a few warlock-inspired shortcuts to get the signatures on the page. Anyway, fill out the rest of the application and take the papers when you go. You'll need the signatures to get in."

Alice opened the envelope to look inside.

"And there should be enough money to cover the cost for the Academy program," Penny said. "Should be plenty for these two."

"THREE!"

Everyone in the room jumped. They turned to the leather couch, where they had all but forgotten about the paralyzed Dez.

"*Three* of us are going to the stupid Academy camp thingy!" Dez was still motionless, but he appeared to have the use of his tongue again. "You're not leaving me here to get eaten by the Big Evil Monkeys!"

"Big Evil Monkeys?" Spencer said.

"What else could BEM stand for, Doofus?"

CHAPTER 9

"HE'LL MESS EVERYTHING UP!"

Dez wouldn't stop talking until someone propped him up on the couch. Although he'd been lying paralyzed for almost half an hour, he'd heard every word that was said. But hearing and understanding were two different things—especially for Dez.

In the last hour, Dez had been tied up with a mop, floated to the ceiling, held hostage by a stranger, caught in a paralyzing chalk explosion, and hauled helplessly to Spencer's house in the back of a dark janitorial van. Sure, the bully was tough and insensitive, but even Dez had his limits.

Spencer tried to explain about the janitors from the Bureau of Educational Maintenance. But Dez had regained enough control to shake his head vigorously, white chalk rising in puffs from his buzzed hair.

"I'm not getting left behind to get picked off by . . ." Dez stammered, "by janitors with superpowers!"

"They're not after you," Walter explained. "The BEM doesn't even know who you are."

"Actually," Daisy said, "they might. Remember? Dez did some dirty work for the BEM back in September."

"I did?" Dez looked around.

"Remember that substitute, Miss Leslie Sharmelle?" Daisy said. "She was part of the BEM. She had you take some magic soap into the boys' bathroom to get Spencer."

"Yeah!" Dez grinned. "You're right! I *did* do dirty work for the BEM. And I'll do it again if you don't take me with you. I'll tell them where you're going!"

Spencer groaned. Dez was such a nuisance! Even covered in chalk dust, slumped on the couch with only the ability to move his head, Dez was complicating things.

Walter rubbed a hand over his face and glanced at his niece. Penny tilted her head and shrugged.

"Fine," Walter said. "You're going with Spencer and Daisy."

"What?" Daisy shrieked.

"No!" said Spencer. "He'll mess everything up!"

Dez's foot suddenly shot out and kicked Spencer in the shin. "All right! I can move my legs again!"

Alice repositioned herself between the two boys. Her hands went to her hips, daring Dez to try it again.

"Dez has seen too much," Penny said. "He's involved whether we like it or not."

"Your old substitute teacher, Leslie Sharmelle, is locked

safely away in jail," said Walter. "But if she used Dez before, then other BEM workers may try to contact him in the future."

"I thought the whole point of sending us to this Academy was to keep us safe," Daisy said. She glared at Dez. "We're never too safe when *he's* around."

"Listen," Walter said. "I know you three kids have had some disagreements in the past."

Spencer rolled his eyes. Wasn't a fistfight in the boys' bathroom more than a disagreement?

"But it's time to set your differences aside. It's just as important to protect Dez from the BEM. I want him to go with you to the Academy." Walter looked at Spencer and Daisy. "And I expect you two to answer any questions he might have."

"We're going to tell him about . . ." Daisy leaned around Alice to glance at Dez. Then she lowered her voice to a whisper. "Toxites?"

"I'm not deaf," Dez shouted from the couch. "Just because I can't move doesn't mean my ears are turned off. I already heard your whole dumb conversation. If you want to make me—"

"I don't think Dez should know," Spencer said, ignoring the comments from the couch.

"Dez knows enough to be curious," Walter said. "If you don't give him answers, he might turn to other sources. It's better for him to hear the truth from you than be told lies by the BEM." Walter dropped his voice while Dez continued ranting. "I need you to gain his trust. Until you do, what will stop Dez from betraying us?"

Walter was right. They had to get Dez on their side. It would be easy for the BEM to trick him. The bully was already inclined to make chaos. He could be dangerous in the hands of the enemy. Dez would never help the Rebels unless he had a reason. But Spencer knew that getting Dez to trust him would be nearly impossible.

"You're not going to give him soap, are you?" Spencer asked. It was the Glopified soap that made it possible to see Toxites.

Walter shook his head. "I don't have any extra soap. And even if I did, I wouldn't give it to him. Not being able to see the Toxites was the only thing that saved Dez from getting picked apart in the library."

"Besides," Alice said, "if anyone's getting soap, it should be me."

Spencer turned to the half-paralyzed bully. Dez's tough-guy commentary hadn't slowed down at all. "And I'm not afraid of your Toxic breath, either!" he shouted.

"It's actually *Toxite* breath," Spencer said. "Unless it's coming out of you."

"Whatever," Dez said. "You better look out. I just wiggled my little finger."

In response, Daisy tried to wiggle her own little finger. "Hey, how did you do it without moving your other fingers?"

"It's wearing off," Penny said. "We need to get cracking so we can take this boy home."

Walter was caught in a sudden thought, causing his

brow to wrinkle. "Dez will need an application to the Academy program."

"Can't we just print a form off the Internet?" Alice said. "From the Academy's website, like you did?"

"Yes," said Walter. "But it's those signatures that he'll need. Otherwise, they'll never let him in."

"What's the problem, Uncle?" Penny asked. "We've got the stuff here."

"But we don't have time," said Walter. "We need to get moving."

"We can leave it with them. They can copy the signatures later."

"Leave what?" Spencer asked.

Penny reached into the box that she'd brought in from the van and withdrew a small bottle, the kind with a squirt cap.

"What's that?" asked Daisy.

"Ink remover," Penny said. "Janitors use it all the time to clean off pen marks and scribbles on the bathroom walls."

"But this has been Glopified," Walter said. "This is the shortcut we took to get the necessary signatures on your applications."

"What does it do?" Spencer asked.

"It copies ink." Walter took the bottle from Penny's hand. "Once we located the Academy signatures that we needed, we used the Glopified ink remover to make a forgery for your papers. I'll need you to do the same for Dez. All you have to do is wet the Academy signatures. Don't spray too much or you'll have soggy paper. Once the ink is damp, you can press Dez's application against it. The ink will absorb, making an identical copy onto his paper."

"I don't see how this is going to work," Alice said. "Won't the Academy take one look at these signatures and know they were forged? They've got to keep records. They're going to remember that they didn't sign these."

"But these aren't simple forgeries," Penny said. "Uncle Walter Glopified the ink remover with that very problem in mind."

"It works like this," said Walter. "The magic in the Glop duplicates the memory of the original signature. For example, I remember signing a check. If someone uses the ink remover to copy my signature from the check onto another paper, then the memory is copied with it. Therefore, I remember signing the check *and* the paper—even though I never actually signed both."

"Whoa!" said Dez, who was now sitting forward on the couch. "That's genius. I could totally spray Principal Fatso's signature and cancel school for a week!"

"That's exactly why we're *not* giving the ink remover to you," Penny said.

"I developed the formula quite some time ago," Walter continued. "It was getting harder and harder to find equipment for the Rebel schools. I used to buy cheap mops and brooms from janitorial supply stores. Problem is, the BEM owns all those stores and has blocked my signature. So now I use someone else's signature to place my orders. The ink remover works against the BEM, and it will work just fine to get you into the Academy."

Walter handed the ink remover to Spencer, who studied the little bottle. It was pretty amazing what Glop could do. "Any questions?" Walter asked. The boy shook his head. "Let's move on, then."

Penny turned back to the box on the coffee table. "Now comes the fun stuff. New supplies!"

CHAPTER 10

"WHAT ABOUT DEZ'S STOMACH?"

"We've got some fresh gear for you to take to the Academy," Penny explained. "We're not expecting any trouble up there, but you might as well have something to fall back on."

"We didn't bring the larger equipment inside," Walter said. "But we've got the usual for you out in the van. Standard broom, mop, pushbroom."

"And I know you're familiar with this." Penny's hand disappeared into the box and appeared with a few Ziploc bags of vac dust. "Freshly charged. Got it out of the vacuum cleaner earlier today."

She set the clear bags on the coffee table and reached back into the box. "A few more familiar friends," she said, tossing a handful of latex gloves onto the table. The first time Spencer had used such a glove, he had been stealing the magic warlock hammer from Walter Jamison. The wearer of the glove would be able to slip through anyone's fingers without getting held down.

"Uncle Walter's been pretty busy working on some new stuff, too." Penny tucked a strand of red hair behind her ear. "You explain it, Uncle. I don't want to steal your thunder." She handed him a chalkboard eraser.

"This isn't new anymore," Walter said. "Like I explained, throw this against a wall and it explodes into a cloud of paralyzing chalk dust." He set it on the coffee table, and Penny added two more. "You have to be extremely cautious with the erasers. They work well in a room full of Toxites, or to escape from the BEM. But," Walter glanced at Dez, "anyone can get caught in the explosion." He turned to Spencer and Daisy. "Don't use them unless absolutely necessary. The erasers should always be your last resort."

Penny withdrew another object from the box and handed it to Walter. He grinned as he held it up. It had a short handle and a red suction cup at the end.

Spencer raised an eyebrow. "A toilet plunger?"

"This little beauty should come in handy." Walter swung it around like a knight testing a new sword. "The handle is short enough to give you good maneuverability. A direct hit from the rubber end will kill most Toxites. But that's not what makes the plunger special."

Walter crossed the room; Alice stepped away as he neared the couch. "What's a Toxite's natural reaction to being detected?"

"Run and hide," said Daisy.

"Exactly," Walter answered. "So let's say you're hunting Toxites in the teachers' lounge. A Filth knows it's been seen, so it scuttles under the couch." Walter thrust the toilet plunger, and the red cup suctioned onto the side of the leather couch. "No problem," he said. "Just move the couch."

With no apparent effort, Walter lifted the toilet plunger. The attached couch came off the floor, Dez and all. The bully let out a yelp and fell sideways onto the cushions. Walter took a few steps and set the couch down in the hallway. With a twist of the handle, the toilet plunger released from the couch. Walter smiled.

"Is this your idea of feng shui?" Alice asked. "I hope you're going to put that back."

The warlock pulled a face like he'd been caught stealing cookies. With one movement, he latched the plunger to the couch and returned the furniture to its original arrangement.

"I don't think I'm strong enough to do that," Daisy said.

"That's the great thing about these plungers. They adjust the weight and balance of whatever you latch on to. A toddler could pick up this couch."

"What about a house?" Daisy asked. "Could you pick up a house?"

"The plunger has its limits," said Penny. "It can only clamp onto something that has a flat spot big enough for the suction cup. It will clamp onto a wall as tight as you'd like, but you won't be able to lift it. The plunger can only pick up freestanding objects."

"What about a fridge?" Daisy asked.

Penny nodded.

"A bed?"

"Yep."

"A piano?"

"Yep."

"A *grand* piano?"

Penny held up her hands. "Do you know what *freestanding* means?"

"Sure." Daisy nodded. "It means it's not hooked onto anything. What about a guinea pig?"

"No."

"But it's freestanding."

Penny sighed. "It doesn't have a flat spot big enough for the suction cup to take hold."

"What about Dez's stomach? It's pretty big," Daisy observed.

"Hey!" Dez's arm jerked out in a spasm. His elbow buckled and his fist returned to punch himself in the mouth.

"We're making these toilet plungers standard issue for the Rebels," Walter said. "You kids should have them too." Walter offered the plunger to Spencer. The boy eyed the red suction cup nervously.

"Has it been . . . used?" Spencer asked.

"Oh, that's another great feature," Penny said. "That thing will knock out the worst clogs."

Spencer stepped away. He could get by just fine without a toilet plunger.

"She's joking," Walter said. "It's brand-new. I took it

straight from the store to my van, touched it to the Glop formula, and brought it here." Still somewhat reluctant, Spencer took the plunger by the wooden handle. He held it for only a moment, to prove that he could, before setting it on the table.

"That's all for new supplies," Walter said. "We'll give you a few mops and brooms for backup." He dusted his hands together. "That takes care of everything."

Spencer paused. A couple of mops and brooms along with the new cleaning supplies did *not* take care of everything. Walter was avoiding the most important thing. Spencer had been patient, but now it seemed that Walter was planning to leave without mentioning it.

"What about the Vortex?" Spencer asked. The room fell quiet. Penny lifted her eyebrows toward Walter. "What about Marv?" Spencer pressed. "You said he might be alive in there."

The old warlock ran a hand over his bald head. "I know what I said," Walter muttered. "And I believe it. More so now than ever."

"We've been running tests on the Vortex," Penny said, "trying to understand the way it works. The more we understand, the better chance we'll have of finding Marv."

"Here's what we've discovered," said Walter. "The Vortex is still highly charged and dangerous. It didn't appear to lose its potency, even after you pierced it. The magic sealed around the hole you made. There's still a rip, but it's stable enough not to suck everything inside."

"So we decided to crack that seal," Penny said. "This time in a controlled environment."

"A couple of weeks ago, we set up a temporary lab at a Rebel middle school in Nebraska. A bare concrete room in the basement. I knew I could pierce the bag and not get sucked in, as long as I held tightly. So I tried to pry open the Vortex and drain it, to get a glimpse inside. My efforts failed. The Vortex was too strong, and every attempt broke down the walls of the lab until it was unsafe to continue. But on our last attempt, we decided to *let* something get sucked in."

Penny nodded smugly and mouthed the words, "My idea!"

"I entered the experiment room with my cell phone and called Penny," said Walter. "She has one of those fancy new smart phones, so she started recording our conversation. Once the recording had started, I pierced the Vortex and let the magic happen. I saw the phone swirl above my head and fly into the bag."

"That's when things got interesting," Penny cut in. "It got really noisy. From what I could hear on the phone, it was like a hundred TV channels playing at the same time. Then the phone went dead and I lost the call." Penny smiled. "But thanks to my new favorite app, I got the whole thing recorded."

"But we couldn't make sense of it," Walter said, "no matter how many times we listened to the recording. There was just too much noise to filter without help. So we went to see a friend of mine. Guy by the name of Kenny—an audio genius. He filtered the recording layer by layer, isolating sound bytes and playing them for us one after another until we heard something we recognized." Walter nodded for Penny to take over.

The warlock's niece reached into her pocket and withdrew her cell phone. She pressed a few buttons, changed the setting to speakerphone, and held out the device. "Listen to this," she whispered.

Penny pressed "play" and the whole room seemed to freeze. Spencer and his mom were tilting forward with anticipation. Dez was picking his nose, and Daisy's big eyes refused to blink.

The recording was a mess of static. It hissed and fuzzed obnoxiously, Spencer counting the seconds as they rolled by.

"I can't . . ." he squinted. "All I hear is white noise."

Daisy squinted too. "How can you tell what color the noise is?"

There was a sudden break in the static wave. The hiss of nothingness fell away to reveal a deep, gruff voice in perfect clarity. "Hahaha! Gutter ball!"

Click.

The recording ended. It was silent in the Zumbro living room. Then Spencer, Daisy, and Alice started talking at once.

"Was that Marv?"

"He's alive!"

"What did he say?"

Walter held out his hands. "Gutter ball." Walter repeated

the recorded message and followed it up with a quick explanation. "It's a bowling term. Marv loves bowling."

"So he's alive in there!" Spencer said. Speaking it with conviction helped to melt away some of the guilt that lingered from Spencer's decision to pierce the vacuum bag.

"That's our Marv." Penny grinned. "No doubt about it."

"So . . ." Daisy said. "Why is Marv bowling in the Vortex?"

Walter threw his hands in the air and gave a clueless chuckle. "All I know is what you heard. Marv is alive . . . and seems to think he's bowling."

"So what are we waiting for?" Spencer said. "If we know Marv can survive in there, then why don't we send someone in to look for him?"

Walter scratched his head as he shook it from side to side. "Too risky," he muttered. "But I'm working on a plan. It's going to take time, but I think—"

A popping sound interrupted Walter's plan. Everyone turned their attention across the room as Dez began to laugh. Somehow, the bully had recovered the use of his legs, and while Walter and Penny explained their progress with the Vortex, Dez had quietly taken a second plunger from the box. Now he stood in the corner of the room, one hand on the toilet plunger as he balanced Aunt Avril's antique grandfather clock above his head.

CHAPTER 11

"ONLY IN AN EMERGENCY."

"Put down that clock right now, young man!" Alice threatened.

"Chill out!" Dez set the grandfather clock back in its place.

Alice shook her head. "I will not be 'chilled out.' That is a priceless piece."

"I wasn't going to drop it." Dez detached the toilet plunger with a twist of the handle. "I'm good."

Daisy rolled her eyes. "I don't think you even *try* to be good."

"Why bother?" Dez spun the plunger in his hands. "Bad is the new good."

"That doesn't even make sense," said Daisy.

Dez shrugged. "I heard it on a TV show." He set the plunger back into the box.

Walter and Penny traded a glance. "We've got to get him home," Penny said.

"Yeah." Dez looked out the window. "Where are we, anyway?"

"Hillside Estates," said Daisy.

Dez turned to Spencer. "I didn't know you were a rich boy!" He rubbed his hands together. "Why haven't I been taking your lunch money?"

"Penny," Walter said, "why don't you take Dez out to the van? I'll join you in a moment."

Penny crossed the room and put a hand on Dez's shoulder.

"Maybe you could drop a few mops and brooms into the garage," Walter added.

"I'll open the garage door." Alice walked out of the room.

Dez leaned over the Glopified objects on the coffee table, but Penny pulled him away. "Hey! I want my share of the stuff!" He reached for a chalkboard eraser, but Walter blocked his grasp. "Don't you guys believe in sharing? Some of it's mine . . ."

"Only in an emergency," the warlock said. "You haven't been trained with this equipment. Spencer and Daisy will keep it safe. If danger arises at the Academy, you'll get your share."

Penny ushered Dez toward the door. She nodded at Daisy and stopped when she reached Spencer. "Nice to finally meet you," she said.

Spencer stared at Penny's face, that bright red hair

curving around her cheeks. She was so familiar. He knew he'd seen her sleeping in the van's passenger seat.

Penny smiled and extended her hand. "The youngest warlock in history."

Spencer tried not to blush. "Only for a moment." He accepted her handshake.

Without warning, Spencer's vision bleached and he gasped. His eyes opened and he saw a stewardess standing in the aisle beside him.

"Sir," she said, "would you like something to drink?"

Spencer glanced out the small black window of the airplane. Then he turned back to the stewardess. He shook his head and held up a dismissive hand. It was a man's hand, with a white pressed cuff at the wrist.

The woman in the aisle pushed her cart away and he leaned his head back against the airplane seat. Brightness clouded his vision and he squinted against it.

"Spencer?"

He felt someone reaching around him. Red with embarrassment, Spencer realized that he had collapsed into Penny's arms. She helped him stand, eyes full of concern.

"Are you all right, Spencer?" Penny asked.

"Ha ha!" laughed Dez. "I've never seen someone so desperate to get a hug!"

"Get Dez outside," Walter said, coming up alongside Spencer. Penny gave the boy one last worried look before dragging Dez out the front door.

Daisy and Walter helped Spencer to the couch just as Alice reentered the room. She raced to her son. "What's wrong, Spence?" His face was pale and he was shaking slightly.

"Nothing," Spencer said. "I'm okay now." He rubbed his forehead. Were these visions actual glimpses of real life? Was it the future? The past? Or was he imagining things that didn't exist? There was only one way to find out.

"Walter?" Spencer said. "Where were you today at noon?"

"We were driving to Welcher, fast as we could," the warlock answered.

"Did you come through Cheyenne, Wyoming?"

"Yes, we *were* there at noon." Walter put a hand on his bald head. His tone was very serious. "But how could you know that?"

If there were one person who might have answers, Spencer knew it would be Walter Jamison. As crazy as his experiences sounded, Spencer needed to tell all.

"I saw you. No . . . I saw *through* you. Penny was sleeping. You were whistling along to a song on the radio."

"And where were *you?*" Walter asked.

"In Principal Poach's office, picking up a behavior form."

"Did it happen again just now?" Walter gestured to the spot where Spencer and Penny had shaken hands.

Spencer nodded. "I was in an airplane, 35,000 feet above Grand Island, Nebraska, heading west." Spencer held a hand to his head. How did he know that? He'd never even been on a plane before. But somehow he knew the exact location: altitude, latitude, and longitude. Spencer had a perfect fix, tight and sure as a GPS, on the mysterious person seated on that airplane.

"What?" Alice muttered.

"I've never even heard of Grand Island, Nebraska," said Daisy.

"Neither have I," Spencer replied.

"Can you tell me what caused it?" Walter asked. "Can you tell me anything else?"

Spencer shook his head, swallowing against the fear in his chest. "Maybe it was nothing," Spencer tried. "I could have imagined it." But the look in Walter Jamison's eye quickly dismissed that hope.

"Penny and I must go," Walter announced abruptly. "We'll drop Dez at his house and continue out of town. Mrs. Zumbro, let me thank you in advance for taking the children to the Academy program. It should give the Rebel reinforcements time to make Welcher safe again." He zipped his jacket and headed for the door.

Spencer stood up, still shaking. "Wait! Aren't you going to explain what just happened to me?"

The warlock paused at the door and drew in a deep breath. His face looked grim. "I wish I could."

"Well, why can't you?" Daisy asked.

"I don't *know* what's wrong with him."

The thought pierced Spencer. If Walter Jamison didn't know, then who would? And why did Walter say something was *wrong* with him? Wasn't that the word Spencer's mom used about his brother's broken toys?

"Don't speak of your experience to anyone," Walter

said. "Remember, once you get to New Forest Academy, find Roger Munroe. He'll keep you safe."

"When will we see you again?" Spencer asked.

Walter opened the front door. "As soon as I find out what happened to you."

CHAPTER 12

"I DON'T LIKE WHERE THIS IS GOING."

Spencer felt someone shaking him. He rolled over and pulled a pillow onto his head. Was it time to get up already? He knew he'd stayed up too late packing his bag for the coming week at the Academy.

"Spencer," Alice whispered. Her voice didn't have the usual impatient tone of a wake-up call. "They're here."

The words injected immediate alertness into Spencer. He threw off the pillow and sat up, heart thumping. "Who's here, Mom?"

Alice glanced toward Spencer's second-story window. The pale light of dawn was filtering through the blinds. "The BEM. Five men are waiting in the yard outside."

Spencer didn't know why he was surprised. It was Monday, the day they were leaving for the weeklong program at New Forest Academy. Walter had said the BEM would arrive in Welcher today, but Spencer hadn't thought it would be so early. And he certainly hadn't thought they would come straight to his house!

With a shudder, Spencer remembered why the enemy was here. The BEM thought he had something important. They were coming to get it from him. Spencer felt incredibly vulnerable, surrounded in his own house.

"Get your things," his mother said. "We have to go."

"What about Daisy and Dez?"

"I already phoned over to the Gateses and explained that we'd be leaving earlier than planned. Daisy's parents were fine with it. Never takes much to convince them."

"And Dez?" Spencer asked. "He used to have a cell phone." As soon as he said it, Spencer remembered how Mrs. Natcher had confiscated the phone when she caught Dez playing games during science.

"All we have for Dez is an address," Alice said. "It's not too far from the Gates home. Daisy said she'd walk over and get him. We're supposed to pick her up there."

Daisy's courage always surprised Spencer. A few months ago, she'd been terrified of Dez. Now she was willing to make an early-morning visit and pound on his front door until the bully woke up.

Alice glanced nervously at the window again, as if she expected a BEM janitor to come crashing through the glass on a broom.

Spencer tossed away the blankets and put his feet on the floor. His bag was ready to go, so all he had to do was change his clothes. Alice left the room as Spencer slipped into some jeans and a T-shirt. He tied his shoes, grabbed his luggage, and headed down the stairs without even making his bed. That was a first.

Spencer found his mom and three-year-old brother standing in the kitchen. Max was still in his pajamas, a wide yawn stretching his little face. Max was up earlier than usual and had no idea he was about to take a long car ride to Colorado. Since Alice had been planning for an early-morning departure, she'd called in a favor and sent Spencer's other siblings to sleep at a friend's house.

Spencer walked into the living room and peered through the wide window into the front yard. Parked on the street was the vehicle the BEM workers had arrived in. It was an industrial van with a painted logo on the side: *Flood Damage Cleanup & Repair*.

Five men were strategically staggered through the yard: one near the porch steps, one by the side gate, another on the frosted lawn, and two more on the driveway next to the Zumbros' shiny new SUV. The men wore heavy coats and knit beanies. Their breath escaped as puffs of white in the cold November morning. In their gloved hands, they held frostbitten mops and pushbrooms, eager to lash out at something.

Alice suddenly appeared at Spencer's side, staring through the window at their only chance of escape—the SUV.

"You know," Spencer said, "we wouldn't be having this problem if you had let me clean out the garage so we could actually park in it."

"Garages aren't for parking," Alice said. "They're for storage."

"We need a plan," Spencer mused.

"The latex gloves," Alice said. "We could slip past the BEM and get into the car."

"I don't think so," Spencer said. "The gloves won't stop us from getting snagged in their mop strings. Besides, if any of them have on a latex glove under their winter gloves, we're caught for sure."

"A mop, then," Alice tried. "Can't we grab the car with the mop strings and drag it closer to the front door?"

"Not going to work," Spencer said. "I've never seen a mop strong enough to move a car."

"I should just call the police," Alice said.

Spencer shook his head. "The police won't help. Remember last time you called?"

"This is different," said Alice. "There are strangers staked out in our front yard."

"Not strangers. *Flood Damage Cleanup & Repair*." Spencer pointed to their van. "They've got mops. They look totally legit."

Spencer scanned the yard and driveway. There had to be a way to get safely into the Zumbro vehicle. "Do we have all the Glopified equipment in the house?" An idea was forming in Spencer's mind.

"The small stuff is in that cardboard box. The mops and brooms are still in the garage."

"Let's get everything upstairs into the toy room," Spencer said.

"The toy room?" his mother said. "I don't like where this is going. You've got your father's scheming look in your eye."

Spencer walked back into the kitchen, gathered his luggage, and found the cardboard box stocked with equipment. Max was scratching his messy hair, still trying to wake up. Alice slipped past him and quietly entered the cold, dark garage. She reentered the kitchen a moment later, arms laden with brooms and mops.

Spencer ushered Max up the stairs and into the toy room. The first rays of sunlight pierced through the window. Alice carefully set down the Glopified supplies.

Walking over to the huge toy box, Spencer started digging. He found what he was looking for buried at the bottom, forgotten since the weather turned cold. Four of his sisters' jump ropes were tangled together in a mess.

"No," Max said. "I don't wanna play jumpy rope. Let's play trucks!"

Spencer took a moment to untangle the ropes. Then, with his very tightest knots, he tied the jump ropes together in a long line. Crossing the room, he reached into the box of Glopified supplies and pulled out a toilet plunger.

"Time to put Walter's equipment to the test." Spencer picked up the jump ropes and tied one end squarely to the handle of the toilet plunger.

"Whatcha doing?" Max asked. Spencer crossed the room without answering his little brother. He opened the large window and peered outside. The toy room window had lost its screen last summer when Max pushed too hard. Now

Spencer could lean over the open sill and get a perfect view of the driveway directly below.

"This is not a good idea," Alice muttered. But she didn't try to stop Spencer as he leaned out the window. In fact, Alice was reluctant to come within ten feet of the high, open window. Her fear of heights had kicked in as soon as Spencer opened the glass.

He would have to be quick. If the BEM sensed any movement from above, it could ruin his whole plan. Spencer held the plunger in one hand and the end of the jump rope in his other. The alignment couldn't have been much better. The SUV was parked directly below the toy room window.

Holding his breath for luck, Spencer took aim and dropped the toilet plunger.

CHAPTER 13

"ARE YOU TRICKIN' ME?"

The red suction cup made a resounding *pop* as it clamped onto the top of the SUV. The five BEM workers in the yard jumped at the sound, bringing their Glopified weapons to the ready. By the time they spotted the jump ropes dangling from the toy room, Spencer was already heaving.

The automobile felt lightweight as Spencer pulled the jump ropes hand over hand. Unfortunately, he hadn't considered the angle of ascent. As soon as the four tires lifted from the driveway, the SUV swung inward like a pendulum, smashing the passenger side of the vehicle into the garage door below. Spencer winced at the sound. Max laughed and clapped his hands.

Alice started jabbering in a nervous monologue. Her speech consisted mostly of the word *stop*. Alice repeated it over and over again, sometimes in short staccato, sometimes drawn out like she was talking in slow motion. Spencer's mother even went so far as to spell it. "S-T-O-P!" Like phonetics might help get her point across.

But Spencer didn't stop. And he knew Alice wouldn't interrupt him, either. Spencer was using his mom's fear of heights, giving him space to carry out his half-baked plan.

Each tug on the rope lifted the car higher, scraping and grinding the right side of the vehicle as it dragged up the front of the house.

A vacuum sound came from the driveway below. A puff of vac dust from one of the BEM men struck the bottom of the rising car. The suction force on the SUV jerked Spencer forward. He slammed into the windowsill and felt the jump rope dragging him over.

Just when Spencer thought he was going to swan dive onto the concrete driveway, Alice broke her panicky monologue, leapt forward, and grabbed his legs. Her eyes were closed with fear, but she pulled with all the desperation of an overly protective mother.

Mop strings, cast from below, whipped against the toy-room window and licked at the underside of the dangling SUV. But the car was too high for the mops to get a solid grip on such a large object.

The vac dust subsided, causing Alice and Spencer to stumble backward. The SUV grated against the last few feet of brick and came to rest at the base of the toy-room window. The top of the car was level with the windowsill, like a perilous balcony.

"Okay, Mom," Spencer said. "You're not going to like this, but I need you and Max to climb onto the roof of the car." To show that it was secure, Spencer picked up his luggage with one hand and tossed it onto the car. The SUV wobbled unconvincingly, but at least the plunger's grip was trustworthy.

Alice's face was white, her hands shaking. She swallowed hard and shook her head. This was going to take some serious convincing.

"Max," Spencer said. "Can you be brave and show Mom what to do?"

"No, Max," said Alice.

Spencer hated going against his mom like this, but it was their only chance of escape. "Max. I need you to climb out the window and lie down on top of the car."

His little brother pulled a face. "Are you trickin' me?"

"No, I'm serious. If you do it, I promise I'll give you all my leftover Halloween candy." It wasn't much, but the offer of candy settled it for Max.

The little boy ran to the windowsill, and Spencer boosted him with a knee. Alice gave a shriek as her youngest son crawled onto the top of the hanging vehicle.

That seemed to spur her motherly instincts. She raced to the window. Max was clinging tightly to the car, a mischievous smile on his face. "Spencer Alan Zumbro!" Alice shouted. "Are you out of your mind?"

Spencer heard shouting from the BEM workers below. One said, "They're climbing out the window!" Another called, "Get the brooms from the van!"

If the enemy had brooms, Spencer's advantage would be ruined. Spencer pointed at the pile of Glopified equipment. "Please, Mom. I need you to get all that stuff on top of the car."

More shouting from the driveway below.

"If we don't get out of here, they'll . . . they'll . . ." Would the BEM actually kill him if they had the chance?

"They'll what?" Alice shouted.

"They'll take me." He lowered his voice. "Just like they took Dad." Spencer didn't know for sure if the BEM was behind his father's disappearance, but he hoped the implication would be enough to spur his mom into action.

Alice's face was tight. Spencer knew the look. She was trying to hold back her temper. "You're going to be in so much trouble if we survive this!"

Alice grabbed the box of Glopified equipment and shoved it recklessly onto the roof of the car. Max giggled as the SUV teetered and grated against the house.

Spencer used his foot to scoot a broom within arm's reach. He'd need a broom in order for this plan to succeed. Spencer gestured to the rest of the pile. "Quick, Mom." He glanced at the BEM men below, already headed back from the van with Glopified brooms.

Muttering incoherently, Alice gathered up the load of mops and brooms. Then, closing her eyes against the height of the open window, Alice extended her arms and pushed the supplies onto the car. She cracked one eye open.

"I can't do this," Alice whispered, suddenly dizzy. "I can't climb out there."

"You've got to," Spencer urged. "It's the only way."

Max turned to the open window. "It's fun," he said. Then, to Alice's horror, the three-year-old stood up. Once she got over the urge to faint, Alice found the courage to climb onto the windowsill.

"Sit down, Max!" she said. "You sit down right now!"

Instead, the little guy took two shaky steps forward and reached a hand out for his mother. "Come on," he said. "It's okay out here."

Alice grabbed Max's hand and slid off the windowsill. The car shifted with her weight and Max toppled into her arms. Holding her son tightly, Alice went spread-eagle on her stomach, gripping the car top rack with white knuckles.

In the driveway below, the BEM workers were spreading out with their brooms, gauging the distance and angle of the flight that would get them to the window. Spencer knew he had one chance to get safely away. If he failed, it could cause immeasurable damage to property, not to mention serious injury to his mom and brother.

Holding the SUV easily with one hand on the rope, Spencer bent down and picked up the broom he'd scooted aside. He backed across the toy room, feeding the jump ropes through his hands as he went. He'd need lots of momentum for this to work.

Spencer had his back to the wall, the jump ropes stretching across the toy room and the SUV still dangling at the windowsill. Suddenly, two BEM workers soared into view on brooms, closing on the toy-room window from both sides. Spencer hefted the broom in his left hand and drew a deep breath.

He sprinted forward, kicking and scattering toys in his way. The jump rope went slack and the SUV plummeted toward the driveway. Spencer heard his mother scream as he vaulted through the open window and slammed the bristles of the broom against the sill.

Spencer shot forward like a bottle rocket, narrowly missing the airborne BEM workers and angling up and away from the house. The jump rope went taut and the SUV swung over the driveway, barely escaping mop strings from another BEM worker below.

Max was laughing, Alice was screaming, and Spencer breathed a sigh of relief. It worked! The Glopified toilet plunger had adjusted the car's weight so the broom was easily able to bear the load away.

They soared over the street and Spencer squinted against the light as the sun peered over the neighbor's roof. Eyes widening, Spencer realized that he'd breathed that sigh of relief too soon.

From his angle on the broom, Spencer would easily clear the roof of the house across the street. But the SUV, dangling so many feet below, was on a flight path straight for the neighbor's second-story window!

Spencer fought the urge to panic. He glanced over his shoulder and noticed that the three BEM workers from the driveway had struck their brooms and launched in pursuit of the escaping SUV.

Instinct told Spencer how to react. He swung the rope

up, looping it over the flying broom. Using one hand, he began to pull frantically.

He seemed to be hoisting the car in slow motion. Despite the cold, Spencer's hands grew sweaty as the time to impact drew nearer.

Glancing down, he saw the SUV only feet away from the neighbor's house. Closing fast, the nearest BEM worker reached out, almost seizing the vehicle's bumper.

Desperately, Spencer gave one final pull on the rope, as hard as he could. The dangling car lifted above the gutter, but not quite high enough.

The SUV tires squealed as they dragged along the roof's shingles, leaving four tracks of black rubber across the frosted rooftop. Spencer's broom jerked and he almost lost his grip. But the Glopified broom was powerful, and the toilet plunger was still working its magic on the payload.

The SUV bounced off the roof, cleared the peak of the house, and sailed freely over the neighbor's backyard. The pursuing BEM workers did not share the same fortune. The unalterable course of their brooms sent them slamming into the side of the neighbor's house. Spencer cringed at the sound of shattering glass; he could only assume that one of the BEM workers had sailed right into the neighbor's second-story bedroom. *Flood Damage Cleanup & Repair* was going to have a lot of explaining to do.

The ground dropped suddenly as the Zumbros' flying vehicle soared away from the steep slope of Hillside Estates. There were no obstacles now, just the open farm fields of small-town Welcher.

The Glopified broom gradually descended. The SUV touched down first, bouncing and skidding into a freshly harvested field of potatoes. The jump rope went tight, angling the broom into a nosedive. Spencer let go just before he hit the cold ground.

Spencer rose to his feet and dusted off his knees. In contrast to the rush of flying and the anxiety of their escape, it seemed peaceful and quiet in the middle of the potato field. Spencer couldn't have asked for a much better landing pad.

"Spencer?" his mom called from the top of the vehicle.

"I'm okay, Mom," he answered.

"Well, you better enjoy your last few moments of being okay, because as soon as I get down from here . . ."

CHAPTER 14

"DON'T GET ALL TECHNICAL ON ME."

Alice actually calmed down a lot faster than Spencer thought she would. In no time, they had the car loaded and running. Spencer clipped on his seat belt as they drove through the bumpy field of potatoes.

Max made some noise, strapped into his car seat, but other than that, the drive to Dez's was remarkably silent. The passenger side of the SUV was scratched terribly, the side mirror broken completely off. Spencer apologized again, but the look on his mom's face said she wasn't ready to accept it yet.

Spencer sighed. Maybe he had been wrong. Maybe there had been a better way to escape than flying the SUV recklessly through Hillside Estates. His mom had shared a few ideas, but Spencer had quickly dismissed them. He'd taken on the situation alone, just like when he'd pulled the fire alarm, or rushed into the library to rescue Dez from the chalk bomb.

"This is it," Alice said, pulling the car into a tight parking lot.

"Dez lives here?" Spencer scanned the area in disbelief. It was a row of dingy, small apartments. Trash littered the parking lot; rust stains dripped down the walls. Paint peeled off the doors, like it was trying to get away. Rickety metal stairs led to a second floor of apartments.

Alice put her hand on the horn, but before she could honk, a door at the top of the stairs opened. Daisy came out, suitcase in hand. Her coat was zipped to her neck and she wore winter gloves. She reached the SUV and tossed in her suitcase as Dez appeared at the top of the stairs, pulling the apartment door shut.

"I'm glad you guys finally got here," Daisy said. "It was *so* hot in there."

Spencer saw that Daisy's hair was clinging to her forehead with sweat. "Why didn't you take off your coat?" Spencer asked.

Daisy lowered her voice. "There was nowhere to put it." She shuddered. "You would have died in there, Spencer."

Daisy glanced up the stairs to where Dez was struggling to lock the apartment door. She jumped into the SUV and started describing the apartment in fast-forward, trying to tell as much as possible before Dez reached the vehicle.

"The whole place smelled like the inside of a shoe, and there was garbage and stuff all over the floor, and it looked like nobody has ever tried to clean up. The TV was on, but it was playing a channel that I'm not supposed to watch, so I didn't, but I saw Dez's dad asleep on the couch. All he was wearing were little shorts—no shirt. All around him were empty cans. He must have been really thirsty, 'cause there were a lot of them. Then, all of a sudden, he just sat up—like a zombie coming out of the ground. He shouted five bad words and threw one of those Coke cans across the room, hard as he could. Then, *bam*, back to sleep on the couch."

"Um," Alice said, "I don't think those were Coke cans."

"Well, it didn't look like Sprite," said Daisy.

The car door suddenly opened as Dez reached the vehicle. It was like someone pressed a mute button on Daisy. Her stream of commentary about Dez's home life ended instantly.

"What took you chumps so long?" Dez threw in his bag and climbed into the SUV.

"We flew!" Max said.

"Oh, seriously?" Dez moaned. "I have to sit by the little kid?"

"No, you don't *have to*," Alice said. "Spencer would be more than happy to strap you on *top* of the car, if you might like that better."

"No, thanks," Daisy said. "Too windy up there."

"Mom," Spencer begged, "I said I'm sorry."

"Sorry for what?" Daisy asked.

Alice peeled out of the parking lot as Spencer tried to explain how they'd escaped from the BEM at Hillside Estates.

"You flew the car over your neighbor's house?" Daisy's eyes were wide when Spencer finished the story.

Dez rolled his eyes. "Come on, Gullible Gates," he said, bringing back his old nickname for Daisy. "Don't tell me you believe that junk." Dez suddenly reached up and pinched Spencer's arm.

"Ow!" Spencer jerked away. "Why would you do that?"

Dez shrugged. "This whole conversation about flying cars is so *Twilight Zone* . . . I had to make sure I wasn't dreaming."

"Um . . . don't you usually pinch *yourself* to see if you're dreaming?" Daisy asked.

"You think I'm dumb?" said Dez. "I don't want to hurt myself."

"Look," Spencer said, trying to regain control of the conversation. "No one's dreaming, and no one got hurt."

"What about me?" said Alice. "Deep wounds here, Spencer." She pointed to her head. "Serious emotional damage to your mother." Her face went tight again. "We all could have died."

"Wasn't there another way out?" Daisy said.

"I had a few ideas," Alice said. "Apparently they weren't risky enough for Spencer."

Spencer slumped against the passenger seat. The SUV filled with awkward silence. It was going to be a long drive to Colorado.

"Here." It was Dez who broke the silence. "I filled out that application you printed for me." He handed the

Academy paperwork to Spencer. "Why'd they have to ask such hard questions?"

"Well, let's see . . ." Spencer unfolded the papers. "Yep. You got your name right. Wait. Here's a tricky one. *What is your birthday?*"

"Hey! Stop looking at my answers!" Dez shouted. "Spencer's cheating!" He lunged for the application, but Spencer pulled away.

"I've still got to spray the signatures," Spencer said.

"Well, hurry up and do it."

Spencer unfolded his own application and looked at the list of signatures at the bottom. Most were so extravagant that they weren't even legible—big loops and indecipherable scribbles. They would have been impossible to forge by hand, but they didn't stand a chance against Walter's Glopified ink remover.

Spencer reached between the seats and grabbed the small bottle from the box of supplies. He pulled off the plastic cap and gave a few sprays onto the signatures. A fine mist settled, and the paper barely wrinkled from the moisture. The handwritten names seemed to absorb the Glopified spray.

Before it could dry, Spencer took Dez's application and pressed it tightly against the damp ink. When he peeled the papers apart, the original signatures looked untouched, but an identical copy had bled through onto Dez's page.

"So," Dez piped up. "What kind of stuff are we going to do at this sissy Academy?"

Alice glanced at him in the rearview mirror. "You're going to stay out of trouble and do what you're told."

"Oh, please," Dez said. "You're starting to sound like the mother I never had."

"Not true," said Daisy. "If you never had a mother, then how were you born?"

Dez stuck out his tongue. "Don't get all technical on me."

Spencer blew on Dez's copied signatures, but the replica was already dry. Folding the application, he handed it back to Dez.

"Perfect copy," said Spencer.

"Good," said Dez. "Now you can give me that spray stuff so I can change a few things."

Spencer pulled the ink remover away as Dez lunged for it from the backseat. "You heard Walter," Spencer said. "You're not getting any of the Glopified supplies unless there's an emergency."

Dez suddenly crossed his legs and rocked back and forth, pretending like he had to use the bathroom. "What kind of emergency?"

"It's for Toxites," Daisy said. "Or in case the BEM finds us."

"You keep saying that," Dez said. "But it sounds lame."

Spencer and Daisy shared a quick glance. Walter had told them to answer Dez's questions. It was better that he learn it from them than any other source. Taking a deep breath, Spencer started explaining the basics.

He told how the invisible Toxites inhale kids' brain

waves and exhale sleepiness, distraction, and apathy, so that kids couldn't learn in school. But the Toxites didn't affect all the kids in the same way. Daisy was more prone to the distracting breath of the Grimes, while Spencer had a hard time resisting the sleepiness from the Filths. Bullies like Dez had a higher tolerance for the Toxites overall, since the creatures wouldn't waste their breath on kids who didn't really want to learn.

Spencer went on to tell how the Bureau of Educational Maintenance had protected schools for centuries by hiring janitors who could see and kill the little monsters. For no apparent reason, the BEM had recently withdrawn all support from the schools and were letting Toxites run wild. They were destroying education and, with it, the future. Other janitors, like Walter and Marv, had banded together to form a Rebel Underground, dedicated to go against the BEM and continue to fight Toxites in schools.

The more Spencer explained, the faster Alice seemed to drive. Time passed quickly, with Daisy adding her own comments about the situation. Dez sat quietly through most of it. His expression was unreadable. Surprisingly, he didn't have any questions.

Dez listened passively as Daisy described the sludge-like Glop that gave the janitorial equipment magical powers. She explained about the three Founding Witches who had discovered Toxites. When they died, they placed their magic into three bronze hammers, each with a matching nail. The bronze hammers were passed down among the

BEM for years until Walter stole one for the Rebels and made himself a warlock.

Spencer jumped in again, adding any final details that he could think of. At last, exhausted, Spencer and Daisy leaned back, having explained everything they knew.

Dez rode silently for a moment, staring out the window at the passing mountain landscape. "So . . ." he said at last. "When do I get my share of the stuff?"

Daisy slumped back against the headrest. "Not unless there's an emergency!" she said. "That's what we just finished explaining."

"Sorry," Dez said. "I kind of zoned out after a while. You guys talk way too much."

CHAPTER 15

"IT'S JUST CLEANING STUFF."

Alice almost missed the freeway exit, darting across two lanes of traffic and onto the off-ramp without even using the car's blinker. The movement caused Spencer to jolt awake.

"Everything okay?" he asked. His mom's eyes were glazed after so many hours behind the wheel.

"Fine," she said. "We'll be there soon."

The great metropolis of Denver lay to the southeast. But the directions to New Forest Academy took them through the residential outskirts, winding westward toward the mountains.

Alice mostly ignored the speed limit, and soon they were driving a long road at the base of the mountains. The late autumn scenery was amazing. Most of the trees were already bare for the winter. Dead leaves whipped across the road.

Alice slowed down at an intersection and quickly consulted the scrap of paper that bore Walter's directions to New Forest Academy. A car behind them honked and swerved around the Zumbro SUV. Alice checked the street sign and then turned onto a narrow, twisting road that rose steeply up the mountainside.

"You told me we were going to a school." Dez watched the mountains through his window. "Aren't schools usually in cities?"

"We're not lost, if that's what you mean," said Alice. As if on cue, they crested a hill and the road flattened out. Before them was a wide parking lot dotted with cars. A huge sign hung on the side of the road, as big as a billboard.

WELCOME TO NEW FOREST ACADEMY
HOME OF THE OVERACHIEVERS

As Alice pulled the vehicle into the parking lot, Spencer got his first look at New Forest Academy. A tall brick wall fenced in the large campus, blocking any view other than the tops of the school buildings. Behind the man-made structures, the mountain continued to rise in a forested incline.

The whole school seemed to be nestled quietly into the mountainside with the city far below. It was remarkable how removed the campus felt, even though Alice had just been driving through neighborhoods not ten minutes ago.

Alice drove toward a wide gate in the brick wall. The gate looked sturdy, and the man in the operating booth looked even more so.

Alice rolled down her window. The outside air was chilly, and Spencer was glad he'd brought his heavy coat. The man in the booth leaned out.

"Hi," Alice said. "I'm here to drop off some kids for the New Forest Academy recruitment program."

The man checked his watch. "You're early."

Alice shrugged. "We're overachievers." She gave a gesture for him to open the gate.

"You have your registration papers?"

Spencer felt a twinge of nervousness as his mom passed the applications through the window. How good was Walter's Glopified ink remover? Would the man know that the official Academy signatures had been forged?

The man disappeared into the booth for a moment. He returned with a furrowed look. "We don't seem to have your information on file."

"We were a bit late with the registration," Alice bluffed. She handed the man the envelope of money that Penny had given her. "But they said there wouldn't be a problem. They said as long as we had the applications signed, that we'd get in."

Alice was starting to get upset. Spencer had never considered his mother much of an actress, but she was doing a decent job at it.

The man nodded apologetically. "I'm going to call down the program director. If there's a problem, we'll fix it." He smiled congenially. "If you'd like to park over there, ma'am." He pointed across the parking lot. "For the safety of the students, only authorized vehicles are admitted into New Forest Academy."

Alice threw the car in reverse and spun around. There were several cars in the parking lot, but Alice found a spot near a maintenance shed and a couple of dumpsters.

"If they're not going to let our car in," Spencer said, "how are we supposed to get our Glopified stuff into the Academy? Won't it look kind of suspicious if we go walking in with janitorial supplies?"

"It's just cleaning stuff," Dez said incredulously. "It's not like we're trying to smuggle guns and knives."

Their attention returned to the brick wall as the gate swung open mechanically. A black car idled in the gateway, the driver conversing with the man in the booth. After a moment, the gatekeeper pointed toward the Zumbro SUV.

"I don't want to risk it," Daisy whispered, as if the black car were close enough to hear. "I mean, what if they examined our stuff and took it away?"

"We have to try," said Spencer. "We can't just send the supplies home with my mom." The Academy car pulled away from the gate booth.

"How about this," Alice said. "I'll leave the stuff behind these dumpsters. You can come out and get it later, when the coast is clear."

"What if someone finds it before we get back?" Spencer asked.

"I'll hide it under a bush."

"What about squirrels?" Daisy said. Everyone turned to her with puzzled expressions. Daisy shrugged. "Well, we *are* in the mountains. What if squirrels steal our stuff?"

Spencer shook his head. "Why would squirrels steal cleaning supplies? You think they mop and vacuum?"

The black car came to a stop behind the SUV. A Latino man with dark hair and sunglasses stepped out. He was well dressed, with a striped collared shirt and a sport coat.

The man waited with a broad white smile as the three kids gathered their backpacks and luggage from the SUV. A moment later, all of them were standing in the parking lot, the cold mountain air nipping their faces. The man from the black car extended a handshake to Alice.

"Welcome to New Forest Academy! My name is Carlos Garcia." His voice carried the hint of a Spanish accent. Spencer recognized the name. It was one of the signatures he'd forged with the ink remover.

"Alice Zumbro," she said. "This is my son Spencer and his friends Daisy and Dez."

Garcia shook each of their hands, his expression warm and friendly. "My apologies about the confusion at the gate. Not sure why your information wasn't on file. I remember signing your applications."

Spencer glanced at Daisy, hopeful that she wouldn't say anything. The ink remover was amazing stuff. Just as Walter had explained, the Glopified solution had created a duplicate memory, making Carlos Garcia think that he remembered signing the applications.

Garcia went on. "As the director of New Forest

Academy, I hope you will have an enjoyable week with us. This recruitment program is a wonderful opportunity for you to learn what our school is all about. At the same time, we can evaluate your performance and decide if we want you to study with us as a regular, full-time student."

Dez groaned. "I liked everything until the part when you said *study*."

"Studying doesn't have to be boring. I hope we can help you learn to love it." Director Garcia smiled again, a warm gesture. "Let's head in, if you have everything." He nodded to Alice. "A pleasure meeting you. Your children are in good hands here."

"I see that," Alice said. She pulled Spencer into a half hug. "You'll call me tonight?" she asked.

Spencer glanced questioningly at Director Garcia. Did they even have phone service here in the mountains?

"Of course," Garcia said. "It is our policy to have each of the recruits call home on the first evening."

Max shouted something from inside the SUV, still strapped into the confines of his car seat. Alice took a hesitant step back toward the vehicle. "Better get going," she said. Then, turning to Spencer, she gave her son some very clear instructions. "Be safe."

CHAPTER 16

"JUST COME THIS WAY."

The campus of New Forest Academy was much nicer and more modern than Spencer had expected. Driving through the gate was like discovering an oasis of civilization in the mountains. On the other side of the brick wall, the landscape provided an enormous open area, dotted with buildings and playgrounds.

The brick wall ringed in the front half of the campus, while the natural incline of the forested mountain closed in the back half. It was like the school grounds were nestled into a pocket in the mountain. It certainly felt safe, all boxed in.

"How did you find this place?" Spencer asked.

Director Garcia grinned. "It didn't always look like this. We made some major modifications before building the school. Dynamite blasting, excavation, more blasting . . .

this campus is many years in the making. And we're still doing alterations." He pointed out the window. "Can you guess what we're putting in over there?"

Spencer looked across the campus and saw a backhoe and a crane near the trees. He could just glimpse a large area roped off with yellow caution tape.

"A swimming pool?" Daisy guessed.

"No," said Dez. "It's a giant Porta-Potty!"

"Nothing like that," Garcia said. "We're putting in an underground parking garage. We should be finished with construction in a week or two."

"Why did you choose to build the school here?" Spencer asked. "Why not down in the city?"

"There's something enchanting about going into the mountains to learn," Director Garcia said. "Our students are far from distractions and the corruption of civilization. It's safe and remote. Research has found such environments to foster the greatest learning."

"Sounds like a snooze," Dez muttered. "I should have brought my pillow."

Spencer elbowed Dez in the ribs. They were supposed to act like ordinary students. Dez's attitude was going to blow their cover.

Director Garcia didn't seem to notice Dez's commentary. There was a stirring energy about the man, the way he talked about the Academy, the way he gazed proudly out the car window. Director Garcia's enthusiasm was contagious, and Spencer felt a twinge of excitement in his stomach.

"Does this place even have electricity?" said Dez. "Or do we have to use those weird plug-in lights?"

"New Forest Academy sports an eco-friendly campus. We're equipped with the finest facilities and state-of-the-art technology. And everything is solar-powered," answered Garcia. "Only the best of the best for our students."

The director stopped the car at a crosswalk as a group of uniformed students headed from one building to another. The students looked clean and sharp. Despite the strict uniform, they found ways to express themselves. The boys had stylish haircuts; the girls were covered in expensive-looking jewelry. They carried themselves with an air of self-importance that bordered on arrogance.

"So, parents have to drive clear up here to drop off their kids every day?" Spencer asked.

"Many do," Garcia said. "We draw largely from families in the Denver area. No more than an hour drive to get here. Many parents strongly believe that public schools are failing to educate their children. They believe, as I do, that New Forest Academy is the solution. They're willing to make the commute so their kids can get a proper education."

The car rolled forward again. "For the older kids, we have a boarding program. Grades five through nine can actually live on campus in our comfortable dormitories."

"I can't think of anything worse than living at school," Dez said.

"What about getting paper cuts on your eyeballs?" said Daisy. "That would be worse, don't you think?"

"Since you're a few hours early," Garcia said, pulling the

car into a small parking lot, "I'm going to drop you kids at the computer lab. You can keep yourselves entertained until the recruitment dinner."

"Yeah!" Dez said. "I love computer games!" He put an imaginary bazooka on his shoulder and started making explosion sounds, bits of spit flecking from his mouth. "Do you have *Slaughterguts 900?*"

Director Garcia turned a disapproving glare on Dez. The bully, unaffected by such stares, threw an imaginary grenade as he strode past Spencer and Daisy.

Garcia led the three kids into the warm building. Spencer peered into the first classroom and saw rows of tables with top-of-the-line flat screen computers. Academy students sat attentively at each monitor. Spencer had never seen such a well-behaved class. It was the extreme opposite of his class in the Welcher Elementary library last Friday.

"Let's make sure they have room for three more," said Garcia. He slipped into the computer lab to talk to the media specialist, leaving Spencer, Daisy, and Dez alone in the hallway.

"So," Dez said, "when are we going back for the stuff your mom hid in the bushes?"

Spencer and Daisy hushed him simultaneously, glancing around to make sure they were really alone. "We'll talk about it later," Spencer whispered.

"I just want to make sure I don't get left behind." Dez folded his big arms.

Spencer yawned, his mouth stretching wide and his eyes squinting closed. He had a right to be tired, after getting up so early to escape Hillside Estates. But as Spencer shook his head to clear out the sleepiness, he saw Daisy pointing down the hallway and he knew that this sudden twinge of fatigue was not natural.

A Filth had rounded the corner, scurrying like an overgrown rat. Dusty quills shook as it limped sideways. The creature slammed into the wall, righted itself, and kept running toward them.

"What are you looking at?" Dez squinted in the same direction as his peers.

"It's injured," Spencer whispered.

"What?" said Dez. "What's injured? Your brain?"

"I thought Walter said there weren't Toxites here!" Daisy said.

"No," Spencer corrected. "He said that Roger Munroe was supposed to have killed them all off."

As if in response to this comment, a wiry man leapt around the corner at the end of the hallway. From his left hand came a well-aimed funnel throw of vacuum dust. A suction sound ripped down the hallway and the Filth collapsed. The little monster quivered on the floor as a mop from the man's other hand stretched out to crush the Toxite.

The kids stood in surprised silence, watching the mop strings retract from the spot where the Filth had been destroyed. "Let me guess." Dez tapped Daisy on the arm. "He just killed a . . . thingy."

"Toxite," Daisy corrected.

The thin man approached the kids, walking cautiously

along the wall of the hallway. He had oily black hair that came to a sharp widow's peak but slicked straight back from his broad forehead to form a straggly mullet. His skin was pale and pocked from old acne. A pair of thick glasses, desperately needing to be washed, sat heavily on his large hooked nose.

Spencer waited for some kind of greeting from the janitor. When it didn't come, he looked at the man's face for any sign of recognition. But the beady black eyes behind the dirty glasses just shifted back and forth nervously.

"Roger!" Spencer finally said. It had to be him. This was New Forest Academy's Rebel Janitor that Walter had told them to contact.

"Where are you kids supposed to be?" the janitor said, pointing an accusatory mop handle at them. His voice carried a slight country drawl, but it wasn't friendly like Daisy's dad. This man's voice was too crackly, almost like a raven's caw.

"It's okay," Spencer said. "Walter told us to find you. Roger Munroe?"

The janitor's entire expression changed. His eyes flicked down the hallway. The man swallowed, his sharp Adam's apple sliding along his throat. "Why don't you kids come with me?"

Spencer stepped forward, but Daisy grabbed his sleeve. "Shouldn't we wait for Director Garcia?" She glanced at the computer lab. "He'll wonder where we've gone."

"It don't matter," the janitor said. "Just come this way. We need to talk."

The door to the computer lab suddenly opened and Director Garcia reappeared, looking surprised to see the Academy janitor in the hallway. "Hello, Mr. Fletcher."

"Mr. *Fletcher?*" Spencer muttered.

The janitor wiped his nose with the back of his hand. His lips were quivering as though he wanted to say something but didn't dare. Instead, he nodded respectfully to his boss.

"Are you the janitor here?" Spencer tried to ask with tact, but Daisy cut him off bluntly.

"Where's Roger Munroe?" she asked.

"You know Munroe?" Garcia raised his eyebrows.

"Uh . . ." Spencer swallowed. "Yeah. Roger is Daisy's uncle."

Daisy's mouth fell open in surprise. "He is?"

Spencer nodded unconvincingly. "Remember? Second uncle, once removed."

"Removed from what?" Daisy said.

"Removed from New Forest Academy," answered the wiry janitor, swinging the mop over his shoulder. "Munroe *quit.*"

"Quit?" Spencer's legs felt suddenly weak.

"Last Friday," Director Garcia said. "Mr. Munroe resigned suddenly. Fortunately, Mr. Fletcher was able to step in quickly to this new position. He's our computer technician, but he's had some cleaning experience and was willing to fill in as our custodian."

"Please," said the janitor, wiping a hand across his greasy black hair. "Call me Slick."

Spencer and Daisy looked at one another, trying not to let their shock betray them. Slick wasn't just an average temporary custodian. He was a janitor! Slick had seen that Toxite and executed it with precision and skill.

"I thought we were gonna play some computer games." Dez broke the silence.

Director Garcia nodded. "There's a computer ready for each of you." He gestured for them to enter the lab. "I'll drop your bags at the dormitories, and someone will come get you when it's time for the recruitment dinner."

Dez pushed into the lab and Daisy followed close behind. Spencer stood rooted in place as Slick turned away from the computer lab and sauntered down the hallway, his mop strings still dangling over his thin shoulder.

It didn't seem right. Roger Munroe was gone, having suspiciously resigned only three days ago. Now Slick had taken over as New Forest Academy's janitor. Spencer knew nothing about Slick, but the whole situation seemed unsettling.

"Is everything all right?" Director Garcia's voice startled Spencer. The boy nodded, pasting on a false smile. But everything was not all right.

CHAPTER 17

"DID YOU GET STRANGLED TOO?"

Spencer dragged his last slice of steak through a dab of A.1. sauce and popped it into his mouth. It was the best cafeteria food Spencer had ever tasted, and the Academy claimed it was organic and healthy, too.

It was a welcome dinner for the students who had arrived for the recruitment program. They totaled fifty kids, ranging from fourth grade to seventh. Lots of them picked at their dinner hesitantly, faces creased with nerves for the week to come.

Daisy was leaning back in her chair, studying the other students while Dez picked over his sautéed green beans. It was an added measure of comfort to be surrounded by two friends. Well, one friend and one nuisance.

Director Carlos Garcia suddenly stood up and clapped

his hands for attention. A few conversations had broken out among the recruits, but they ended instantly.

"Welcome to New Forest Academy!" He opened his arms in a warm gesture. "You're all here because you have an interest in attending this great school."

"Not *all* of us," Dez muttered under his breath.

"New Forest Academy is in its sixth year and growing rapidly. Our mission is to provide a successful education to any student who qualifies.

"At the end of this week, some of you—and I hope it will be many—will receive an invitation to attend New Forest Academy. That invitation has the power to change your future. But such an invitation must be earned. This week will be challenging. We plan to test you in every way: academically, socially, mentally, physically."

Spencer noticed that Daisy had a plastic spoon to her mouth, chewing nervously on the end. She saw him staring and whispered, "What if I don't pass?"

"It's okay, Daisy," Spencer said. Her spoon suddenly snapped between her teeth. Spencer ducked as a piece of it went shooting over his head. "We're not here to get accepted, remember?" Daisy set down the broken spoon and nodded, relieved by Spencer's reminder.

"The first thing you must do is divide into teams," Director Garcia explained. "There are fifty handkerchiefs on the table in the back of the cafeteria." He pointed, and all the students turned to look. "There are five different colors, so, five different teams. When I clap my hands, you have exactly three minutes to get the color you want and group yourselves into color-coordinating teams."

Director Garcia lifted his hands and swung them together into a single clap that resonated through the large cafeteria.

The students sat silently for a moment until one kid suddenly scrambled out of his chair and dashed toward the back table. Like a small stone that starts an avalanche, forty-nine students instantly scrambled after him, their voices rising to a squall.

"Let me through!"

"Give it to me!"

"That one's mine!"

Someone checked into Spencer and he skidded sideways, toppling into Daisy. They were in a tight press of bodies crowding the table with the colored handkerchiefs.

"Which color are we supposed to get?" Daisy asked.

"Don't think it matters." Spencer shoved against a large kid. "Let's just try to get two of the same. That way we'll be on a team together."

Spencer strained forward, stretching his arm dangerously close to somebody's armpit. He grasped a handkerchief, but he couldn't see the color until he stumbled away from the crowd.

"Red," Spencer shouted to Daisy. "I got red!"

Daisy staggered backward, gripping a handkerchief of her own. "Green!"

Spencer lunged back into the fray, squeezing forward until he could see the table. By this time, most of the handkerchiefs had been snatched up. There were no greens or reds remaining. Spencer grabbed two blues, threw his red back onto the table, and leapt out of the way.

"Here," Spencer said. "I guess we'll be blue." Daisy accepted the handkerchief and turned to throw her green one back on the table.

The students were spreading out, trying to find other kids with the same color. Many held their handkerchiefs protectively. A few tug-of-war fights had broken out. And Dez . . . Dez had a blonde girl pinned against the wall!

Spencer took off in Dez's direction, getting an elbow to the ribs as someone jerked a handkerchief away from another student. "You look real tough, Dez, picking on a girl," Spencer said.

The bully turned to glare at Spencer. Dez had taken a long green bean from his dinner plate and put one end up each nostril. The green bean hung in a loop, like a metal ring in the nose of a bull. Dez was probably trying to make himself look more intimidating, but the green hanger from his nostrils just looked disgusting.

"I don't care if she's a girl or a . . . whatever," Dez said. "She's got the color I want."

"I don't!" the girl said, clutching the handkerchief behind her back. "I dropped the brown one back there. I have red now!"

Dez sneered, green bean waggling. "Then I guess I want red!" Dez was in one of those moods. In a new crowd like this, he needed to establish himself as Alpha Bully before anyone else had the chance.

"Let her go," Spencer said. He was trying to decide how far he would go for this stranger. Was it worth another fist-fight with Dez?

The bully shoved the girl against the wall. She scrunched up her face and closed her eyes, her whole body tense. Spencer rolled his handkerchief from end to end and stepped forward.

Dez lowered his voice. "Just give me your hankie and no one has to get—"

Spencer looped his handkerchief over Dez's head and pulled on the corners. It jerked around the bully's throat, sending him into a fit of gurgling gags.

"Ghhaaa!" Dez gave a great huff, and the green bean launched from his nose. It sailed into the air, twirling like a boomerang in flight.

"Time is up!" Director Garcia shouted over the din of the cafeteria. "Find your teams!"

Spencer released Dez and leapt away. The cafeteria quickly fell into order as the students assembled into color-coordinated groups of ten. At least for a moment, Dez couldn't give chase.

"What were you doing over there?" Daisy whispered to Spencer as the blue team came together. "Trying to strangle Dez?"

"He was picking on a girl."

"And why was that *your* problem?"

"Dez is always *my* problem," Spencer said. He scanned the room for the blonde girl. When he spotted her across the cafeteria, Spencer was surprised to see that she was staring right at him. She gave a timid wave, and Spencer hurriedly looked away.

"Your face is turning red," Daisy pointed out. "Did you get strangled too?"

Spencer didn't want to explain why he was blushing. He was grateful when Director Garcia called for attention once more.

"Some of you may be wondering why we bother with teams," Garcia said. "This helps us test your social interactions and teamwork skills. Your team is the key to your success." He paused for effect. "Only *one* team will be invited to attend New Forest Academy."

A murmur of surprise and complaint rippled through the fifty recruits. Glares were exchanged between groups. Why hadn't the director mentioned that before? Students were studying their handkerchiefs, wondering if they'd picked the winning color.

Director Garcia continued. "Let me explain the rules. Academy instructors will be monitoring you closely during the week. We will make changes to the teams by adding or removing students until we have the perfect group. That winning group could be any size. It may be more than half of you. It may be only a handful. Everything depends on your performance. You are all bright, I'm sure. But New Forest Academy can accept only the very best."

Spencer glanced at the various groups. Dez had staked out a place among the brown team. The green team was mostly girls, and the red group was primarily boys. The yellow team looked far too energetic for its own good.

Spencer turned to his own team. There were one or two fourth graders, but most of the kids looked twelve or thirteen years old. One of the boys was tall with reddish hair. Another was thin, with prominent Asian features.

The other recruits on the blue team were here to win; Spencer could see it in their eyes. This enthusiasm was the common thread, uniting everyone in the room with the desire to get accepted to New Forest Academy. Everyone except Spencer, Daisy, and Dez. They were only there to kill time until Welcher was safe again.

If the Academy staff planned to watch the teams, then surely they would notice this difference in enthusiasm. Spencer and Daisy would stand out. And hadn't Walter sent them here to blend in and hide?

"We can win this," Spencer said to his teammates. He was pleased at how convincing his interest sounded.

Daisy wrinkled her forehead. "But I thought you said we weren't here to—"

Spencer elbowed her softly. "Blue team rules!" he shouted.

The Asian boy at Spencer's side scanned the room. "Our odds of winning at this juncture are equivalent to the other four teams. To assume dominance based solely on the color of a handkerchief is juvenile at best."

Spencer and Daisy shared a quick puzzled glance. "Um . . ." Spencer said. "Is that your way of saying *go, team?*"

The Asian boy looked back at Spencer. "I'm not trying to be insulting," he said. "I'm just dealing with the facts."

He held out a hand for Spencer to shake. "My name is Min Lee. I'm your team captain."

"Says who?" the redheaded boy cut in. "Every one of us is smarter than the average school kid. That's why we're here. So what makes you think that you should be in charge?"

Min raised his eyebrows. "Perhaps a quick spelling bee could resolve your concerns?"

Someone tapped Spencer on the arm. He turned away from his bickering teammates and found himself uncomfortably close to the blonde girl Dez had been threatening.

"Hi." She had a huge smile. "I'm Jenna."

Spencer took an awkward step back. "Spencer." His face was going red again.

Jenna held up her hand and Spencer saw a blue handkerchief dangling between her fingers.

"I thought you were green, or red, or . . . whatever," Spencer stammered.

"I was. But then I . . ." Jenna lowered her voice and leaned awkwardly close. "I traded." She pointed across the cafeteria. A former blue team member was heading away from the group, a red handkerchief in her hand.

Spencer wanted to point out that a last-minute hankie swap wasn't exactly following the rules. But then she smiled at him, and Spencer lost his train of thought.

Jenna shrugged. "I guess I'm on your team now."

CHAPTER 18

"LESS CHANCE OF FALLING."

Spencer lay on the top bunk in the dark dormitory, the ceiling only arm's reach away. The soft sounds of sleep drifted over from the bunk where Min and the other boys from the blue team were sprawled under their covers.

Spencer's mattress suddenly seemed to hiccup. The springs squeaked and a lump rose under his back.

"Is it time yet?" Dez's hoarse whisper drifted up from the bottom bunk. He kicked harder, and Spencer's mattress bulged even more.

All evening, Dez had been persistent and obnoxious about going to get the Glopified janitorial supplies. He had even forgotten his revenge on Spencer for choking him in the cafeteria. Then Dez had threatened one of the blue team boys, making him give up his bed so Dez could sleep in the blue dorm, with one eye on Spencer. This kind of calculated patience was unusual from Dez, and Spencer couldn't help but worry about the bully's ulterior motives.

Spencer glanced over at Min and his teammates to make sure they hadn't heard Dez's whisper. They were peculiar boys who considered themselves too smart for a typical public school. Getting into New Forest Academy meant everything to them.

After breaking into color groups, they had spent the evening in team-building and getting-to-know-you games. Spencer and Daisy found themselves constantly yielding to the overbearing personalities of the other recruits. Everyone wanted to take control and show his or her brilliance. Well, everyone except Jenna. She seemed wholly content to stare at Spencer wordlessly.

Then the promised phone call happened. Spencer had a brief moment in the front office to call his mom. With the secretary right there, Spencer had to be subtle.

Spencer tried to tell his mom that "Uncle" Roger Munroe was gone. He wanted her to pass the information to "Grandpa" Walter. But Alice just seemed confused and rushed. Fate would have it that Aunt Avril happened to call at the same moment. Every time Spencer said something important, the call-waiting bleeped it out. In the end, Alice had to answer the international call from Avril, leaving Spencer frustrated and discouraged.

Spencer felt another dull stab in the back as his mattress heaved.

"Come on, Doofus," Dez said. "I know you're not asleep."

Spencer checked his watch. It was close enough. He

leaned his head over the edge of the bed and whispered down to Dez, "Get your coat and be quiet."

A moment later, Spencer was delicately closing the dormitory door while Dez blundered ahead in the darkness. His flat-footed steps echoed harshly in the hallway.

"You're not very good at sneaking, are you?" Spencer said, rolling his feet silently along the floor.

"Never had to be," Dez said. "When my dad's asleep it's usually 'cause he drank too much. He never hears a thing."

Spencer remembered Daisy's vivid description of Dez's apartment. Trashed and littered with empty beer cans . . . Dez's dad asleep on the couch. Spencer couldn't imagine living like that. It must be horrible for Dez, going home after school to that smelly place, just waiting for his dad to shout and throw things.

Spencer thought of Aunt Avril's home in Hillside Estates. Yes, the Zumbros had cluttered it plenty, but he always wanted to go back to his family because there was love at home. Always had been, even when Spencer's dad disappeared and things got tough.

The two boys slipped out the door and into the crisp night. With the mountain's altitude, the early November air was very chilly. Spencer zipped up his coat, a thing he hadn't done inside for fear of being overheard.

"This way." Dez set off across the lawn between two dormitory buildings.

"No," Spencer said. "We wait for Daisy!"

Dez groaned and leaned against the building. "She probably fell asleep."

Spencer looked toward the girls' dorms and checked his watch. "She couldn't have."

"Why not?" Dez said. "She forgot her blanky and her binky?"

Right then, the door cracked open and Daisy appeared in her puffy coat and gloves. She glanced around nervously. "Are you sure we should go?"

"Psh, yeah!" Dez said. "How else are we going to get the stuff?"

"It's just . . ." Daisy went on. "Walter said to stay with the group, not to go anywhere alone."

"We're not alone," Dez said. "There's three of us."

"Yeah, but the three of us are alone," said Daisy.

"That doesn't make sense." Dez shook his head.

"We'll be fine," Spencer cut in. "Besides, my mom said it was okay this time." It was good justification and seemed to soothe Daisy.

The three of them set off silently across New Forest Academy's campus. Ringed in by the trees, the grounds seemed extra dark, showing the moon overhead as a perfect half. The trio easily avoided the few outdoor security lights. It took several minutes, but they eventually reached the brick wall that closed in the front of the Academy campus.

Spencer stopped in the shadows, breathing heavily from their silent dash across the grounds. The gate was nearby, bathed in spotlights.

"All right," Spencer whispered. "This is the hard part. Once we have our brooms, we can fly back. But we're going to have to get out the traditional way."

"Climb over the wall?" Daisy glanced up. It was probably fifteen feet high at least.

"Either that or run through the spotlights and try to jump the gate before anyone catches us."

"I'm going for the gate plan," said Dez. "Less chance of falling." Without another word, he stepped into the spotlights and sprinted down the road that led to the gate.

"Wait!" Spencer tried to call, but it was too late. There was no choice but to race after Dez.

It was a terrible feeling, running the distance to the gate while spotlights shone down on both sides. For a moment, Spencer had the ridiculous notion that an alarm would sound and a net would fall out of the skies, trapping them hopelessly.

There was a metallic clang as Dez leapt onto the gate and started climbing.

"Oh, man!" Dez shouted as Spencer and Daisy jumped onto the gate below him. "It's got Barbie wire at the top!"

Spencer glanced up and saw the coils of metal wire, sharp points glinting in the spotlights. There was no time to explain to Dez the huge difference between *Barbie* and *barbed* wire.

They were stuck. There was no way they could get over the gate without tearing themselves to shreds! The carefully calculated safety procedures that made New Forest Academy so secure also made it a prison for those inside.

An electronic beep cut through their panic. The gate suddenly shifted, and Spencer almost lost his grip.

"It's opening!" Daisy shouted.

Sure enough, the gate was swinging slowly away from the brick wall, Spencer, Daisy, and Dez holding on for the ride.

"Is there a car coming?" Daisy asked. Spencer looked in all directions, but only the darkness of the mountain was visible.

"Maybe it opens automatically at midnight," Daisy rambled nervously.

"Yeah," Dez said, climbing down the moving gate, "to let all the bad guys in." He jumped off the gate and bolted across the parking lot. Spencer and Daisy leapt down and ducked past the gate booth. But all was dark inside, as if nobody was there.

Dez had reached the maintenance shed by the time Spencer and Daisy caught up to him. The big kid was searching in the darkness, but Spencer was determined not to let the bully find the Glopified supplies first.

"Gotta be around here somewhere." Dez peered between the two dumpsters that flanked the shed.

"The bushes," Daisy said, running to the edge of the parking lot. Spencer and Dez joined her, rummaging through the tangled mountain shrubs.

"Here's something," Spencer said. Clearing away some dried leaves, he grabbed a bundle of wooden handles and dragged them back to the parking lot. There were brooms, mops, and pushbrooms, the handles tied together with a bit of yarn that Alice must have found in the SUV.

"What about the rest of the stuff?" Dez asked.

"She must have hidden the box somewhere else."

Spencer and Daisy turned back to scour the bushes at the edge of the parking lot. The slapping sound of running feet jerked Spencer around.

Dez was sprinting away from them, back toward the open gate. In one thieving hand he gripped a broom; the other clumsily held a mop and pushbroom.

"Dez!" Spencer shouted, but the bully didn't turn. Instead, Dez touched the broom bristles to the blacktop. He rose, completely out of control but laughing with delight.

"We've got to catch him," Daisy said. She retrieved a mop and broom for herself. The yarn was shredded from where Dez must have gnawed through with his teeth.

"You go after him," Spencer said. "Leave me a broom. I'll find the box and meet you back inside."

Daisy nodded bravely and grabbed a second mop and pushbroom in her left hand. Dez drifted clumsily over the brick wall, scraping his shoes along the top. Daisy ran a few steps, angled her body, and slammed the broom against the ground. She shot across the parking lot in pursuit.

Spencer hurried back to the bushes, frantic now to find the box and get back into campus. He dropped to his hands and knees in the autumn leaves, refusing the idea that his mom had forgotten to leave the rest of the stuff. Or worse . . . that someone else had found it.

At last he spotted the tattered cardboard box shoved deep into a prickly shrub. It took him a moment to work it free. By the time he did, Daisy and Dez had disappeared beyond the brick wall.

Spencer quickly scanned the contents of the box to

make sure everything was still intact. There were several bags of vac dust, chalkboard erasers, latex gloves, and three toilet plungers, their handles sticking out. There was something else, too. Peering inside, Spencer saw that his mom had thrown the Glopified ink remover into the box with the other supplies.

Spencer tucked the box securely against his hip with one arm and headed back toward the dumpsters. As he stooped to pick up the last remaining broom, Spencer heard a muffled cough.

He jumped back, heart racing. His eyes scanned the dark parking lot and his hand instinctively went into the box for a chalkboard eraser.

The stillness of the night settled around him. Just as Spencer's heart began to slow, he heard it again. A muffled cough, like someone was trying to hold it back. Spencer circled the dumpsters, ready to hurl the Glopified chalk bomb. But the parking lot was vacant.

"Hello?" Spencer called into the night. His back was pressed against the dumpster so no one could sneak up behind him. "I know you're here. I heard you coughing, so you might as well show yourself." Spencer was surprised at the steadiness of his voice, but his hands were shaking to make up for it.

A third time the cough rang out. Spencer staggered away from the big dumpster. Impossible! Spencer stared at the metal bin.

The cough had come from inside the dumpster!

CHAPTER 19

"WHO DID THIS TO YOU?"

Spencer took a cautious step forward. "Hello?" He rapped gently on the side of the dumpster. It resonated like a hollow drum. "Is someone in there?"

"Get out of here, kid," came the muffled reply.

Spencer jumped back again, his stomach caught in his throat. "Who are you?"

"Just get away. And forget about this."

Spencer looked at the black lid of the dumpster. A silvery strip of duct tape ran all around the edge of the lid, taping it closed.

"You're trapped in there," Spencer said. The man coughed again. Spencer set the chalkboard eraser back into the box and lowered the parcel to the ground. Reaching up, he grabbed the curled corner of the duct tape and tugged.

The tape held fast. Spencer repositioned himself and strained against the tape with all his might.

"Forget it," the prisoner said. "You'll never get it open."

Spencer stepped away. "The tape is Glopified, isn't it." There was silence from within the dumpster. "It's okay," Spencer said. "I know all about it."

"What's your name, kid?" the dumpster prisoner asked.

"Spencer Zumbro."

Again, there was silence. Then, "What do you know about Glop?"

"A lot," said Spencer. "I know about Toxites, too. And the BEM. They locked you in here, didn't they?"

Spencer heard a shuffling sound from inside the dumpster. He could only assume that the prisoner was scooting closer to him.

"Listen. I don't know how long I've been in here or where I am. The duct tape they use to seal the dumpster is Glopified, like you guessed. The tape is indestructible. Can't cut it, tear it, break it . . . believe me." He gave a bitter chuckle. "I've tried everything. This Glopified duct tape is fingerprint sensitive. The only person who can remove it is the same person who taped it down."

"Who?" Spencer asked. "Who did this to you?"

"I don't know. I can't see anything from inside." He coughed again, and Spencer thought of how cold the prisoner must be. "They've been moving me a lot lately, never keeping me in one place for more than a few days."

"Where are they taking you?"

"I don't know, but you have to leave. When they dropped me here, they said they'd be coming back tonight."

"No," Spencer said. "I won't let them take you." He pulled a toilet plunger from the box. "I'm getting you out of here."

Spencer stuck the plunger to the side of the metal dumpster. The suction was good, and he lifted the dumpster easily. Spencer glanced across the parking lot. He didn't know where to take the garbage bin, but if he could just hide it for tonight, then the BEM wouldn't be able to relocate the prisoner. Spencer could hide him and tell Walter at the end of the week.

"Put me down," the man said, but Spencer wasn't listening. Maybe he could fly the weightless dumpster into the darkness of the trees. That might be the safest place.

"You have to put me down!" The prisoner raised his voice. "I'll die if they don't find me."

The urgency of the man's voice cut through Spencer's plotting. He lowered the dumpster slowly to the ground. "What do you mean?"

"I'll starve to death," the man said. "Every day, the BEM gives me food. It isn't much, but I survive. Whoever taped this dumpster shut has to be there to open it. If they lose me, I'll starve."

"But we'll get you out," Spencer said. "We'll break open the dumpster."

"It's useless." The man coughed. "The whole thing is Glopified. The only way in is through that duct tape."

Spencer popped the toilet plunger off the side of the dumpster. "I can't just leave you here. I want to help."

"You want to help? The best thing you can do is get out of here." The prisoner paused. "Wherever *here* is."

"We're in Colorado," Spencer said. "In the parking lot of a private school. New Forest Academy."

"Academy?" the prisoner said.

Spencer nodded, even though he knew the man couldn't see him. "New Forest . . ."

"I know the name," interrupted the prisoner. "I've heard BEM workers talk about it. They've got somebody working there. Somebody dangerous. They call him Fletcher. He's a henchman for one of the BEM warlocks."

Spencer swallowed the sudden lump in his throat. "Slick."

Headlights suddenly cut across the parking lot, and Spencer heard the purr of a large engine. Peering around the dumpster, he saw a big truck entering the lot next to the WELCOME sign. The vehicle was headed straight toward the dumpster.

"Someone's coming," Spencer said.

"Go. Get out of here!"

Spencer's head was swimming. Wasn't there a way he could rescue this poor stranger from his prison? But the garbage truck was dangerously near, and Spencer staggered away from the dumpster. The approaching truck lowered a mechanical arm with two prongs to grip the garbage bin. The truck beeped as it reversed to the right angle.

"I'm sorry," Spencer muttered. Then he picked up the

box of Glopified objects, scooped up his broom, and sprinted away.

Spencer took flight, not daring to look at the dumpster again. He ran the whole way back to his dormitory, tossing paranoid glances over his shoulders. The pockets of shadow that filled New Forest Academy's campus seemed as deep and dark as Spencer's fears.

CHAPTER 20

"IT'S A SCIENCE BOOK."

The fifty recruits were perusing the Academy library. It was the last stop on their tour of campus. They'd been to the computer labs, the science labs, the art building, the recreational center, and the main school building. Now lunch was only a half hour away.

Colored handkerchiefs were tied around arms, looped through backpacks, or worn like bandannas. Spencer had his dangling out of his jeans pocket. Each recruit was supposed to check out a book or two so they could have something to read in the dorms during the week. Spencer didn't imagine that he'd get any light reading done, but he checked out a short sci-fi because the robot on the cover looked cool.

"Did you find anything good?" Spencer asked as Daisy joined him in the checkout line. She held up a few nature and outdoor magazines. Min marched past, his arms laden with heavy books about advanced chemistry and computer programming.

Dez's face suddenly popped around a bookshelf, his brown handkerchief tied around his forehead. He stuck out his tongue at Spencer and Daisy, then ducked out of sight again.

Daisy glared in his direction. "He still won't tell me where he stashed his mop and broom," she said.

While Spencer had been busy with the dumpster prisoner, Daisy had been trying to catch Dez. By the time she had reached him, the bully had already hidden his Glopified items, determined not to give them up. Dez had gone inside and Daisy had hidden her equipment under a dormitory porch, the place she and Spencer had already decided would be the new stash.

"If Dez won't give up his supplies, then he probably plans to use them on his own," Spencer said.

"I hope he doesn't do something dumb," said Daisy.

"*Dumb* is his middle name."

"I didn't know he had a middle name," said Daisy.

"If Dez gets caught with Glopified supplies," Spencer whispered, "then *Slick* might know we're armed." He said the janitor's name to try it out in the context of an enemy.

Spencer had told Daisy everything about his conversation with the dumpster prisoner and how he'd said Slick was part of the BEM. Daisy wanted Spencer to have a plan, but he felt just as hopeless as ever. They needed to contact Walter, but the strict rules of the Academy program wouldn't permit it. Distractions from home life were supposed to be left behind for the week, allowing the recruits to perform at their very highest.

"There's one thing I can't figure out about Slick," Daisy said. "Remember yesterday, by the computer labs? If Slick is working for the BEM, why did he kill that Filth in the hallway? Aren't BEM workers supposed to let the Toxites run wild?"

"I've been thinking about that too," said Spencer. "It was probably just an act. What if Slick killed that Toxite to trick us into thinking he was a Rebel?"

"Well, he didn't trick me," said Daisy. "Which is saying a lot."

"Garcia said that Slick used to be the computer tech until Roger Munroe resigned," said Spencer. "Now Slick's been promoted to head janitor. It's the perfect position to turn New Forest Academy over to the BEM."

"That's not his only position," said Daisy. "Slick's also in the perfect position to capture *you*. And isn't that what the BEM really wants? That mysterious something that you're supposed to know about?"

A shiver passed through Spencer. He remembered Walter's warning about staying with the group. There was safety in numbers. Glancing around the library, Spencer was grateful to be surrounded by other Academy recruits. But could the blue team protect him from Slick if the janitor attacked?

Spencer and Daisy finished checking out of the library

and headed for the door. As they passed a bookshelf, suddenly Jenna was walking alongside Spencer.

"Hi," she said. Her short hair curled around her cheeks, shimmering slightly. It looked almost silvery in the sunlight shining through the window. The same pretty smile from last night was on her face. "What you reading?" She glanced at the book in his hand, but Spencer tucked it away, suddenly embarrassed by the robot on the cover.

"It's a science book," Spencer said. "Don't know what it's called. I just grabbed it."

"I got this one." Jenna held out her book. "It's by Asimov. One of my favorites." On the cover was a robot looking pensively into space.

"Hey," Daisy said, "that kind of looks like the one Spencer checked out."

The conversation was growing more and more uncomfortable. Spencer had to shift the topic before he short-circuited.

"Ready for lunch?" he asked Jenna. "Chicken tenders, I think."

"I only like them dipped in ranch," Jenna said.

Spencer nodded. "Yeah, me too."

"Perfect," said Jenna. "So, can I sit by you? Share some ranch?"

"I . . . umm . . ."

Didn't the cafeteria make individual dressing cups for a reason? Double dipping was an absolute sin in Spencer's personal rule book.

"Maybe," he floundered. "I think that's okay?" Spencer swallowed hard. "Is that all right, Daisy?"

Jenna stopped and eyed Spencer and Daisy standing side by side. "Oh, wait a minute. Are you two . . . ?"

"No!" Spencer said. "No, we're not."

"Are we what?" Daisy asked.

"Uhh," Spencer stammered. "Related! She wants to know if we're related!"

Daisy chuckled. "Of course we're not," she said to Jenna. "But Spencer is the closest thing I have to a brother."

Spencer needed a breath of fresh air to put this whole awkward conversation behind him. He stepped toward the library's carved wooden doors and grabbed the rustic metal handle. Before he could jerk the door open, a harsh whiteness overwhelmed his vision.

He was seated at a desk with a glass tabletop, rocking gently in an office chair. On the desk was a copy of *The Janitor Handbook*. Spencer recognized the brown cover with a large ring of keys embossed into the front.

The walls of the office were painted with sharp lines in neutral grays and blues. Above a filing cabinet was a framed crest of the Bureau of Educational Maintenance—a circular seal with the United States eagle, *e pluribus unum* written on a banner in its beak. In one talon it held a broom; the other clutched a dustpan.

The man swiveled in his office chair and Spencer was staring out a high window. A bustling city stretched before his view. Spencer somehow recognized it as the nation's capital, Washington, D.C.

"Are you all right?"

Spencer blinked hard and opened his eyes. He was slumped at the base of the door, Jenna's worried face surprisingly close to his. Behind her, a cluster of recruits had gathered to check on him.

"It happened again, didn't it?" Daisy said. Spencer nodded.

"You mean, passing out is a regular thing for you?" asked Jenna. "What causes it?"

The girls helped Spencer to his feet as Min approached. "Likely causes would include dehydration or low blood pressure. Let's get him to the cafeteria."

"I'm fine," Spencer said. But despite his protests, Min organized the blue team to surround Spencer and escort him safely to the cafeteria.

CHAPTER 21

"HOW IS THAT A DEAL?"

Spencer emptied his tray into the trash can just as the bell rang. Lunch hadn't been chicken tenders after all. Instead, Spencer had choked down a very dry, parmesan-encrusted fish fillet. He would have liked a bit of tartar sauce with it, but the fear that Jenna would double dip forced him to eat it plain.

Spencer and Daisy were ever watchful. They hadn't caught a glimpse of Slick since yesterday, and the janitor's absence was unsettling.

"Where are we going now?" Spencer asked. Daisy already had her schedule out and was studying the campus map. But it was unnecessary, since Min was within earshot and already had an answer.

"Room 104 of the main building," he said. "We're

combining with the green team for a lecture from Director Garcia."

A lecture didn't sound like fun, but as long as Spencer and Daisy stayed with the blue team, Slick would have a hard time attacking. Just like Walter had said, there was safety in numbers.

The blue team had diminished from its ten initial members to eight. The Academy administration was making frequent changes, and Spencer couldn't help but worry that he might be separated from Daisy at any point.

Through some unspoken rule, the team members stayed together. There was a sense of security knowing that everyone in the team was either going to make it into the Academy . . . or not.

Jenna, especially, seemed glued to Spencer's side, talking through most of lunch. She seemed so happy all the time. It reminded Spencer what it was like to be an ordinary student. Jenna didn't have to worry about Toxites, or stress about the BEM's corrosive plan. She was a regular thirteen-year-old. And the fact that she was a bit older than Spencer didn't seem to bother her a bit.

Min led the blue team out of the cafeteria and into the hallway, admonishing them about being tardy to Garcia's lecture. They were halfway to room 104, just passing the bathrooms, when Dez burst out of the boys' bathroom, a handful of guys from the brown team right behind him.

All eight members of the blue team came to a halt as Dez and his comrades spread across the hallway, blocking their passage. Dez cracked his knuckles and glanced at his new friends. How had Dez made himself the ringleader? Weren't these Academy recruits supposed to be smart kids?

"Where do you think you're going?" Dez asked.

"To hinder us will profit you nothing," Min said. "If you think to gain an advantage over us by making us tardy . . ."

Spencer knew Dez wouldn't like Min's big words. Before the blue team leader could finish, Dez grabbed him by the collar of his shirt and threw him backward. Min stumbled into his teammates, who caught him before he hit the ground.

Dez's backup crew glanced around the hallway. Their expressions showed a mix of anxiety and excitement. Throwing kids around was probably something they'd always wanted to try. Until Dez had showed up, they'd been smart enough not to do it. But Dez's careless behavior opened doors to the other boys . . . and gave them someone to blame if the need arose.

"What do you want, Dez?" Spencer pushed to the front of his group.

"There you are, Doofus," said Dez. "Me and my friends have a preposition to make."

Spencer made a face. "It's actually *proposition*, not preposition."

"Whatever." Dez shrugged. "My homies here," he pointed to the guys behind him, "they really want to get into this stupid Academy. That means your team can't win. Deal?"

"How is that a deal?" Daisy asked. "It sounds more like a demand."

Min stepped forward, more upset than Spencer had

thought possible. "I will not be manipulated like this! One more threat and I'm going straight to Director Garcia!"

"Boo hoo!" Dez faked tears. "Blue team's full of tattletales."

"Why does it matter, Dez?" Spencer stared at the bully. Dez knew perfectly well that the Academy was only a temporary place for them. No matter the outcome of the recruitment program, the three of them would return to little old Welcher, Idaho.

Around the corner, Spencer heard someone give a quick two-note whistle. Another student repeated the sound, and it echoed down the hallway until it reached Dez.

"Teacher's coming!" Dez said to his friends. "Scatter!" And just like that, the brown gang vanished. Dez disappeared into the bathroom, two boys merged into a lineup at the drinking fountain, and the other three slipped into a nearby classroom.

The announced teacher walked by, urging the blue team not to be late to the lecture. No one could find the words to speak against the brown team, not even Min. Dez's gang was still too close. Still listening.

The confrontation was clearly premeditated, something Dez never could have figured out alone. Brown team members had been strategically placed throughout the hallway to whistle the chain of warnings. Spencer couldn't decide if Dez was using the brown team or the brown team was using Dez. The genius of the recruits combined with the careless brutality of Dez made for a dangerous symbiosis.

Whatever Dez's motive, the brown team was determined to win.

CHAPTER 22

"A NEW FOREST WILL RISE."

Director Garcia's lecture started off with a PowerPoint slide show and a broad smile. Due to the blues' confrontation with the browns, the green team had arrived at the classroom first. It didn't bother Spencer to be a moment late, but Min was annoyed that he couldn't have a front-row seat.

"Let us start with a question," Garcia said.

Spencer saw many of the recruits already taking notes. What could they possibly be writing down? The question hadn't even been asked yet!

"Who can tell me, what is ecological succession?"

Most of the recruits' hands shot into the air, the students desperate to prove their knowledge to Director Garcia and earn their way into the Academy. Spencer had never heard of *ecological whatever* and he exchanged a clueless look with Daisy, seated at his right.

"Min." Director Garcia pointed.

The Asian boy stood up beside Daisy and raised his voice so the whole class could hear. "*Ecological succession* refers to the changes that occur after an ecosystem is disturbed."

"Thank you," said Director Garcia. "A great example of ecological succession can be seen in forests." He clicked the PowerPoint controller and a picture of a tall green forest appeared on the screen.

Suddenly, a folded paper skidded onto Spencer's desk. He looked around for the deliverer and caught Jenna's eye. She quickly turned away.

"For an example," continued Garcia, "take this forest not far from here."

Spencer tried to act casual, unfolding the paper and holding it so no one else could see.

I think U would B a better team leader than Min.

What? Why would Jenna think that? Spencer felt his face turning red at the praise.

"Many years ago," Garcia lectured, "lightning struck this forest, starting a series of large wildfires." He clicked to the next slide to show raging fires engulfing the trees in thick smoke and deep orange flames.

Spencer took a pencil from his pocket and wrote back.

No way. Min's a lot smarter than me.

He carefully folded the paper and tossed it onto Jenna's desk.

Spencer tried to tune into the lecture again. "These fires burned for weeks, destroying thousands of acres. But the wildfires were not the end of the forest." Director Garcia clicked to the next slide. Here, the charred trees from the fire rose like spears through a thick growth of new green.

The note came back, and Spencer opened it up.

It's not just about being smart. U stood up 2 the Browns.

Spencer had a quick response.

I'm crazy, I guess.

"As you can see," Garcia said, "new trees and brush have risen out of the ashes. A new forest will replace the old one. It is younger, stronger, healthier."

Jenna's note fell onto Spencer's desk again.

U R brave. I like that.

Spencer felt his face flush redder than ever. He quickly decided not to pass the note back. Jenna didn't need any encouragement. Instead, Spencer tried to turn all his attention back to the lecture.

"This," Garcia pointed to the screen, "is the very philosophy behind New Forest Academy. The old forest of traditional public schools is failing. Politicians and educators are trying to fight the fire, but nature is running its course. Those who say all hope is lost do not understand ecological succession. A new forest will rise."

For as eloquent as the speech was, Spencer knew it was wrong. Toxites were burning out the public schools. But what Director Garcia didn't understand was that New Forest Academy would fall just like the others. With the Rebel Janitor Munroe gone, it would be too easy for Slick to let the Toxites take over the Academy.

As idyllic as this new Academy seemed, nothing could save it but the janitors. They were the key to success in every school. And unless the BEM started fighting Toxites again, every form of education would collapse forever.

Garcia went on with the lecture, but Spencer was caught up in thought. He pondered his situation, essentially trapped in New Forest Academy, cut off from the outside world while Slick was probably preparing a cunning trap to catch him. It was a terrible feeling. If Spencer had wanted this kind of anxiety, he might as well have stayed home in Welcher. But circumstances had brought him here. And New Forest Academy wasn't turning out to be the safe haven that Walter had expected.

Walter. They needed the warlock's help, but how could they contact him? A quick phone call would be enough, but the Academy rules would never permit it. Recruits weren't allowed to call out unless there was some kind of health emergency.

Spencer looked to his right. Daisy was looking a little paler than usual . . .

CHAPTER 23

"WE LOST HIM."

Spencer and Daisy moved quickly down the hallway. Behind them, the cafeteria was still abuzz with conversation and laughter as the recruits finished their dinners. No one had noticed Spencer and Daisy slide out the side door.

"I can't believe how sick you are," Spencer said to Daisy.

"I'm not . . ." she started. Then Daisy remembered the plan. Doubling over, she began to moan. Her acting had to be good enough to convince the secretary to let them make a call home. Unfortunately, Daisy's fake groaning sounded more like a dying cat.

Spencer shook his head. "You're overdoing it," he whispered. "You sound . . . constipated."

"Isn't that okay?" Daisy said as they rounded a corner. "I mean, I'm trying to sound sick. Being constipated is serious business, you know. One time, my dog swallowed a tennis ball and she couldn't go—"

Spencer reeled backward, frantically shoving Daisy back around the corner. "Sorry," she said. "Was that too much information?" But Spencer shushed her with a finger to his lips. Peering cautiously around the wall, the kids saw Slick emerge from a dim janitorial closet. He looked both ways, wiped his hooked nose, and then reached back into the closet for something. As the door to the closet swung closed, the object in his hand came into sight.

Slick was holding an Agitation Bucket.

Spencer could see wings, tails, and quills bristling over the Bucket's rim as the angry Toxites made a futile attempt to climb out.

"Where's he going?" Daisy whispered as the BEM janitor exited the school building. It was the first time they'd seen him all day, and the anticipation of the moment was thick.

"Nowhere good," said Spencer. "If Slick dumps that Bucket, we're done for." He took off down the hall, heading for the opposite exit.

"And where are *you* going?" Daisy said, falling in step with him.

"To the stash. We've got to get some supplies to stop Slick."

Daisy didn't argue. If Slick overturned the Agitation Bucket, then New Forest Academy would be in the same danger as Welcher Elementary: full of angry Toxites.

They raced across campus. Outdoor lights flickered on

as twilight shadows started to fill the area. In a moment, they reached the stash under the dormitory porch.

Spencer and Daisy each donned a latex glove and pocketed a chalkboard eraser. They were armed and ready to stop Slick, but Daisy pointed out the obvious problem.

"Now what?" she said. "Which way did he go?"

"Let's find out," Spencer said. Taking a broom in both hands, he gripped it tightly and slammed the bristles straight down.

He streamed upward, higher and higher. With his new aerial view advantage, Spencer scanned the campus below. Movement at the gate caught his eye. The spotlights illuminated Slick, carefully carrying the Agitation Bucket through the front gate of New Forest Academy.

Spencer touched ground again, a puzzled look on his face. "He's leaving the campus." Daisy suddenly bent over and moaned in pain. "Are you all right?" Spencer reached out.

Daisy nodded. "I almost forgot to be sick."

Spencer exhaled. "Forget it, Daisy. That's not the plan anymore. We've got to find out what Slick's up to with that BEM Bucket!" Spencer took off, striking his broom against the ground.

They flew along the perimeter of campus, passing the filled construction pit where the cranes and machinery glinted like dinosaur skeletons in the faint light. In no time, they had landed near the front entrance. Spencer tapped his broom on the ground and rose to the top of the Academy's brick wall.

From his new position balancing on the wall, Spencer

watched Slick approach the large maintenance shed, near the spot where the dumpster prisoner had been the night before. The janitor set down the Bucket and pressed a button to open the shed's garage-type door.

The shed was a cave of darkness, and Slick stepped inside for a moment. He returned, pulling something into the parking lot. In the last glimmer of daylight, Spencer could see that it was a janitorial cleaning cart, the kind that Marv had often used when cleaning classroom after classroom.

Slick hefted the Agitation Bucket and stepped onto the cart. He leaned slightly, and the cart rolled smoothly across the parking lot, picking up speed and turning toward the exit. In a matter of moments, Slick and the cleaning cart were swallowed by the darkness as he drove down the mountainside away from New Forest Academy.

Spencer readied his broom. "Wait," Daisy said at his side. Spencer hadn't even noticed her fly up. "I don't think we should go down there. It's good enough that he took the Bucket away from here."

"Not good enough for me," Spencer said. "If Slick's taking that Bucket someplace, we need to know where." Leaving Daisy to follow, Spencer took flight toward the maintenance shed.

He was there in a few seconds. Stepping through the open garage door, Spencer saw a large truck with a snowplow on the front. Other outdoor maintenance objects cluttered the shed: a riding lawn mower, a weed whacker, an edger, and a couple of hand shovels. But tucked against the wall was the item Spencer was hoping for.

Spencer wheeled the janitorial cart into the parking lot as Daisy landed. The cart had four sturdy wheels on a rectangular black base. There was plenty of room to stand on one side, while the other side sported a rack with a few shelves. A built-in yellow garbage sack dangled off the front.

"Glopified?" Daisy asked.

"Definitely," said Spencer. "Didn't you see how Slick was riding it?" He pushed the cart toward Daisy. "There's another one in there." He disappeared into the maintenance shed and reappeared with another cleaning cart.

Spencer clipped his broom onto the rack and stepped onto the flat side of the cart, holding on to the shelves in front of him. He couldn't help but think that it looked like a Roman chariot without horses.

"Shouldn't we just use our brooms to follow him?" Daisy asked.

"Too hard to steer," Spencer said. "Besides, brooms don't do long distance."

"Well, then there's something I should probably tell you." Daisy stepped cautiously onto the flat side of her cart. The wheels rolled forward, and she gripped the rack with white knuckles. "I don't have my driver's license!"

Spencer rolled his eyes. "Come on, Daisy. It's just a cleaning cart."

He leaned forward with all his weight. Instantly, the cart shot forward, burning across the parking lot at high velocity. Spencer could barely hang on. He regained balance on the footboard and threw his weight backward. The cart came to a screeching halt.

"It's all about shifting your balance," Spencer called. But there was no need to explain. Daisy went rolling past, taking a corner and exiting the parking lot. Spencer shifted his weight and zoomed after her.

"Wow, Daisy! You're pretty good."

Daisy shivered against the cold on her face. "I've played a balance game like this on the Wii!"

The two kids sped down the canyon road, Spencer taking the lead once he got used to the balance of the cleaning cart. It was amazing how fast they could go. As speeds exceeded anything possible on a bicycle, Spencer thought of how upset his mother would be if she knew what he was doing. He wasn't even wearing a helmet!

The ride was surprisingly smooth. The four little wheels of the cart managed to absorb the bumps without offsetting the driver's balance. It was a little scary on the tight corners, speeding forward without even a headlight to illuminate their way.

They caught glimpses of Slick far ahead, leaning into his cart. It was hard to keep a safe distance without losing sight of him around the corners. Spencer and Daisy pressed forward, gritting their chattering teeth against the cold wind and squinting painfully. Their hands were white and numb.

At last, the mountain road leveled and they came into a residential neighborhood. A dog barked in someone's yard. Through lighted windows, Spencer could see families clearing the dinner tables.

Daisy shivered. "We lost him." Her speech was a bit slurred, as the cold wind had numbed her face.

They drove their carts to a side street and peered down the dim lane. The janitor could have taken any number of roads.

"There!" Daisy pointed away from the roads. Spencer turned and saw Slick cruising through a dark field. Spencer leaned sideways, spinning his cart toward the meadow. He didn't see how the small wheels could possibly handle the off-road terrain, but Slick seemed to manage.

The going was rough. The two kids took a serpentine path across the field, carefully driving around shrubs and bushes. Twice, Spencer's wheels jarred on hidden rocks, causing his cart to jerk in an unexpected direction as his balance shifted. And once, Daisy leaned too far and actually tipped her cart on a bit of uneven ground.

At last they arrived at a small road on the far side of the field. An errant breeze sent a few dry leaves whipping around the cleaning carts. "Some shortcut," Daisy murmured, glancing back at the treacherous field.

"Hey," Spencer said. "Look where it brought us."

The road wound around a long chain-link fence. Peering through the links, the kids saw a flat, grassy soccer field and the silhouette of playground equipment. Beyond that was a low building with lots of windows.

"It's a school," Daisy said.

Spencer nodded. "A public school for all the kids that live around here. The kids who don't go to the Academy."

"And Slick came here?" She glanced around. "Where'd he go?"

"Must have gone around to the front of the school."

Spencer stepped off his cart and unclipped his broom from the rack. "And I'm afraid I might know what he's planning."

The first flight from their brooms landed them on the soccer field. The second sent them soaring onto the roof of the school. They tiptoed around skylights and roof vents, making their way to the front of the building. They arrived just in time to see Slick lean around the street corner and stop his cleaning cart by the school's front entrance.

Dropping to his hands and knees, Spencer could see clearly. Slick wiped his runny nose with the back of his hand. He grabbed the handle of the Agitation Bucket and lifted it from the cart. With a ping of dread, Spencer remembered the Welcher Elementary library and the devastation an Agitation Bucket could cause.

With one swift motion, Slick upended the bucket as though he were tossing out dirty water. But instead of harmless water, dozens of agitated Toxites spewed onto the school's front lawn.

As soon as the bucket was empty, Slick shifted his weight on the cart and sped away. A few of the monsters leapt after him, clicking and grunting, but the chase wasn't worth it.

The angry Toxites had been a doorstep delivery. They smelled the school and tasted the students' residual brain waves lingering from a hard day of learning.

In a bristling mass, they flooded up the school's front steps. They were home.

CHAPTER 24

"WE'VE GOT TO STOP THEM!"

We've got to stop them!" Spencer said as the first Toxites reached the front of the public school.

The Grimes had no problem entering. They compressed their lizardlike bodies and squeezed through the tiniest crack. Many of the bristling Filths burrowed into the lawn like rabbits to await the school's opening. The winged Rubbishes lit on windowsills, croaking like ravens and pecking at the glass.

Spencer gripped his broom and prepared to leap into the fray. It didn't seem like the smartest idea, but hadn't Jenna praised him for his bravery?

"Are you crazy?" Daisy grabbed his arm. "Those things just came from an Agitation Bucket! They'll kill you!"

"But we can't let them inside!" Spencer said. "We've got to stop them!"

Daisy pushed Spencer away from the edge and reached into her coat pocket. Stepping forward, she lifted her arm, and Spencer saw the weapon in her hand.

A chalkboard eraser.

Daisy hurled the eraser downward. It struck the front step of the school and instantly began gushing white chalk dust. The Toxites skittered to escape, but without walls to contain the explosion, the chalk cloud was rising too fast.

A few Rubbishes turned skyward, wings flapping wildly. The white cloud seemed to reach up and swallow them. Limp, paralyzed bodies plummeted to the school grounds. But the rising chalk cloud seemed bent on ensnaring more than just the Toxites.

"Run!" Daisy screamed. The explosion was stretching across the roof of the school in less than a heartbeat. Spencer and Daisy sprinted away, wisps of chalk dust wrapping around their ankles like hungry ghosts.

Side by side, Spencer and Daisy slammed their brooms against the roof. The magic activated in their brooms, propelling them across the soccer field and over the fence. They landed clumsily in the meadow and scrambled back to their waiting carts.

The public school was enveloped in a milky haze. Tendrils of chalk dust spiraled heavenward, given an eerie illumination by the rising half moon. The explosion was subsiding, but the paralytic effect on the Toxites had been devastating.

"Phew!" Daisy swallowed hard. "That was close."

But Spencer was shaking his head. "It didn't kill them,"

he said. "Walter said the chalk bombs wouldn't kill the Toxites, only paralyze them for a day or so."

"At least we stopped them," said Daisy. She started to say something more, when out of nowhere a pushbroom pierced the air like a javelin and struck her in the side. Daisy screamed as she lost gravity, soaring out of sight over the dark field.

Spencer leapt onto his cart, cutting a hard turn as he shifted his weight. Where was the attacker? Where was Slick? Blindsided by a blast of vac dust, Spencer toppled from his cleaning cart. Suction force held him to the road as Slick coasted into view, his cart rack full of Glopified supplies.

"Glad you could join me out here," the greasy janitor said. "Much more convenient. I was having a devil of a time figuring how to catch you without making a stir on campus. The other students are quite sensitive. Don't want to ruin their education."

Slick wheeled closer on his cart. Spencer strained against the vac dust. His hand reached out to the side of the road and closed around a heavy rock. But what use was a rock against Slick's Glopified arsenal? Spencer could barely lift the rock, let alone throw it.

"Now that I've got you alone," Slick said, "why don't you tell me 'bout the package? That's all the BEM really wants from you." He rolled even closer, the cart's wheels almost smashing Spencer's arm. "Just tell old Slick what was in the package that Daddy sent."

Heaving against the vac dust, Spencer lifted the rock

and rolled it onto the back of Slick's cart. The added weight caused a sudden shift in the balance, jerking the cleaning cart backward across the road.

Spencer jumped up as the vac dust subsided. Slick's cart was spinning in tight, uncontrollable circles as the janitor tried to kick the heavy rock away and regain balance control.

Daisy appeared at Spencer's side, shaken but unhurt. The pushbroom that Slick had used against her was still on the road, and she picked it up just as the janitor abandoned his out-of-control cart.

Slick came running toward the kids as his cart zoomed off in the opposite direction. Daisy leapt onto her cart, leveled the pushbroom, and charged like a jousting knight on horseback.

The flat bristles caught Slick under the chin and he flew off the ground. His feet clipped the top of the school's chain-link fence, and the action sent him spinning head over heels through the dark night.

Without a moment's delay, Spencer and Daisy were navigating their carts back through the bumpy field, desperate to reach the Academy before Slick had a chance to recover.

Without a doubt, Spencer and Daisy knew that Slick was an enemy. Their safety at the Academy was compromised. But where else could they go? They were many hours from home with no one to drive them. And Spencer didn't think the cleaning carts would be too safe in freeway traffic.

"We need to get a message to Walter," Spencer said as they sped up the road.

"A phone call?" Daisy asked. "Should I be sick again?" She gave another unconvincing moan that sounded like a frog throwing up.

"No," Spencer said. "Slick will expect us to try a phone call. We need something different. I have Walter's e-mail. We'll tell him what happened to Roger Munroe. Tell him that Slick is working for the BEM."

"Then what?" Daisy asked. "We're still stuck at the Academy."

"Walter will send help if he finds out we're in trouble." Spencer squinted against the cold. "All we have to do is stay alive."

CHAPTER 25

"CAN WE START OVER?"

A ball bounced off the back of Spencer's head.

"Ha ha!" Someone from the brown team laughed.

"Jail time for Doofus!" Dez shouted across the gym. Spencer glared as he crossed the dodgeball line and entered the brown team's prison. Daisy was waiting for him at the back of the gym, anxiously observing the game.

Morning P.E. was supposed to be energizing and exciting. It was supposed to prepare the kids for a full day of classes. But things looked grim for the blue team. Only Min and Jenna remained. Jenna cowered near one of the corners, and Min seemed to be calculating the velocity of every ball thrown toward him.

Min hurled a ball at Spencer, intending for him to catch it and return to the game. Spencer reached up, but the soft ball passed over his head, his hands closing too slowly to grasp it. The ball rolled out the doorway and into the hall.

Stepping out of the gym, Spencer saw the ball under the drinking fountain. He was just bending down to grab it when a hand closed over his mouth and a rough arm shoved him against the wall.

Eyes watering with panic, Spencer twisted to see his captor. It was Slick. His filthy glasses pressed down on his hooked nose, and his greasy hair was matching every expectation of his nickname. His face was scratched, and a rash from the coarse pushbroom covered his neck.

"Spencer?" Daisy's voice rang out from inside the gym. Of course she had noticed that he had been gone too long. Spencer tried to warn her, but Slick's dirty hand was tight across his lips. Spencer tried not to think of the plentiful germs that were probably leaping off the janitor's hand and onto his face.

"Move along," Slick said into Spencer's ear. The janitor pushed him down the hallway until they reached a janitorial closet. The door was partway open, so it was easy for Slick and Spencer to step inside. Spencer barely glimpsed Daisy coming out of the gym before the closet door closed, leaving Spencer and Slick alone in the dark space.

Slick bent close to the boy's ear again. "Thought you could get away from me so easily? The BEM didn't hire me to fail."

Suddenly, the closet door jerked open. Daisy locked eyes with Spencer. Then she quickly stepped inside the closet and pulled the door shut again.

"Nice hiding spot," she whispered in the dark. "Who are we hiding from?"

"Me," said Slick.

Daisy jumped a full foot. She tried to push open the door, but Slick caught the handle.

"Spencer!" Daisy said. "Slick got you!" Spencer rolled his eyes. Luckily Daisy had arrived to point out the obvious. "I thought you were hiding out. I didn't even see him in here!"

How could she have missed Slick? Spencer didn't usually stand in dark closets with a hand clamped over his mouth. Now they were both trapped!

"Not another word from you, Missy," Slick whispered, "or Zumbro gets hurt."

Daisy held up her hands like she'd seen people do on TV. "Okay," she said. Then she clamped her hands over her mouth. "Oops! I said a word! I didn't mean to say that! Can we start over?"

The bell rang, officially ending P.E. All the teams started pouring out of the gyms and into the hallway, following Director Garcia's directions to meet at the main building after dodgeball.

Spencer started to fidget. Help was only feet away. All he needed was a quick shout and someone would surely open the janitorial closet.

It was as if Slick had read Spencer's mind. "Don't even think 'bout screaming. Either of you." His crackly voice was barely audible above the noise of the kids in the hall. "If you want to scream, we'll save it for later. This closet's full of Glopified supplies that will make you squeal."

A scream was certainly what they needed. But Slick seemed to be the only one allowed to speak. So how could Spencer get Slick to raise his voice above a whisper?

An idea came to Spencer. A horrible, disgusting idea. Spencer closed his eyes against the nasty task. Then he opened his mouth and bit down hard on one of Slick's dirty fingers.

The janitor let out a wail and jerked his hand away. He blundered through the darkness, causing more of a ruckus as supplies crashed and fell.

Spencer started spitting and gagging. Desperate to sanitize his mouth, he grabbed his blue handkerchief and started wiping his tongue.

Daisy reached for the exit, but before she grabbed the handle, the closet was flooded with light from the hallway. Min stood with his hand on the door, Jenna at his elbow. Spencer and Daisy tumbled out of the closet.

"Sportsmanship," said Min.

Spencer looked back into the closet for Slick. The janitor's thick glasses had fallen among the rubble of supplies, but Slick was nowhere to be seen. Spencer squinted into the dimness. Was there another way out? A secret passage in the back of the closet?

"Frankly, I'm disappointed in you," Min continued. "You must develop a better sense of sportsmanship. Do you expect to hide in a closet every time we lose a game of dodgeball?"

"We weren't hiding . . ." said Spencer.

"It was . . ." said Daisy, pointing into the closet. But she couldn't say *Slick* since the janitor had somehow managed to vanish.

"We heard you shout," Jenna said to Daisy. "Are you okay?"

Slick might have been offended that his scream was mistaken for a girl's, but the janitor was nowhere to be seen.

"We're . . . fine," Spencer said. "Thanks for finding us."

"As blue leader," Min said, "I have to watch out for my team." He strode up to Spencer, who stood clutching his handkerchief.

"The Academy isn't a place for hide-and-seek, Spencer. You need to start thinking of how your actions will affect the group," Min said. "Behavior like this jeopardizes everyone. And I cannot let that happen." Min pulled the blue handkerchief out of Spencer's hand and let it fall to the floor. "I'm requesting a team change for you, Spencer."

CHAPTER 26

"YOU CAN SIT RIGHT BY ME!"

The teacher suddenly stopped talking, and Spencer froze as he leaned over to whisper something to Daisy.

"I'm not going to ask again," Mr. Lund said. "Lunchtime is over. You two need to stop talking or I will separate you."

Spencer sat up rigidly, aware of everyone on the combined blue and red teams staring at him. If only Mr. Lund knew what he was talking about. It was so much more important than the afternoon history lesson the teacher was giving.

Spencer and Daisy had been deciding how to tell Director Garcia about Slick. The problem with the janitor had escalated much higher than an ominous warning from a dumpster prisoner. Slick had attacked them . . . twice!

Mr. Lund resumed his lesson. Spencer glanced at Jenna, secretly hopeful that she might pass him a note to get his mind off the problems. But Jenna was paying attention to the teacher.

The classroom door opened and Mr. Lund stopped talking again. He was growing impatient with all these distractions until he saw that his boss, Director Garcia, stood in the doorway.

"Welcome, Director." Mr. Lund gestured for Garcia to take command of the class.

"I'll only be a moment," Garcia said. "I'm here to make a change in the blue team."

Spencer felt his heart thumping. He glanced over at Daisy, who sat biting her pencil. Min took a quick look over his shoulder at Spencer.

"An anonymous request has been made for Spencer Zumbro to leave the blue team," said Garcia. "We don't often get requests, and we rarely choose to honor them. But after much deliberation, the committee has decided that this one should pass."

Spencer glared at the back of Min's head. For as smart as that boy was, he sure didn't know the kind of danger he was creating by separating Spencer and Daisy.

Director Garcia reached in his pocket and pulled out a new handkerchief. "Spencer, please come forward and claim your new team."

The handkerchief dangled in Garcia's hand, wrinkled and unappealing.

It was brown.

Spencer shuffled forward, turned in his blue cloth, and took the brown one. He was dead, for sure. If Slick didn't get him, Dez and his gang certainly would. Spencer took one last look at his old teammates. Daisy's eyes were saucers and it looked like she'd nibbled off half of her pencil. It was some consolation that Jenna had a frown on her face. But Min refused to make eye contact.

Spencer followed Garcia into the hallway. At least this would give him a moment alone with the director. Now was probably his best chance to talk about Slick. But as Garcia pulled the classroom door shut, Spencer froze.

Slick was standing near the drinking fountain, wiping the shiny metal with a rag. The greasy janitor held up a hand. Director Garcia took the gesture as a wave and greeted Slick with a nod. But Spencer knew what the janitor was really doing. Slick was showing off his bandaged finger. It was a discreet threat, but Spencer got the message. If he said a word to Garcia, Slick would be waiting for revenge.

"Good luck with your new team," the director said, ushering Spencer into another classroom. Garcia poked his head inside just long enough to introduce Spencer as the newest brown team member.

Dez stood up, a huge grin on his face. "Old buddy! You can sit right by me!" The brown team members passed Spencer down the aisle until Dez took him by the shoulders and plopped him into a desk.

"Welcome to the team, Doofus," Dez said as the teacher resumed the lesson. "Brown team is the toughest, baddest team ever!" Dez's whisper was anything but quiet. "First of all, brown is a rockin' awesome color! Just think about how many cool things are brown."

"I'm not sure," Spencer said. "Are you referring to mud or . . ."

"Never mind." Dez shrugged it off. "Let's just say that being on the brown team will protect you from a lot of things—atomic wedgies, wet willies, spitwads—just to name a few. But that means you have to do what I say." Dez made two fists and bumped them together. "Trust me. You don't want to get on the brown team's bad side. We're not just a bunch of tough guys, you know. My team is smart, too."

"Like what? They all know their times tables?" Spencer said.

Dez nodded gravely. "*And* division."

CHAPTER 27

"THIS ONE'S GOT A VIRUS."

It was an hour after dinner, and Director Garcia had given all the recruits a bit of free time in the computer lab before lights-out. For Spencer, it was a much-needed break from his new team.

The whole dynamic of the brown team was different from the blues. It wasn't a matter of brains. The brown team recruits were plenty smart. But they were conniving. Dez was having the time of his life, but Spencer could see what was really happening. The browns were using Dez: learning his tricks, keeping him around as a scapegoat. For now, they let Dez rule the roost. But if the need ever came up, Spencer had no doubt that the brown team could easily outfox the bully.

Dez didn't like the brown group to sit apart. He'd forced Spencer to eat dinner with the browns. But when Spencer saw an open computer next to Daisy, he quietly slipped into the seat.

Escaping the browns wasn't Spencer's only motive for sitting next to Daisy. This was his chance, as good as any, to send an e-mail to Walter Jamison.

Spencer nudged Daisy to get her attention. She turned away from her computer to look at his. "Read through this," Spencer said. "Tell me if you think I should add anything."

Daisy scooted her chair closer, took control of his computer mouse, and began reading. Spencer stood up, looking around the computer lab to make sure that no one else was rubbernecking a peek at his e-mail.

Spencer took a few casual steps to block his computer from view of the other students. Jenna watched him from the end of the table, a half smile on her face. They hadn't seen each other for a few hours, and apparently, Jenna missed looking at him. Spencer accidentally made brief eye contact. Before Jenna could see his face redden, Spencer turned back to Daisy.

"It's good," Daisy said. "Send it."

Spencer sat back down at his computer and gave the e-mail one final read.

To: WalteRebel@janmail.com
From: SpenceZ@wahoo.com
Subject: Academy in danger

Dear Walter:

New Forest Academy is not safe! Roger Munroe is gone. He's been replaced by a BEM worker named Slick. He tried to get us twice already, but we got away. Please send help from the Rebel Underground ASAP.

We still have our cleaning supplies, so we should be able to defend ourselves from Slick if we have to.

Spencer and Daisy

Spencer clicked the *Send* button and waited for confirmation. The Internet seemed painfully slow. Suddenly, a pop-up appeared on the screen.

MESSAGE FAILED. UNABLE TO SEND. BLOCKED DOMAIN.

"Daisy," Spencer said. "Look."

She glanced back at his computer. "What happened?" She took control of the mouse and hit the *Send* button. The same pop-up appeared. "Go get help," she said, pointing toward the media specialist.

"Yeah, right!" Spencer whispered. "The first line I wrote says the Academy isn't safe. We can't let anyone see this." He tried to send the e-mail a third time, but the pop-up multiplied.

"Why won't it send?"

"The page is blocked," Spencer mused. "Someone must not want us to send an e-mail to Walter."

"I bet it was Slick," Daisy said. "He used to be the Academy's computer technician, remember?"

Spencer clicked on the computer's menu and pulled up the control panel. "We've got to get through." He browsed through tabs and folders, frantically looking for some kind of web filter.

The media specialist stood up, and Spencer hurriedly closed out. Did she know that he was trying to hack the system?

"One more minute," she announced. "Please wrap things up and shut down your computers for the night."

Desperately, Spencer clicked *Send* once again.

MESSAGE FAILED. UNABLE TO SEND. BLOCKED DOMAIN.

Students were logging off and powering down their computers. They headed toward the door of the lab, conversing casually.

"Maybe something's wrong with the computers," Daisy said. "Looks like Min's got some kind of virus."

Spencer turned to where Daisy was pointing. Min's computer screen showed hundreds of numbers separated by commas and dashes.

"Min!" Daisy whispered. "We're having computer trouble too! What should we do?"

"Trouble?" Min said, logging off and shutting down without delay. "I was programming a computer game." Of course. Min didn't just play computer games, he *made* them. "It's a physics-based puzzle game. Should be quite entertaining once I've finished."

Spencer glared at Min. How could he seem so unsympathetic? Min didn't care at all that he'd gotten Spencer transferred to the brown team.

"Maybe you can help us," Daisy said.

"No!" said Spencer. "We don't need his help!"

"We might not get another chance to send this!" Daisy said.

"Send what?" Min asked.

Daisy pointed to the computer, and Min took a step closer. His dark eyes scanned the pop-up. "The site is blocked," he said, commandeering the mouse.

"Don't read the e-mail," Daisy blurted.

Min scanned the address. "The filter won't allow you to send e-mails to a janmail account."

"We need to," Daisy said. "It's very important. Can you get it through?"

"You want me to *hack* through the Academy's security firewall?"

"Hack? Isn't that what they say when a cat coughs up a hair ball?" Daisy made a grossed-out expression. "I don't want you to hack up anything. I was just hoping you could send that e-mail."

Min shook his head, black hair bouncing. "That could get me expelled from the Academy."

"You haven't even been accepted yet," Spencer happily pointed out.

"Then getting expelled would certainly ruin the odds of my acceptance." He folded his arms. "I decline."

Spencer was trying to control the frustration he was feeling. "Forget it, Daisy. Min's just selfish. He doesn't want to help someone from a different team."

"This has nothing to do with teams," Min said. "It is simply a question of ethics."

"This has everything to do with teams!" Spencer said.

"That's why you requested for me to get traded. You thought I was ruining the blue team's chances—*your* chances!"

"That's not true," Min said.

"Then why'd you do it?" Spencer said. "You thought I looked better in brown?"

Min suddenly dropped into the chair and took control of the mouse. Spencer looked at Daisy, not even trying to mask his surprise at Min's sudden compliance.

In just a few seconds, Min had found the source of the blockage. "It requires an administrator password to disable the firewall. It will take me a few moments to overwrite it. We'll have to restart the computer for it to take effect."

"Wow," Daisy said. "You're good."

"Did you ever think I wasn't?" Min typed a few letters and numbers into the keyboard.

"All right, you three!" the media specialist called. Spencer looked up, trying to mask the guilty look on his face. "Computer time is past over."

All the other recruits had set off toward the dorms, leaving Min, Spencer, and Daisy alone. The media specialist started toward them. "Turn it off."

"Hurry," Spencer urged. Min was typing furiously.

Daisy backed away from Min and Spencer until she reached a different computer. "This one's got a virus!" she shouted to the media specialist. The distraction was enough for Min to quickly restart Spencer's computer.

The woman approached Daisy. "What's wrong with it?" the specialist asked.

Daisy pointed. "The screen's all black."

"That's because the computer is *off*, dear."

Spencer's computer rebooted, and Min opened the e-mail draft and clicked *Send*.

YOUR MESSAGE HAS BEEN SENT.

"Sounds like a bad virus to me," Daisy said, trying to keep the woman's eyes away from Spencer and Min. "A virus that turns the whole computer off?"

Spencer made a celebratory fist, but Min wasn't finished yet. He quickly pulled up the control panel and began erasing his steps, leaving no trace of his unauthorized hack.

The media specialist shook her head at Daisy. "The virus didn't shut off the computer. The student did. Just like those two boys should be doing!"

She whirled back to Spencer and Min. The boys were standing side by side, the computer behind them successfully shut down.

Under the stare of the media specialist, the three kids hurried out of the computer lab into the cool night. Min didn't say a word until they were crossing the road headed toward the dorms.

"So," he said. "Who's Walter?"

"Hey!" Daisy glared at him. "You weren't supposed to read that e-mail!"

"Hard not to, when the subject line says *Academy in danger*."

"It's not dangerous for you," Spencer said. "Forget about it."

Min stopped in the middle of the dark street, dry leaves fluttering past him. "You two are different from the other recruits. You don't actually *want* to get accepted into the Academy, do you?"

"Is that why you wanted me off the blue team?" Spencer asked. "Is that why you sent the request to Director Garcia?"

"Actually," Min said, "it wasn't me." In the silence that followed, Min folded his thin arms.

"What?" Spencer said.

"I only threatened to submit your change after P.E. I didn't actually do it," Min said. "In truth, I was frustrated to see an asset like you leave the team."

"But . . ." said Daisy to Spencer. "If it wasn't Min . . . then who else would want you off the blue team?"

"Perhaps that is not the question," said Min. "Perhaps we should ask who would want you *on* the brown team."

"Dez?" Daisy lifted an eyebrow. "I don't think so."

"Slick," Spencer whispered.

"But why?" Daisy asked.

Spencer had spent enough time with the brown team to have an idea why Slick would want him there. "The brown team lets a lot of things happen that shouldn't happen. Slick knows he'll have a better chance of getting me if I'm surrounded by browns. The blue team was too protective."

Min cocked his head. "You believe the custodian is . . . out to get you?" He didn't look convinced.

"He's not a custodian," said Daisy. "He's a janitor."

"Look," Spencer said, "I know it sounds crazy, but we might be in danger. We didn't come to the Academy to get accepted. We came to get away from some problems back home."

"And now you're afraid the problems have followed you here," Min assumed.

Daisy nodded. "That's why the e-mail was so important. Walter will tell us what to do."

"Truly fascinating." Min continued walking. "But if you really are in danger, I don't suggest that you continue sneaking away from the team."

"What do you mean?" Spencer tried to sound innocent.

"Two nights ago, you secretly left the dormitory at a quarter to midnight," Min explained. "Then last evening, you left the cafeteria toward the end of dinner and didn't return until twenty minutes before lights-out."

"Wow," Daisy said. "How did you see us? I thought we were pretty sneaky."

"I watch my team closely," said Min.

"That's why I'm worried." Spencer looked toward the shadowy dorms. "I'm not on your team anymore."

CHAPTER 28

"COME ON, NOW."

Spencer awoke to a soft *click*. He was lying in his new bed, surrounded by the boys of the brown team. Dez was snoring in the bunk below him.

Spencer lay very still. Had he imagined the noise? It sounded like a door opening. But maybe it was just the heater clicking on. Or maybe he had dreamt it.

How had he fallen asleep? Spencer had been determined to stay awake in case Slick tried to enter the brown team's dorm, but fatigue had overwhelmed him.

Now the heater clicked on, providing a soft background hum and proving to Spencer that the first sound he'd heard was something else. Spencer ducked his head under his blanket and hit the glow button on his watch.

2:18 A.M.

Using the glow like a flashlight, Spencer searched through the sheets. It was there when he fell asleep . . .

No sooner did he find what he was looking for than Spencer's covers were suddenly ripped away, his sheet slipping to the floor. Spencer let out a sharp cry and rolled over. Slick stood on the bunk ladder, a short-handled dirty mop pointed directly at Spencer.

"Go ahead," the janitor said. "Give another little girly scream. Every boy in this room is sleeping on fifty dollars. Fifty dollars that I gave them after dinner if they promised to sleep through the night, no matter what kind of ruckus they heard."

Spencer slid back against the wall. Fifty bucks? That was the going rate? He glared at the brown team members, their faces down in their pillows, pretending to sleep on. Below, Dez's snoring had ceased. These scumbags were even worse than Spencer had suspected! If they'd sell out a fellow student, there was no telling what else they might do.

"Come on, now," Slick whispered. "You're going to come with me, and we'll talk 'bout that package."

He ordered Spencer down from the top bunk. The boy dropped barefoot onto the chill wood floor. Slick's hand wrapped around Spencer's neck like an iron clamp, and the janitor dragged the boy to the doorway.

Spencer kept his head down as they entered the hall, letting Slick drag him without resistance. Spencer's heart was hammering in his ears. Each thump told him to pull away and run. But he forced himself to wait for the right moment. He might only have one chance to make a good escape.

They were almost outside when Spencer saw what he was looking for. Instantly, he pulled away. Slick let out a surprised gasp as the boy slipped easily through his fingers. Spencer reached the wall and turned, showing Slick the latex glove he had slipped on when he ducked under the blankets.

Slick shifted his mop, preparing to ensnare Spencer, whose glove would be useless against the Glopified strings. But the janitor hesitated as Spencer reached for something on the wall.

"You might be able to pay off the brown team," Spencer said. "But it's going to get expensive when everyone else wakes up."

Then, for the second time in a week, Spencer pulled the fire alarm.

CHAPTER 29

"IT'S KIND OF SLOPPY."

Nothing could have been more awkward than breakfast the next morning. Spencer sat at the edge of the brown team's table, aware of all the eyes on him. He'd made a stir with the fire alarm last night. Slick had ducked out before anyone saw him. To avoid discipline, Spencer claimed that he had pulled the alarm in a half-dreaming, delirious state of mind. Even Daisy believed him.

Only the brown team knew that something more had happened. Likely, Dez was the only person who understood why the janitor would want to capture Spencer in the middle of the night. But at breakfast, Dez seemed unaffected by last night's dealings. He was at the opposite end of the table, having a belching contest with the two newest brown team recruits.

In all, Dez's disorderly team had reached eighteen

people! The yellow team had dissolved completely, green and red fluctuated frequently, but the blue team stayed stagnant.

Spencer was dumping his breakfast leftovers when Director Garcia took him aside.

"How are you adjusting to your new team?" he asked.

"Honestly?" said Spencer. "I'm not."

Garcia nodded, as if expecting this answer. "Then you'll take this as good news. I've decided to trade you back to the blue team." He pulled out Spencer's old handkerchief.

Back to the blue team! Back to the watchful eyes of Daisy and Min! Spencer took the blue cloth and followed Garcia out of the cafeteria. He didn't glance back at his crude brown team members, but Spencer assumed they would be equally happy to see him go.

Walking alongside Garcia, Spencer gathered the courage to mention Slick. But the opportunity died as another recruit joined them. She was a talkative fourth-grade girl named Alex. She had a long, blondish ponytail and a story about everything. Garcia was transferring her to the red team, but her nonstop talking made it impossible for Spencer to tell Garcia about Slick's threats.

The director led Spencer and Alex outside the main building, across campus, and up the steps of the art building. Teams were spending the morning integrated into New Forest Academy classrooms, learning alongside the full-time Academy students.

Alex was just finishing a crazy, made-up story about a giant bug when Director Garcia dropped her off at the red team's classroom. The art room was just across the hall, and before Spencer could say anything, Garcia ushered him through the doorway.

"Blue team," Garcia announced. "You all remember Spencer? He is rejoining your company."

Spencer held up his blue handkerchief happily. There was scattered applause, more obligatory than heartfelt. Regardless, it was good to be back with teammates he could trust. Spencer found Daisy instantly.

"Glad you're back," she said. She had a dozen stamp pads in front of her, but somehow, most of the ink seemed to be on her hands and not on the stamps she was using.

"Me too." Spencer looked down at Daisy's paper, quickly filling with stamps and smudges from her fingers. "So . . . what exactly is that?"

"Art." She tilted her head to see it from a new angle. "Actually, I'm not really sure. I just started stamping things. But now I think I want to do handprints."

Before Spencer could tell her that it didn't sound like a good idea, Daisy pressed her hand onto the red stamp pad.

"We need to talk," Spencer whispered. "Slick tried to get me last night. The browns let him do it."

But before Daisy could respond, Jenna was pressing in on their conversation.

"I was hoping you'd come back! I wanted to show you this." She handed him a piece of paper. "What do you think?"

The drawing was amazing, as far as quality. Jenna was apparently quite a talented artist. The content, however, made Spencer feel hot and uncomfortable. It pictured two people holding hands, walking down a dirt road. The whole thing was framed in a giant pink heart.

"Gee . . ." Spencer didn't know what to say. "Looks like two people holding hands." Spencer forced a smile and handed the artwork back to Jenna.

He turned away and saw Director Garcia walking slowly around the art room, greeting students and commenting on projects.

Spencer noticed the discipline of the full-time Academy students in the classroom. Each one spoke a formal greeting and extended a handshake to the director.

Garcia paused behind Min. Using scissors and colored paper, the Asian boy had snipped out dozens of geometric shapes. Min was in the process of gluing the shapes onto a larger piece of paper.

Min shook the director's hand and explained his project. "It is a beta-glucan polysaccharide, as seen at the molecular level."

Garcia nodded, impressed. "How very interesting."

Director Garcia passed several students before stopping behind an unassuming Daisy Gates. He cleared his throat and held out his hand for the formal greeting. Daisy whirled around, taken completely by surprise. Before she realized what she was doing, and before Spencer could stop her, Daisy thrust her filthy hand into Director Garcia's.

All eyes shifted to the handshake as Daisy realized what she'd just done. They released hands with a squelch of red stamp ink. The whole class held its breath as Director Garcia studied his hand.

At last, his familiar smile cracked the look on his face. "It appears I caught you red-handed." The students broke into relieved laughter.

"That's okay," Daisy said. "I just started doing handprints." She pointed to her sloppy artwork. "Here's a good spot."

Director Garcia leaned down and pressed his hand onto the blank area on the page. The art teacher, Ms. Bennett, was suddenly at Garcia's side with a moist paper towel.

"I'm so sorry," she said. Ms. Bennett tried to wipe the director's hand while shooting a glare at Daisy. "Clearly, this recruit didn't follow directions. I told them each to create an art project that best represents their personalities." Ms. Bennett turned to Daisy and pointed at her paper. "You think this mess of a project represents *you?*"

"Well . . ." Daisy made a face at her paper. "It's kind of sloppy."

The art teacher followed up with an immediate question. "Do you think we have room for sloppy projects at New Forest Academy?"

Garcia finished wiping his fingers and held up a hand to calm the art teacher, as if his broad smile wouldn't do that. When Ms. Bennett stepped back, Garcia turned to Daisy.

"Remind me of your name," he said.

"Daisy Gates."

Director Garcia nodded and faced the art teacher again. "I think Daisy Gates understood your directions very well," he said. "The assignment wasn't to make a clean project. It was to make something that reflects the student's personality. If Daisy feels like she is sloppy, then shouldn't her project represent that?"

The art teacher floundered in front of her boss, evidently trying to think of a professional response.

"Not a single project here is wrong," Director Garcia said to the class.

"Phew!" Daisy wiped a hand across her forehead, leaving an inky smudge above her eyebrow.

"To say that a project is right or wrong would be to suggest that some personalities are right and others are wrong," said the director. He turned once more to the art teacher. "Are you ready to make that judgment?"

Then Director Garcia grinned at Daisy. "Congratulations."

"For what?" Daisy asked.

"For creating a masterpiece." Director Garcia held up the sloppy artwork, and Daisy blushed as red as the ink.

CHAPTER 30

"I THINK YOU'RE FORGETTING THAT."

Daisy poured exactly 300 milliliters of clear liquid into a beaker.

"I can't stop thinking about last night," said Spencer. They were paired off in the science lab, working on a chemistry project that was much harder than the usual sixth-grade curriculum. "I mean, Slick would have had me without that glove."

Daisy adjusted her goggles. They squished down on her nose, giving her a comical look. "Well, that's why Walter gave us the stuff. For emergencies. You survived."

Spencer was tired of simply *surviving*. He had lived the past few days in a state of never-ending fear. "Where is Walter, anyway? Shouldn't he be here to rescue us by now?"

"We barely e-mailed him yesterday. Who knows how far away he is?" Daisy pointed to a scale and a bag of white powder. "Can you measure 43 grams of that potassium stuff?"

How could Daisy focus on this science experiment? Wasn't she as uptight as Spencer? How could she even think about grams and milliliters while Slick was doing work for the BEM at New Forest Academy?

Spencer grabbed the bag and started spooning powder onto the scale. "You know what freaks me out the most?" he said quietly. "Slick wants me for that package my dad supposedly sent. But I still don't know anything about it!" He realized that he'd put too much powder on the scale, so he skimmed his spoon across the top of the pile. "I just expect Slick to be hiding behind every corner."

"We haven't even seen him today and it's almost dinnertime," said Daisy.

"That's what scares me. It's like he's waiting for tonight to strike again." He passed the 43 grams to Daisy.

"You have to remember," she said, "we're here to watch out for each other. You don't have to fight Slick alone."

"I was all alone last night. Dez and the brown team would have let anything happen. Those guys give me the creeps. I mean, they're smart, no doubt about it. But they're not as cool as Dez thinks. They're a bunch of sellouts. Slick bought them for fifty bucks apiece!"

"You're not on the brown team anymore!" Daisy poured another 300 milliliters of liquid into the beaker and started stirring in the powder. "You'll be safer tonight with the boys from our blue team."

"Min's a genius and all," whispered Spencer. "But he

doesn't really know about the BEM. He doesn't know about the danger."

"But *I* do!" Daisy stared at Spencer through her foggy science goggles. "I'm here to help you. I think you're forgetting that."

The chemistry teacher stood up at the front of the lab. "All right, boys and girls. At this point, you should be ready to add the diluted hydrogen peroxide to your solution."

Daisy picked up a graduated cylinder and carefully poured the premeasured hydrogen peroxide into the large beaker. She and Spencer watched with anticipation to see the outcome. Daisy was holding onto her goggles as if the solution might explode.

All around them, other students were oohing and aahing over their successful experiments. Min and Jenna had a perfect result. The liquid in their beaker was changing colors dramatically—from clear, to amber, to deep blue.

Spencer looked back at their unchanged experiment. "Isn't it supposed to *do* something?"

Daisy's shoulders slumped. "Forget it." She pushed the beaker away and pulled off her goggles. "Walter will come soon. But until then, all we have is each other. And if Slick's going to take you, then he'll have to take me too. We're in this together, both of us."

"*Three* of us," Spencer reminded her. "We've still got Dez to worry about. I should probably tell him that Walter's on his way. In case we have to make a quick getaway." Spencer sighed. "Dez probably won't listen to us anyway."

Daisy shrugged. "We have to try. Let's talk to him at dinner. Remember how Walter told us to gain Dez's trust?"

"Yeah," said Spencer. "But I don't think it's working. Maybe I can just buy his trust for fifty bucks."

"That's kind of expensive," said Daisy. "Hopefully it will be on sale."

CHAPTER 31

"DO YOU SMELL THAT?"

Dez wasn't at dinner. Spencer could easily have imagined the bully roaming the campus with his brown team gang. But all the members of the brown team were seated together in the cafeteria.

"I don't like this," Daisy said. "Where could he be?"

They sat down at the table and started eating. Dez's absence wasn't a good sign. If the bully was off on his own, then he was probably hoping to try out some Glopified supplies.

Just then, a girl from the brown team came up behind Daisy. She was tall, with a mousy face and a sly expression. Spencer hadn't learned her name during his time on the brown team, but he knew she was one of Dez's cohorts.

The girl bent over, putting her head between Spencer

and Daisy. She spoke softly. In the noise of the cafeteria, no one could overhear.

"Looking for Dez?" she asked. "He has a proposal for the two of you. Wanted to meet somewhere quiet to discuss it. He said he'd wait for you in the janitorial closet of the rec center." Her message delivered, the girl from the brown team withdrew and strode casually back to her dinner table.

Spencer stopped chewing. "Can we trust her?" Daisy asked.

Spencer glanced at the girl who'd delivered Dez's message. "There's no way she could know anything about Glopified stuff. It's Dez that I don't trust."

"But Dez wouldn't set a trap for us." Daisy looked unconvinced by her own statement. "Would he?"

"Trap or not," said Spencer, "we've got to go. Dez has probably gotten himself into some kind of trouble. And I wouldn't be surprised if Slick is involved."

They quietly dumped their half-eaten dinners and headed into the hall. Pulling on their coats, they moved outside and jogged toward the recreation center.

Spencer reached into his pocket and withdrew a latex glove. Since last night, he and Daisy had decided to carry them everywhere. A small baggie of vacuum dust filled his other pocket, and he adjusted it for quick access.

"First sign of trouble and we're out of here," Spencer said as they pulled on their gloves and stepped into the rec center.

It didn't take them long to find the closet by the gym, the same closet where Slick had held Spencer hostage. Just remembering the taste of the janitor's dirty finger caused Spencer to shudder, and he vowed never to bite anyone again—no matter how desperate he was.

Spencer grabbed a pinch of vac dust and motioned for Daisy to pull open the door. She nodded bravely and jerked on the handle, Spencer's fist already in position for a funnel throw.

The closet looked much different with the light on. It was a long, narrow room with a hard floor. Dingy shelves lined the walls, and cardboard boxes were stacked almost to the ceiling. The back wall was covered in rows of wooden cupboards.

Dez jumped up from the cardboard box he'd been sitting on, the corner crumpled from his weight. "About time you chumps got here," he said.

Spencer and Daisy stepped into the closet, still scanning the long room, searching for another person.

"What?" Dez looked around. "Was somebody else supposed to be here?"

"You tell us," Spencer said. "Seems like the perfect place for a trap."

"Whatever!" Dez looked confused. "It was your dumb idea to meet here."

"*Our* idea?" said Daisy. "You're the one who—"

The closet door slammed shut. Spencer threw himself against it, but the knob was instantly locked.

"It *was* a trap!" In anger, Spencer flung his vac dust at Dez. The bully went down, a stack of boxes toppling onto him.

"What the . . . ?" Dez shouted through the suction. "You can't trap me! I'm on your side!"

"Wait a minute," said Daisy. "We're not trapping you. *You're* trapping *us!*"

"What are you talking about?" Dez strained into an upright position. "If I was trying to trap you, I would've used bait. Like cheese or something. That seems to catch *rats* like you!"

"I heard peanut butter works too," said Daisy. "But I wonder if mice hate the way it gets stuck on the roof of your mouth."

"Hey!" Spencer shouted, slamming his shoulder into the door. The vacuum suction ended and Dez rose to his feet.

"So what did you want to talk about?" Dez asked, like being trapped in a janitorial closet was a great time to discuss the weather. "One of the girls on my team said to meet you guys here. Said you wanted to talk about something."

"What?" Spencer shook his head. "She told us the same about you." He shoved against the door again but it wouldn't budge. "Looks like we've both been tricked."

"No, no, no!" said Dez. "Brown team wouldn't trick me. I'm their fearless leader. They wouldn't do that to me! Those guys are my friends!"

"Looks like their friendship went to a higher paying customer," Daisy said.

"We've got to bust out of here," Spencer said, giving up on the door. "There's got to be something we can use in this closet." Overhead, the heater clicked on.

"Hold on a sec," Daisy said. "Do you smell that?"

"It wasn't me," said Dez. "You smelt it, you dealt it."

Spencer sniffed. It wasn't so much a scent as it was a change in the air. It smelled dusty—no—it smelled *chalky!*

Suddenly, a plume of white chalk dust streamed through the ceiling vent. The heater circulated the air, swirling the chalk cloud around them and dimming the light.

Slick must have thrown a chalkboard eraser into the vent! The explosion wouldn't take long to consume the small closet.

Spencer, Daisy, and Dez pounded on the door, throwing their whole force against it, pushing and pulling frantically. But anyone that might have heard them was still eating dinner across campus.

In the haze of the janitorial closet, they felt the chalk dust engulf them. It stung their lungs and sent them into bouts of choking coughs.

"Not this again!" Dez shouted, but Spencer and Daisy wisely held their breath. The white chalk settled into their hair. It clung to their shirts and pants, turning their clothing white.

With only an ounce of breath left in his lungs, Spencer remembered his first experience in this closet. Slick had mysteriously disappeared when Min had opened the door. That meant there had to be some kind of secret escape passage!

Spencer ran his fingers along the walls of the closet, searching desperately for any weakness that could lead to escape. Unable to hold out any longer, he gasped for air.

But the chalk-tainted air did not satisfy. His feet were going numb. He tried to speak, but his tongue felt heavy.

There was a thump as Dez fell to the hard floor. Daisy was moving clumsily, stumbling over boxes. Spencer's hand slipped from a shelf, and he collapsed onto his face.

Hadn't he fled Welcher to escape this fate? Now it seemed the BEM had him at last.

CHAPTER 32

"LIFE AIN'T FAIR."

Spencer awoke to the sound of a squeaky door. The floor beneath him was rock hard and dreadfully uncomfortable. He tried to move, but his whole body seemed full of lead. He attempted simply to wiggle a finger, but even that action was denied him. Spencer could only manage to open his eyelids. But as soon as he did, the overhead light caused him to squint blindly.

Spencer heard footsteps, accompanied by a drawling voice. "Lovely morning, ain't it?"

Morning? How many hours had passed in this chalk-blasted closet?

Spencer opened his eyes again as the speaker stepped forward, blocking the light. The voice had already given him away, but seeing the janitor made Spencer's stomach twist in anguish. Slick had a malevolent grin on his pocked face.

Spencer tried again to move. He had a shout of defiance for the janitor, but the chalk explosion from last evening still held him paralyzed.

Slick strode across the long closet and opened one of the cupboards on the back wall. As the little door swung open, a dim light shone from beyond. From his place on the floor, Spencer could see that the cupboard was not full of shelves, as he had expected. It appeared to be an entrance into a hidden tunnel.

If only he could have discovered that when the room was filling with chalk dust!

Returning, Slick stopped in front of Spencer. "The Bureau only needed one of you, but I could think of a good reason to catch all three."

The chalk bomb had left the inside of the closet in a fine white coating, like freshly fallen snow. Slick grabbed Spencer under the arms and dragged him toward the cupboard, leaving tracks in the white dust. "You are the obvious one." He hoisted Spencer's limp body through the cupboard door and into the dim tunnel. "You've got information 'bout the package that the Bureau's searching for." He set Spencer into a waiting wheelbarrow, the metal edge digging uncomfortably against his neck.

Dusting residual chalk off his hands, Slick stooped through the cupboard door and approached Daisy. "Course, we couldn't have you running around trying to play hero."

He dragged her into the tunnel and set her in the wheelbarrow next to Spencer. "So I had to nab you, too."

He returned and started lugging Dez toward the cupboard. "And you . . ." Straining, he lifted Dez into the tunnel. "I've got my own ideas for you."

Spencer and Daisy grunted unintelligibly as Slick plopped Dez on top of them. Dez moaned, clearly trying to say something.

"I know," Slick said. "Life ain't fair. You thought you was the brown team leader, till they sold you out." The janitor chuckled. "They were never really your friends. Just users. Couple hundred bucks and they set this whole thing up for me. It was the only way I could get the three of you alone together."

Slick picked up the wheelbarrow and started down the long, dim tunnel.

"A true friend is hard to come by these days. Too bad, right? You should pick your friendships as careful as you pick your nose."

CHAPTER 33

"DO YOU FEEL IT?"

Spencer had no idea what time it was when he finally regained the use of his voice. In his paralyzed state, the passage of time was excruciatingly slow. He drifted in and out of nervous sleep for what seemed like days.

"Hello?" was the first word Spencer tried. When that proved successful, he tried another. "Help!"

The last moment worth remembering seemed like hours ago. Slick had pushed the wheelbarrow out of the tunnel into an adjoining janitorial office in the Academy's main building. He'd dumped Spencer, but had taken Daisy and Dez out of sight up some stairs.

Spencer turned his head clumsily from side to side, a skill he had recently recovered. "Hello?" he tried again. "Anybody?" He was alone.

The janitor's office was cluttered with cleaning supplies.

Some of the stuff had to be Glopified. If he could just get something to help him escape . . .

Spencer tried to lean forward. His head swung, chin coming to rest on his chest. He was slumped in a hard chair, unable to summon the strength to stand and run. He was a prisoner, held not by ropes or chains but by the paralyzing effects of the chalkboard eraser.

"You're one stubborn fool." Slick's voice cut through the room. Spencer lolled his head around to find the janitor standing in the doorway. "It didn't have to be like this. I gave you plenty of chances to tell me 'bout that package. But you refused to cooperate. Now it's a big mess and you dragged your friends into it."

"Where's Daisy?" Spencer's speech was still slurred, and his tongue felt thick and foreign in his mouth.

"Why don't you leave the question-asking to me?" Slick dragged a hand across his greasy hair. "I'm gonna start simple. The questions only get hard if you make them hard, okay?"

"What questions?" Spencer said.

"Are you the son of Alan Zumbro?" Slick grinned. "See? Not too hard."

Spencer tried to nod his head, but Slick grabbed him by the hair and looked into his face. "Not like that. You've got to speak it out so there ain't no confusion 'bout what you're saying."

"Yes," Spencer said. "I am."

"Have you seen or spoken with your father since his mysterious disappearance two years ago?"

"No."

"Have you received any gifts or packages from your father during his absence?"

"No."

"Try again."

"I said no."

Slick sighed and pushed up his glasses. "I see you want to make things complicated." He walked out of sight and returned a moment later, trailing an orange extension cord in one hand.

"I brought a little friend to help jog your memory 'bout the package your daddy sent in the mail."

Slick tugged on the extension cord, and Spencer saw a Filth stumble around the corner. The creature's breath instantly caused Spencer a moment of drowsiness. He blinked against the fatigue as the Toxite tried to scurry into hiding. But for some reason, the Filth couldn't get away. Then, with a twinge of horror, Spencer saw the reason. The extension cord was plugged directly into the Filth's back!

"He's a little shy right now," Slick said. "But as soon as I plug him in, he'll warm up to you." Slick carried his end of the extension cord over to an electrical socket in the wall and inserted it.

The moment the electricity hit the cord, the Filth stopped squirming. It turned to face Spencer, an almost serene expression on its face. Then the creature began to hum and pulsate gently. Its breath came in deep, intoxicating rushes.

Spencer's head lolled forward and his eyes drooped. But

exerting every muscle in his body, Spencer willed himself not to sleep. His eyes traced the line of the orange extension cord back to the Filth. What he saw shocked him.

The Toxite was evolving!

It had expanded to the size of a small dog. A spike-studded tail was already beginning to emerge, and the sharp quills along the creature's back were lengthening. It didn't seem possible, but the Glopified extension cord was sharpening the Toxite's most dangerous characteristics while growing it to an unnaturally large size.

"Now," Slick said, "we can go on like this all day, but the bigger this critter gets, the more potent its breath. Funny thing how Toxites don't affect adults. But you ain't an adult." Slick leaned forward. "Do you feel it?"

Spencer squinted hard and tried to hold his breath against the Toxite corruption. He felt his mind wandering aimlessly, hopping between one thought and the next, unable to separate his random imaginings from reality. His mind had slipped into that limbo somewhere between waking and dreaming.

"With enough exposure, Filth breath has a way of loosening the tongue." Slick's voice rattled at the edge of consciousness. Then, like a loud noise breaking through a dreamy haze, Slick unplugged the extension cord.

The Filth scurried around the corner, Slick giving it just enough slack on the cord to do so. Spencer's eyes opened and his head rolled around to face the janitor. The air felt fresh again, but the aftereffects of the overgrown Filth's breath lingered in his system like a bad dream.

"Let's go over this part one more time," the janitor said. "What was in the package that your father sent you?"

Spencer swallowed against the fear in his throat. There was no package. What could he say? He felt the heat of the bare lightbulb overhead, the tingle of numbness in his fingertips, and the grip of hunger on his insides. The Filth's foul breath had scattered his mind.

Package. Was there a package? But as hard as he tried, Spencer could not think of a single thing he'd received from his dad in the last two years.

"There is no . . . package," Spencer said.

"Wrong answer."

Slick jerked on the extension cord, and the large Filth stumbled back around the corner. With a faint hum, electricity flowed down the Glopified line and filled the Toxite with a pulsating glow.

"Why don't I leave you two alone for a while?" Slick headed for the doorway. "Think 'bout what I said."

Spencer's eyes closed. He was alone with the growing monster. His mind wandered again. No, this time it was more than a wander. His mind was lost.

CHAPTER 34

"IT'S GENIUS."

Spencer awoke to a blast of cold water in the face. He gasped and opened his eyes. Aside from being dripping wet, he was seated in a dimly lit office full of janitorial cleaning supplies. His legs felt tingly and weak, and when he lifted his arm, it was stiff and sore, as though he hadn't moved it for hours. An empty pit had opened in his stomach, and Spencer wondered how long it had been since he'd eaten something.

And his mind . . . it felt like his brain had been pulled apart and left for a toddler to reassemble. Fragmented thoughts and ideas drifted hither and thither. It was impossible to focus on anything.

A man was standing in front of Spencer, a dripping pail on the floor beside him. He had slicked-back, greasy hair and thick glasses that pressed on his nose. He looked familiar, but Spencer's brain couldn't seem to make the connection.

"Almost forgot 'bout you down here," the man said. Spencer stared at him, void of expression. "That Toxite was nearly as big as a pony by the time I unplugged it."

Toxite. That was a word Spencer thought he should understand.

"Course, you're no good to the BEM if you can't remember nothing. That's what happens with long-term exposure to Toxite breath. It can really bring you low, turn your brain to mush."

The man stared at Spencer. "Oh, come on," the stranger said. "You were only down here with that thing for an hour or two." He patted Spencer's cheek. "I thought the water would refresh you."

The man wrinkled his forehead. "All right, then. How about a quick rundown? I'm Slick, the janitor at New Forest Academy. You are Spencer, son of Alan Zumbro. Your dad sent you a package in the mail and you're going to tell me about it."

Slick. Janitors. New Forest Academy. Toxites.

Spencer's brain finally made the connections, and it all came rushing back into place. As order returned to his mind, it came with a sharp headache and an inescapable urge to run.

Spencer bolted from his seat, shoulder turned to charge past Slick and make his escape. But he only managed three steps before his legs collapsed. Spencer pitched sideways, but Slick caught him before he hit the floor.

The janitor held him still for a moment. Spencer's head throbbed with each heartbeat, wearing down his defenses. He let Slick guide him back to that uncomfortable seat. Spencer rocked back in the chair, trying to muster the strength for another escape.

"Take it easy," Slick said. "It'll be a few minutes before you get your head on straight." The janitor bent over and picked up something from the floor. It was the orange extension cord, now unplugged from both wall and beast. "You've got a choice now. I can bring another Filth to keep wearing you down." He dropped the cord to the hard floor. "Or I can let you rest, help you build up your strength. Maybe bring you a little bite to eat."

Slick crossed the room and lifted a lunch tray from a shelf. The very thought of food had caused Spencer's mouth to start watering. Now seeing the cafeteria food on the tray was almost too much to resist.

"Hungry?" Slick asked. The janitor took a step forward and Spencer grabbed the tray, half surprised that Slick didn't try to pull it away. Spencer lowered the lunch tray to his lap, eyes flicking across the myriad of cafeteria food that awaited him. He instantly started shoveling meatballs into his mouth without even worrying about the fact that he hadn't washed his hands.

Slick crouched down next to the chair, his beady eyes watching the boy eat. "How old were you when your daddy . . . you know, ditched out?"

"He didn't ditch us," Spencer said between bites. "Something happened to him."

"Must have been meddling in unsavory activities."

Spencer could see what was happening. This was Slick's plan—make Spencer comfortable with relaxation and food to get him talking. But it didn't matter, since Spencer knew nothing about the package that Slick was prying about. "He was a scientist," Spencer said. "A Toxite scientist."

"And a reliable go-to for the BEM." Slick tilted his greasy head. "Course, that was before the BEM changed its philosophy on Toxite fighting. The Bureau assigned Alan Zumbro to a top-secret mission. He was tracing a series of very dangerous clues. BEM didn't expect him to solve it so quickly. Plenty of others had tried before, and they came home in caskets. Alan . . . he made it all the way to the final clue. But the BEM wasn't ready, so they had to intervene. Alan found the final package, but before we could capture him, he ditched it somewhere."

Slick arose, put his hands casually in his pockets, and paced a few steps. "Alan knew he'd be interrogated 'bout the contents of the package. So you'll never guess what that devil of a man did."

Slick let the tension hang for a moment. Then he shouted, "He didn't look!" The janitor shook his head. "Alan didn't look inside the package! Do you get it? If he didn't know what was in there, then the BEM couldn't pry the information out of him." Slick rubbed a hand across his oily hair. "But we got a different lead from him. Just two words, but it told us where he'd sent the package."

Slick lowered his face until it was only inches from

Spencer's. He spoke the two words, his breath as foul as a Toxite's.

"Spencer. Son."

Spencer felt a new numbness, far more intense than the effects of the chalk paralysis. It filled him up, twisting his stomach painfully. Surely his dad would never have said those two words knowing that it might plunge Spencer into a world of danger.

"So that, of course, brings us here." Slick shrugged. "Couple of months ago, the BEM sent a sharp representative to your town. Man by the name of Garth Hadley. Maybe you remember him? Garth was supposed to turn you against the Rebel Janitors and gain your trust in the BEM. But Hadley messed up royal. He had his own agenda that the BEM didn't approve. Thought it would be icing on the cake if he got you to steal Jamison's bronze hammer."

Spencer's eyes fell back to the tray of food on his lap. Slick's story had caused his appetite to flee, but Spencer knew that eating was the best way to gain back his strength. And strength was exactly what he would need to escape from Slick's dim janitorial closet. Spencer took a scoop of mashed potatoes on his fingers and pushed them into his mouth.

Slick sighed. "Long story short," he said, "you ended up joining with the Rebels and fighting the BEM. Then comes the next bright plan. BEM lets your Rebel friend, old Roger Munroe, take a job at the Academy. Then the Bureau tips off Walter Jamison, says a couple of workers are coming to kidnap you. Roger phones in, suggests that you come to the safety of New Forest Academy. It's remote, secure, and Toxite-free. But old Roger didn't know that once the plan was in motion, I would help him . . . *resign*."

Spencer suddenly gagged on his mashed potatoes. He rolled the mash over his tongue, face contorting into pure disgust as he spat the soggy white lump onto the lunch tray.

Slick stared at the expectorated mess and nodded. "I know, I know. It's enough to make you sick. But the BEM has a way of taking care of Rebels."

But it wasn't Slick's story that had caused Spencer to gag. Bracing himself against his own spit and germs, Spencer dug his fingers into the squishy morsel.

"Oh, now you're playing with it?" Slick turned away. "That's just gross."

Spencer's heart pounded in his ears. There was a note! He quickly found a tiny scroll of paper and pinched it between his fingers. Now, if he could just create a brief distraction, he might be able to read it.

Giving a quick jerk with his legs, Spencer bucked the cafeteria tray forward, flipping the half-eaten lunch toward Slick. The tray clattered to the floor, cold meatballs bouncing off Slick's steel-toed boots.

The janitor gave a snarl and bent to grab the tray. Spencer quickly unraveled the note, trying to wipe off excess mashed potato as he silently read the message.

Academy = Danger!
I have a school bus in the parking lot!
óMeredith

"What's that?" Slick took a step forward, squinting at the boy's hand. The janitor gripped the lunch tray in his grubby fingers.

"Potato peel!" Spencer popped the note into his mouth. He shuddered at the texture but forced himself to chew. He tried not to think of the route that the little paper might have taken—ripped from a notebook, passed from dirty hand to dirty hand, scribbled on by Meredith with an unsanitary pen, rolled into the mashed potatoes, and finally, chewed to mush in Spencer's mouth. He closed his eyes and swallowed. The paper went down easy. Tasted like . . . potatoes.

"Time's running out," Slick said, setting the tray on a nearby shelf. "BEM needs that package. As far as they're concerned, you're the link to find it."

"I don't know anything!" Spencer's eyes darted around the closet as he tried to plan an escape. Now that he knew Rebel help was at the Academy, Spencer was desperate to break free. But Slick squinted through his dingy glasses, anticipating any move that Spencer might attempt.

"The Bureau will get what it needs." Slick scooped up the extension cord again, his face sinister. "Whether you're willing or not."

"You're crazy!" Spencer shouted. "The BEM's crazy!" His clouded mind felt like bursting.

"Oh no, son. The Bureau of Educational Maintenance ain't crazy." Slick smiled. "It's genius."

"Did you say something about a genius?" A new voice came from the doorway.

Slick leapt in surprise and spun around, dropping the extension cord in his haste.

Min stood a few feet away, holding a feather duster in his hand like a sword. Slick gave an embarrassed chuckle when he saw who had frightened him. Then the greasy janitor reached toward a pushbroom against the wall.

"I suggest you don't move another inch," Min said, his face like stone.

CHAPTER 35

"DO YOU UNDERSTAND?"

Slick paused. "Ain't never seen a Glopified duster like that, kid. You can't scare me."

Min held up the feather duster. "This is a new product, sent to me straight from the Rebel Underground. It hasn't yet been tested on a human." Min cocked his head. "Walter didn't want me to, but I'd be happy to make you the beta trial."

"You Academy brats are all the same," Slick said. "Think you're so smart."

Min put both hands on the thin handle of the duster. Sighting down the shaft, he closed one eye and took aim at the janitor's face. "A simple twist of this handle will send every feather from this duster into your respiratory system. Entering through any available orifice, they will then lodge themselves in your trachea and bronchus. Pulmonary failure will be imminent. Do you understand?" Min tightened his grip on the feather duster. "Or would you like me to get technical?"

Slick glanced one last time at the pushbroom, but Min clucked his tongue disapprovingly. The janitor lifted his hands in the air and retreated slowly to the back wall. Spencer rose from the chair, testing the strength of his legs, preparing to run if necessary. But Min, ever calm and composed, drove Slick back with the feather duster. The janitor stepped onto a wooden pallet, stumbling in his heavy black boots.

"You . . ." Slick threatened. "You ain't seen the last of me." A chain, extending from the ceiling, was bolted securely into the wooden pallet. Slick's hand darted out. Catching the chain, he gave a hard downward tug. Instantly, the wooden pallet under him plummeted down a dark shaft, carrying Slick out of sight.

Min twisted the handle of the feather duster, but the only movement in the room came as a new pallet fell from the ceiling, clanking down the chain until it fit snugly over the dark shaft.

"What happened?" Spencer shouted. Slick was gone in the blink of an eye. Spencer turned to Min. "The duster . . . why didn't it work?"

"I'm sure it works fine," Min said, tossing the item to the floor, "for dusting shelves."

"But, it's Glopified . . . right? Where did you get it?"

"I found the feather duster upstairs, in the closet where I rescued Daisy and Dez. It seemed improbable, but I tried threatening Dez with it first. He seemed to be genuinely frightened, so I wagered the janitor would be also." Min made a belittling smile. "I find it truly absurd that the man believed I could harm him with a duster."

"What now?" Spencer said. "Is Walter here?"

"Actually," Min said, "I have no idea who Walter is."

"But you said—"

"All part of a carefully calculated fabrication. I used terms and references that I had read in your e-mail to give validation to my threats."

"So you're not really part of the Rebel Underground?" Spencer said.

"Never heard of it until I read your e-mail."

"And the duster?" Spencer pointed to the item on the floor. "What does it really do?"

Min gave a blank stare. "It removes dust."

"Right," Spencer said, realizing that Min still didn't believe that janitorial supplies could be Glopified. Regardless, Spencer was amazed by the boy's ability to come up with such a convincing lie.

"You had the misfortune of not following my advice," Min said.

"What do you mean?" Spencer asked.

"You left the safety of the team again. I saw you and Daisy exit the cafeteria during dinner. When you never returned, I became concerned. Slick told Director Garcia that you had all taken ill and he'd driven you to the hospital in Denver. Having read your e-mail, I knew that you had concerns about your safety at the Academy, particularly in regard to Slick. I put two and two together, took the square root of the sum, and decided that you had been kidnapped."

"How did you know to find me here?" Spencer asked.

"I saw Slick taking lunch trays from the cafeteria. He led me right to you."

"There was more on that tray than lunch," Spencer said, remembering Meredith's mashed-potato message. "Where are Daisy and Dez? We've got to get out of here."

"I sent Daisy and Dez to the recreation center to join the other recruits," Min said.

"I think I know a shortcut to get there," said Spencer. He crossed Slick's office until he came to a panel of cupboards. Remembering which one opened to the tunnel, he reached out and grabbed the little handle.

Whiteness. Blinding flashes that overtook his vision.

He was riding in a swanky elevator with wooden paneling and carpeted floor. His sense told him immediately that he was moving upward, passing the sixth floor of the building. The elevator chimed and the shiny doors parted. Spencer stepped onto the seventh floor, moving with purpose down a wide hallway. He encountered several people, but they all cowered in his large shadow. They looked down respectfully, not daring to speak. At the end of the hallway, a white light grew, flooding the passageway and overtaking his vision again.

Spencer blinked against the whiteness, felt Min helping him back to his feet. Ahead of him, the cupboard door swung on its hinges to reveal the secret passageway.

Spencer shook his head, trying to forget about the

sudden vision. He couldn't allow anything to distract him from the immediate task ahead. Meredith was waiting for them in the parking lot, but they had to get out before Slick showed up again.

"This should lead to the rec center," Spencer said. Together, the two boys stepped through the opening.

CHAPTER 36

"WE CAN'T GO."

Spencer and Min kicked open the cupboard door and stumbled into the rec center janitorial closet. Everything was still powdered in white chalk dust. Spencer and Min left new footprints as they maneuvered past boxes and shelves, emerging at last into the hallway beyond. If Daisy and Dez were with the other recruits, then they must be in one of the gyms because Spencer didn't see anyone in the hall.

The boys checked a few empty gyms before Spencer reached a racquetball court at the end of the hall. He tested the small door, but it didn't budge. Either it was locked or something heavy was blocking it from the inside.

"They could be in here," Spencer called to Min.

"Spencer?" Daisy's voice drifted down a nearby stairwell. In a second, she appeared at the top of the stairs.

"There you are!" Spencer said. "Come on! Meredith's waiting for us in the parking lot!"

But Daisy's eyes were wide and filling with tears. "We can't go," she said.

"What are you talking about?" Spencer ran up the stairs, Min close behind. Dez was at the top of the hallway with Daisy, leaning against the wall.

Daisy pointed to an observation window that overlooked the racquetball court. "We have to get them out." Her voice was choked with emotion.

Spencer stepped forward. When he reached the window and looked into the racquetball court below, his stomach churned, threatening to push out the food he'd just eaten.

There were probably thirty recruits below, wearing handkerchiefs of blue, red, and green. They were crowded into the racquetball court, frazzled expressions on their faces. Some showed signs of crying; others were curled up on the floor.

Thick, orange extension cords littered the floor like wet spaghetti noodles, maybe half a dozen. One end of each cord was plugged into a power strip along the wall of the court. But the other end made a gruesome connection with the flesh of a Toxite.

Filths, Grimes, Rubbishes . . . the monsters hunched invisibly, drinking in the brain waves of the Academy recruits and hissing out breaths of grogginess, distraction, and apathy. Electricity flowed through the Glopified extension cords, fueling unnatural growth in pulsating waves.

CHAPTER 37

"I LOVE BREAKING THINGS."

Spencer backed away from the racquetball court's observation window, horrified by the scene below. The students were trapped down there! Growing Toxites sapped away their brain waves, and Spencer remembered what Slick had said about long-term exposure to the Toxite breath. If the students didn't get out of the court soon, their brains could turn to mush!

Then Spencer saw something that made the whole situation painfully real.

Jenna was down there!

She sat in the corner, shoulders slumped like she didn't care about anything in the world. She had the most awfully bored look on her face, and Spencer could see tears staining her cheeks. Behind her, a Rubbish pulsed and glowed.

Having already expanded to the size of an eagle, the monster had to be spewing terribly potent breath.

A figure suddenly appeared on the stairway. The kids turned to see Director Carlos Garcia striding toward them, his hands casually tucked in the pockets of his slacks.

"You were absent when we passed out the envelopes," Garcia said as he crested the stairs. "It was a tough decision, but the winning team really came forward at the end." He rubbed his chin. "The *brown* team has been accepted to New Forest Academy."

"What?" Daisy shrieked. "The brown team won? Like, *Dez's* brown team?"

But the bully didn't look like a winner. He was unusually quiet and pressed against the wall, far from the observation window.

Min looked crushed, his hopes and aspirations for the Academy coming to a fast close. He must have been rescuing Spencer when the announcement was made. Lucky thing, too, or he would be trapped down in the racquetball court with the rest of the Academy rejects.

"Fine," Spencer said. "I don't really care who won. But there's something bad going on down there." He pointed to the window. "We've got to get them out. Now!"

"These others," Garcia gestured to the window, "did not meet our qualifications to study here." His tone was somber, like that of a parent telling a child that the family dog must be put down. "And now we must let the old forest burn."

Spencer turned to him, cruel realization dawning at last. "You *know* . . . ? You know what's happening!"

"You've been working with Slick all along!" Daisy accused. "You've been helping the BEM take over the school!"

Director Garcia shook his head. "The BEM has no need to take over New Forest Academy." He paused. "They founded it."

Spencer felt a tingle pass through his body. What was Director Garcia saying? The BEM was the *founder* of New Forest Academy?

Garcia looked back to the observation window. "With its left hand, the BEM destroys every shred of competition. It lets Toxites run wild, polluting every traditional school and rotting the brains of anyone who opposes it. Then, with its right hand, the Bureau raises up a safe school, a clean school—an exclusive Academy where only the strongest can attend."

Spencer pointed into the racquetball court. "But *they* are the strongest. *They* are the smartest!"

"Unfortunately, brilliance is not the only criteria," Garcia said. He closed his eyes. "Their personalities are not right. They're . . . too loyal, too honest. They don't have what it takes to fight their way to success. They're too afraid to step on their friends to get to the top."

So that was why the cutthroat brown team had won! The Academy was sifting through everyone, looking for the most self-serving, aggressive, manipulative students. That was who the Academy was choosing to educate while everyone else fell by the wayside, rotted out by Toxite breath. Spencer turned back to the students trapped below.

"Who cares if they didn't make it into your Academy!"

Spencer shouted. "They're innocent! Just let them go home!"

"I can't do that." Garcia stepped away from the observation window. "Those kids down there represent the greatest threat to the BEM's plan. If they go home, they'll continue to learn and develop, doing all they can to resist the Toxite breath. We can't let that happen." Director Garcia put a hand on Spencer's shoulder. "In order for the new forest to rise, the old forest must burn."

"They're not trees!" Spencer jerked away from Garcia. "They're human beings, with thoughts and hopes!"

"*Cálmate*," Garcia held out his hands. "They won't die down there, Spencer. We're just helping them find their place in society's future. They will simply be followers. They will still be able to lead normal lives. But they will never be . . . *great*."

"How can you say that?" shouted Spencer. "How can you decide their future?"

"I have been chosen to judge them," Garcia said. "It is a difficult task. I do not enjoy it, but it is necessary to ensure the BEM's success. The Bureau takes no risks. Everything must burn in order to establish New Forest Academy's dominion over education."

Spencer didn't want to know what other diabolical plans the BEM might have. It was enough to know that they had founded an elitist school to educate a select few while the brains of thousands of kids across the nation were rotting from Toxite breath.

Director Garcia was saying something else, but Spencer

couldn't stand to listen. No one heard the soft snap as the Ziploc bag opened in Spencer's coat pocket. No one noticed as he pinched a bit of vac dust between his fingers.

Spencer leapt forward, hurling the puff of dust toward Director Garcia's face. At the last second, the man turned aside and the dust went past. Garcia lunged, shoving Spencer to the floor. On his way down, Spencer pulled the Ziploc bag from his coat and tossed it to Daisy. Garcia whirled around, but the girl was too fast. The suction from Daisy's palm blast caught Garcia and pulled him instantly to the floor.

"All right." Spencer picked himself up and faced his three comrades. Min's eyes were a little wider than usual as he stared at the suctioned director. "We're going to have to split up if we want to get everyone to the parking lot."

Spencer turned to Daisy. "Take Min to the stash. Gather everything we've got. Once you've got it, do what it takes to get that front gate open."

"What about me?" Dez said, still standing with his back to the wall. It was the first thing Dez had uttered, and Spencer wondered at his silence.

"You're staying with me," Spencer said. "I'll need your help to break into the racquetball court and rescue the recruits."

Daisy handed Spencer the Ziploc bag of vacuum dust. "Don't trust anyone from the Academy," Spencer said. "Students, teachers, not even the old members of the brown team. Remember . . ." Spencer narrowed his eyes. "Academy equals BEM. They're one and the same now."

Daisy headed toward the stairs, but Min extended a quick farewell handshake to Spencer. “It’s odd,” the Asian boy said. “My experience at New Forest Academy has taken a sudden janitorial turn that was quite unpredictable.”

Spencer couldn’t help but grin through the tension of the moment. “I hope that’s your way of saying good luck.”

“I hate to break up this lame friendship moment,” Dez said. “But Director G*racias* is trying to get up.”

Spencer whirled around, digging a second pinch of vacuum dust from the baggie. The attack plastered Director Garcia back to the floor. When Spencer turned again, Min and Daisy had vanished down the stairwell.

“So what’s your genius plan to rescue these chumps?” Dez asked.

“Can you break down the door?” Spencer asked.

Dez popped his knuckles. “Sweet.” He grinned. “I love breaking things.”

“I’ll stay here and keep Garcia pinned with vac dust,” Spencer said as Dez headed downstairs. A moment later, Spencer heard the racquetball door shudder once, twice . . . He could imagine the big bully throwing his whole weight against it.

“Won’t break!” Dez shouted.

“Hit it harder!” answered Spencer, readying another puff of vac dust for Garcia.

“You trying to make me hurt myself?” shouted Dez. “I said, it won’t break!”

Spencer tossed the vacuum dust onto the director’s chest. With a grunt, the man was down again. Garcia rolled on his side, a ring of keys jingling on his belt. Spencer quickly unhooked them.

"What about these?" Spencer called. He ran down the stairs, dangling the keys victoriously.

"I bet you had those the whole time," Dez said, massaging his shoulder. "You were just trying to get me to knock myself out."

"That would have been nice." Spencer tried a few keys before he found the right one. They didn't have much time before the vac dust holding Garcia wore off.

"Ready?" Spencer shoved open the unlocked door.

Most of the students were so influenced by the Toxite breath that they didn't even look up. But Jenna lifted her chin, and for one brief moment Spencer thought he saw a shred of hope in her eyes. Then the Rubbish opened its mouth, and her eyes clouded over.

Spencer suddenly yawned as Filth breath drifted through the open door. The potent Toxite breath was going to make this harder than he'd thought.

"Look out!" Dez shouted, jerking Spencer away from the open door. They rolled away from the entrance just as an overgrown Rubbish flapped through the doorway. It cut a jagged course through the hallway and disappeared around a corner.

"Thanks." Spencer turned to face Dez. "Did you see the size of that thing?"

"Yeah," said Dez. "It was huge." He held out his hands like a fisherman telling about his prize catch.

Spencer lashed out, suddenly shoving Dez against the wall. "Anything else you want to tell me?"

Dez tried to make a puzzled expression. "What are you talking about?"

Spencer raised his voice to an angry shout. "Since when have you been able to see Toxites, Dez?"

CHAPTER 38

"THEY MUST HAVE PLANS FOR YOU."

Dez pushed Spencer off and stepped away from the wall.

"You can see them!" Spencer accused.

"So what!" Dez shouted back. "You can too! I'm sick and tired of you and Daisy seeing things and doing stuff behind my back! I'm just as important as you are. I have a right to see the monsters!"

"Who did it to you? Who gave you the soap? Was it Slick?"

"This morning," Dez said. "Slick gave me some while I couldn't move."

"Why would he do that? Did you make some kind of deal with Slick?"

"No deal. He just gave me the soap for fun."

"The BEM doesn't do anything for fun," Spencer said. "They must have plans for you."

Suddenly, an alarm blared through the hallway, resonating in the racquetball courts and every gym in the rec center. Spencer turned to see Director Garcia on his hands and knees at the top of the stairs. He had crawled to the end of the hall, fighting the vac dust long enough to pull a security alarm.

"We've got to unplug the Toxites," Spencer said. "I'm going in!"

He leapt through the small doorway and into the haze of sapped brain waves that filled the racquetball court. The harsh blare of the security alarm helped keep him anchored, without letting his mind slip into worry-free sleep.

"Come on!" Spencer shouted, but the recruits were too far under the spell of the Toxites' breath to heed him. Spencer staggered across the court until he reached the first extension cord. He bent down and grabbed the cord in both hands.

A huge yawn forced him to his knees. He slumped against the wall and crumpled to the floor. Somewhere in the back of his sleep-muddled mind, Spencer knew he had to unplug the cord. Doing so would frighten the Toxites away and give him a chance to help the students escape. But the temptation to sleep was too strong. Instead of pulling out the cord, Spencer rested his head on the floor, eyelids drooping.

Someone bent over his prone form, grabbing the extension cord from his hands and jerking it out of the wall socket. Spencer squinted to see Dez stepping past him. The big kid was walking along the wall, trying to keep a safe distance from the ever-enlarging Toxites. Dez reached the next outlet. Leaning down, he yanked the plug out of the socket and let it fall to the ground.

The Grime that was attached to the other end scurried up the wall, bulbous fingertips finding easy purchase. The next plug Dez pulled sent a Filth scurrying out of the racquetball court, trailing its extension cord along like a dog on a leash without an owner.

With the Filth gone, Spencer felt revived. He rose to his knees as Dez unplugged another. The bully's high tolerance for Toxite breath was impressive, but even Dez was starting to show signs. His pace slowed and his attitude became apathetic, like he couldn't understand why it was important to unplug the Toxites. Finally, he slumped down, only feet away from the last cord. It was attached to that Rubbish, the big one perched behind Jenna.

Spencer dug out a dash of vacuum dust. His Ziploc bag was almost empty now. It was a long shot across the gym. Positioning his hand with the fingers together, he took aim and flung the vac dust. It ripped across the gym with the sound of a revving vacuum and struck the pulsating Rubbish head-on. The creature fell to the court floor and, for a moment, its foul breath caught in its throat.

Dez recovered his senses quickly. Reaching out, he unplugged the final extension cord. The Rubbish shuddered and took flight for the open doorway.

The thirty recruits seemed very confused. Spencer remembered the terrible feeling of trying to piece his brain back together after inhaling too much Toxite breath. But there was no time for a sympathetic recovery.

"Get up!" Spencer shouted. "Everyone's in danger! We have to go!" The piercing alarm gave his warning validity, and a few of the students seemed to realize what he was saying.

In a moment, Spencer had herded everyone into the hallway and Dez was leading them toward the rec center's front doors. Spencer scanned the hall for any sign of Garcia, but the director was gone, probably rounding up help to stop the escape.

The last student to leave the racquetball court was Jenna. She stared at Spencer and gave him a smile. The eye contact had a strong effect, and Spencer saw Jenna put the pieces back together.

"What are we doing?" she asked.

"Couple of guys headed this way!" Dez shouted from the front doors of the rec center.

"Everyone out!" Spencer ordered. But how could he and Dez possibly get all the students past the bad guys with only one small shot of vac dust? Spencer took a final glance into the racquetball court, but the only things in there were discarded extension cords used to make Toxites evolve. Spencer snatched a coiled cord and took off running toward the group, Jenna at his side.

They burst into the crisp November air. All the recruits were huddled on the steps of the rec center. Dez stood in front of them like an angry shepherd guarding his flock.

Two men were running toward the rec center,

determined to stop the escaping recruits. Spencer recognized one of them as the New Forest Academy math teacher.

"Dez!" Spencer tossed one end of the extension cord to the bully. He caught it with a confused look on his broad face.

"What are we supposed to do with this?"

"Run!"

Holding tight to the ends of the cord, Spencer and Dez sprinted forward. The approaching teachers hesitated as the extension cord went taut between the two boys. There was no chance to turn aside. The cord made an inescapable clothesline, catching the two Academy teachers and flinging them to the ground. The force pulled Spencer and Dez off their feet, the extension cord burning as it slid through their hands and out of their grasp.

The boys were quicker to recover. Before the adults could stand, the thirty Academy rejects sprinted past, following Dez and Spencer to the far side of campus. They ran into the street, Spencer crossing his fingers as the brick wall and gate came into view.

Daisy and Min must have been successful. The gate was wide open. Beyond, idling in the parking lot, Spencer could see the back end of a big yellow school bus. It was there! Just like Meredith had promised in her mashed-potato note.

Spencer fell to the back of the group, quickly scanning over the heads of the recruits to make sure no one had fallen behind. They were moving too quickly for him to do a thorough count, so Spencer could only hope for the best.

The group ran through the gateway, making a mad rush to the safety of the bus.

Out of the corner of his eye, Spencer saw a V of flying figures soar over the brick wall. Silhouetted momentarily against the bright blue sky, their trajectory carried them out of sight behind the wall and into the parking lot.

"Go! Go! Go!" Spencer urged, sprinting down the street and through the gate. If those flying BEM workers beat them to the parking lot, the recruits could be cut off from the escape bus.

The first worker touched down with his broom in the parking lot, only feet away. It was Slick, his dirty glasses slipping down his nose from the rapid flight. Spencer didn't think twice; he pinched out the last puff of vacuum dust and hurled it at the janitor. Slick's legs buckled and he dropped to his knees on the asphalt, temporarily rooted in place.

The bus door was open and the recruits started leaping in one at a time. The bottleneck gave another BEM worker time to land. He touched down near the bus door. But before he could fully regain his gravity, Dez tackled him in a flurry of pumping fists.

The Academy rejects were screaming; the bus engine revved. Spencer waited at the end of the group, determined to fight the BEM enemies hand to hand if necessary.

Slick recovered from the vac dust and rallied the other workers. They were racing toward the bus when Spencer leapt onto the vehicle's bottom step, barely finding space for his foot among the crowd of kids. There wasn't even room to close the bus door—Spencer, half dangling outside, clung to the kid in front of him.

"Go!" shouted Spencer.

Through the throng of students, he could see Meredith's hair, still matted from her hairnet. The lunch lady stepped on the gas and the large yellow bus peeled out as fast as it could.

"Move on back!" Meredith shouted over the din of frightened kids. "Move to the back of the bus and sit down! This could be a wild ride!" Meredith spun the wheel, navigating the giant bus through the cars parked in the lot.

The clog in the doorway began to thin and Spencer leaned into the bus, relieved not to see the asphalt speeding beneath him. But his momentary relief was broken as Daisy shouted something from the back of the bus.

"We forgot someone!"

CHAPTER 39

"I'LL BE RIGHT BEHIND YOU."

The bus was pulling out of the parking lot, preparing for the steep descent toward the neighborhoods below. The big truck with the snowplow came careening out of the maintenance shed, angry BEM workers jumping into the back, readying for the chase.

Spencer pushed up the bus steps. "Who did we forget?"

"Unable to get a visual," Min called from the bus's back window. "No, wait . . . it's Dez!"

"He's running after us!" Daisy called.

How could they have left him? Dez had unplugged those growing Toxites and helped the Academy rejects escape from the rec center. The bully had bought them time in the parking lot, going hand to hand with the BEM worker. But Dez must have rolled out of sight during the fight.

"Stop the bus!" someone shouted. But if Meredith stopped, the BEM would recapture everyone.

"No," said Spencer. "I'm going back for him alone."

"Are you crazy?" shrieked Daisy.

"None of us would have made it through without Dez!" Spencer said. "We can't leave him behind!" He found the stockpile of Glopified supplies that Daisy and Min had gathered from the stash.

"You can't . . ." Daisy said.

Spencer slipped on a latex glove. He paused long enough to take a deep breath, letting the air work past his adrenaline and calm his thumping heart. "I can do this, Daisy."

They held eye contact, and for a moment they might as well have been standing in Welcher Elementary's library, trying to stop a single Toxite from hitchhiking in Dez's backpack. Finally, Daisy nodded. "Don't get caught."

Spencer picked up a broom with yellow bristles and a toilet plunger. Pushing to the front of the bus, he opened the squeaky door.

"Keep going," he said to Meredith. "I'll be right behind you."

"Don't go!" someone shouted, but Spencer raised his broom. "Spencer!" Jenna reached through the crowd of kids and grabbed Spencer's arm just as he brought the broom bristles slamming against the bottom stair.

The broom wobbled, thrown off balance by the sudden weight of two bodies. Spencer and Jenna were pulled out of the bus door like puppets on a string. The broom dipped, and the tip of the handle struck the road, causing both kids to tumble painfully on the pavement.

Spencer grunted against the pain in his shoulder and sat up. He was lying at the edge of the road, loose gravel digging into his legs. The bus was already far past them, the big BEM truck almost touching the rear bumper as they sped around a corner and out of sight.

Spencer seemed to remember Jenna tumbling out of the bus alongside him. But where was she?

There! Crumpled in the middle of the steep road. The girl was trying to rise onto her elbows, but she seemed disoriented from the fall.

The roar of a second diesel truck caused Spencer to look up the hill. The vehicle was speeding down the canyon, trying to catch up to the other truck and bus. It was moving much too fast to stop for the helpless girl in the middle of the road. Jenna saw the danger and froze like a deer in the headlights.

The truck closed the distance and Spencer leapt forward, toilet plunger gripped in both his hands. The red suction cup made contact with the side of the truck. The weight of the vehicle redistributed and Spencer jerked upward.

The truck lifted off the ground. Jenna turned her face as the front tire passed only inches above her pale cheek. The speed of the truck caused a rush of wind over the girl. Clothes whipped against Jenna's body. Her blonde hair streamed, tickling the underside of the vehicle.

The truck's momentum spun Spencer around. He

detached the plunger with a twist of the handle, hurling the truck through the air like a shot-putter. The vehicle struck the trees on the roadside with a crunch, air bags deploying.

Spencer grabbed Jenna's arm. The physical contact helped revive her from the shock of what had just happened. "Are you hurt?" Spencer helped her to the side of the road. Jenna shook her head wordlessly. "I'm going back up to the parking lot for Dez. Stay here where it's safe."

He bent down to pick up the scratched broom from the roadside. Jenna grabbed his arm again. "I have to go with you!"

"I'll be back for you," Spencer said. "I promise."

He ran a few steps and took flight with his broom. Soaring over the crest of the hill, he saw New Forest Academy's welcome sign and parking lot. A group of people stood near the entrance gate. Spencer touched down and ran in that direction, weaving through parked cars.

He drew nearer and saw a ring of Academy teachers and BEM workers surrounding Dez. But they suddenly turned away from the bully when an audible *pop* from the toilet plunger echoed off the brick wall.

Spencer stood at the edge of the group, plunger in one hand. With one arm slightly bent, he held a car above his head. "Let him go," Spencer said. "Or I start throwing things."

The startled adults glanced at each other. Then the ring parted. Dez was standing at the center, but he wasn't alone. Slick was by his side, an envelope in the janitor's hand. Both of them stared at Spencer, not entirely surprised by the fact that he'd returned and was holding a car above his head with one hand.

"Come on, Dez," Spencer urged. "Let's go."

The bully took a hesitant step forward, indecision at work on his face.

Slick held the envelope in front of Dez's face, and Spencer saw that it bore the evergreen crest of New Forest Academy. That was one of the Academy acceptance letters!

"Remember our deal, Dez," the janitor threatened.

So there *was* a deal! Spencer knew that Slick wouldn't have exposed Dez to the Toxites without asking something in return.

"Forget it!" Spencer said. "Come on! Run!"

"We had a deal, Dez!"

Dez looked back and forth from Spencer's face to the letter in Slick's hand. His big feet fidgeted, trying to leave and then pulling him back like he was caught in some awkward line dance.

Slick bent closer. "What's at home for you, Dez? An old apartment. An angry dad with a dark bottle in his hand . . ."

"We have to go!" Spencer shouted.

Dez closed his eyes and breathed deeply. The sunlight hit his face from above, casting his eyes in deep pockets of shadow. Then Dez's eyes flicked open. He reached up and grabbed the envelope from Slick's hand.

"I stay."

CHAPTER 40

"STEP ON MY FEET."

Like a pack of wolves, the ring of adults leapt for Spencer. Only the need to escape could pierce through his shock and disbelief at Dez's decision. Sure, the bully had experienced some success with the brown team, but Spencer had never thought it would lead to this!

Spencer hefted the toilet plunger and flung the attached car straight down in front of him. It landed on its side, glass shattering and chrome flying, creating an effective barricade between Spencer and the approaching enemies.

He'd never catch up to Meredith's bus with a simple broom. Especially since he needed to pick up Jenna on the roadside. What he needed was something fast and maneuverable.

An Academy teacher jumped forward and grabbed

Spencer's arm. The latex glove worked its magic, and Spencer easily slipped through his attacker's fingers.

Tilting his broom, Spencer leapt away, touching down in front of the maintenance shed. The garage door was open and the big truck was gone, speeding down the canyon in pursuit of the escaping school bus. But Spencer wasn't looking for Slick's truck. What he needed was tucked against the back wall.

The BEM workers were rushing toward the shed when Spencer burst out, the wheels of his cleaning cart almost catching air as he tore across the parking lot. His broom and plunger were clipped onto the rack and Spencer leaned hard, gaining as much speed as he could for a head start.

He shifted his weight, exited the parking lot, and started down the long road toward the city. A moment later, Jenna came into view on the roadside. Spencer leaned back, the wheels of the cart skidding to a halt in the gravel.

"Is that a janitor's cart?" Jenna asked.

"Yeah," Spencer said. "But I think they could use them in NASCAR."

Glancing over his shoulder, Spencer saw two men on cleaning carts cresting the hill and descending toward them, picking up extra speed on the downhill.

"Get on," Spencer instructed. He scooted back on the platform and Jenna carefully stepped on. Instantly, the cart started forward. Jenna screamed and gripped the handle rack. The cart spun a sharp circle, backed up, then jerked to the side.

"These carts are balance driven," Spencer said. "Not going to work for two people."

"What do we do?"

"Here," Spencer said, sliding forward. "Step on my feet." Jenna turned so she was facing him and stepped onto his feet, apologizing in case it hurt. "Now put your arms around my neck." He would have blushed under any other circumstances, but Spencer was far from feeling any emotion other than panic.

"We have to act like one person," Spencer said. "When I lean, you have to lean with me. Got it?" Jenna nodded.

The two BEM workers had almost caught up to them by the time Spencer and Jenna regained control of their cart and leaned into the downhill again. Jenna's grip around his neck grew steadily tighter as they picked up speed. Their faces were closer than ever, but Jenna had her eyes clamped shut and Spencer was focused on maneuvering the cart around the canyon corners.

They caught their first glimpse of the yellow school bus on a straight section of road, the big truck driving uncomfortably close behind.

One of the cleaning carts drew alongside them, and Spencer could see the whiskery face of a smirking BEM worker. Spencer and Jenna leaned hard, but they couldn't outdistance him.

Suddenly, the man shifted his weight. The enemy cart jerked sideways, scraping into Spencer and Jenna. The attack almost made Spencer lose control. Two of the cart's wheels came off the road and then slammed down again.

Before they recovered fully, the second BEM worker inched forward on the other side and rammed his cart into Spencer and Jenna. They wobbled again, Jenna letting out a cry of fear.

Spencer edged toward a bend in the road where the whipping canyon wind had gathered dead leaves into a pile. Consistent shade from a huge tree had kept the leaves slick and wet from the night's frost.

The three cleaning carts were in a row now, Spencer and Jenna trapped in the middle. Spencer swerved toward the mat of leaves on the roadside and the two BEM workers followed closely.

"Hang on!" Spencer shouted just before they hit the leaves. He threw his weight backward as fast as he could, grinding the cart to a whiplash halt. The nearest BEM worker jerked sideways, his wheels catching in the slick leaves. Before he could correct, the cart tipped. The driver shouted, skidding across the road and colliding with the second BEM cart in a bone-shattering wreck.

Eyes wide at the close call, Spencer and Jenna leaned forward again, closing the distance between them and Meredith's escape bus.

When they were finally close enough to read the license plate on the pursuing truck, everything got worse. The BEM truck inched closer to the bus, and Spencer saw two windswept passengers lean over the sides, Glopified mops in hand. They cast their mops toward the back of the bus. The white strings shot out, trying to ensnare the back tires.

There was a sound like a gunshot and then a hiss of

smoke. The mop strings fried from the friction and the passengers who had cast them fell back into the bed of the truck.

The truck slowed down, and Spencer and Jenna zoomed past it on the roadside. Finally close enough, Spencer saw the damage that the mops had done. Both rear tires of the bus had exploded. The bus was riding on metal rims, throwing a line of white-hot sparks. Meredith struggled to maintain control, but the bus had lost most of its maneuverability. The Academy rejects were screaming inside.

Then Spencer saw the worst part. There was a sharp curve ahead—and, if Meredith couldn't turn the bus, a huge drop-off.

An idea entered Spencer's mind. It was crazy and extreme, yes. But it was something he'd done before . . . and he was fairly sure he could do it again.

Spencer directed the cart alongside the out-of-control school bus, unclipping the broom and toilet plunger as he did so. "Hold on to this!" Spencer pushed the plunger into Jenna's hands. He didn't give her much time to wonder why a toilet plunger could possibly be so important. Using the momentum of the cleaning cart, Spencer angled the broom and struck the bristles.

Spencer and Jenna shot upward, the cart tumbling as their feet lifted off. The broom carried them above the bus windows and onto the vehicle's roof. Meredith was riding the brakes. The sharp screech of metal from the sparking rims filled the canyon.

Spencer took the toilet plunger from Jenna and clamped

it securely on the roof of the bus. Holding the plunger handle with one hand, he hit the broom just as the front wheels of the bus shot off the edge of the dangerous road, unable to make the curve.

The school bus flew forward, a yellow airplane without wings. The Glopified toilet plunger perfectly reduced the weight of the bus, easily allowing the broom to carry it.

On the road behind them, the BEM truck came to a disbelieving halt at the big curve as the yellow school bus soared safely over the treetops of the canyon.

CHAPTER 41

"THIS ISN'T THE END OF THE ROAD FOR YOU."

It didn't take long for Spencer to realize that he hadn't exactly saved the bus from danger. The threat of the BEM was far behind, but that didn't change the fact that the school bus was actually airborne.

The Academy rejects were still screaming. If anything, their shrill cries increased as the broom began its gradual descent. Spencer glanced ahead, trying to predict where the bus would touch down. None of the options were very good. There was a dirt road farther down, but Spencer didn't think they'd make it that far.

"Are we going to crash?" Jenna cried. She was prone against the top of the bus, clinging to the rooftop emergency exit.

"There's a meadow," Spencer said, carefully avoiding her question. And truthfully, there *was* a meadow, but they weren't going to land in it. Instead, the bus was falling fast toward a stand of tall pine trees. Spencer found himself instinctively leaning toward the bare spot of ground. But as hard as he tried, it was impossible to change the broom's flight path. The unavoidable fact was that they were about to perch the bus in the treetops.

They were close to impact. Spencer tensed his entire body. Would the trees be strong enough to hold them? Or would the bus crash through the limbs and roll earthward?

The screams of the frightened students escalated as someone inside the bus lowered a window. Suddenly, white mop strings shot through the opening. The Glopified strings crossed the meadow and entangled the leafless branches of a distant aspen. Then, only seconds before impact, the mop strings retracted, dragging the floating school bus away from its dangerous perch.

Spencer saw the mop release and withdraw through the open bus window. The change of course had been exactly what they needed to touch down in the meadow. But even with a good lineup, the bus's landing was anything but graceful.

Spencer slammed against the roof of the bus. Jenna bounced up, barely holding on. The long vehicle tipped and swayed. At last it came to a standstill, front bumper mashed against a big rock.

The students started pouring out of the bus, their faces pale and streaked with tears. They had certainly been through a lot more than they'd ever expected.

No sooner had Spencer and Jenna descended from

atop the bus than Daisy burst through the crowd and gave Spencer a huge hug. Min gazed back toward the big curve in the distance.

"I thought for sure we were in the trees," Spencer said.

"Given our initial velocity and descent, we would have been," Min said. "We were fortunate to have Daisy modify our course with that mop."

Daisy started beaming from the praise, but then she noticed something. "Where's Dez? Didn't you get him?"

Spencer remembered Dez's shadowy eyes. "He didn't want to come." The betrayal was hard to believe and Spencer did not want to think about it. The hurt surprised him. Wasn't Dez just a bully? So why did it matter if he stayed?

Jenna peered around Spencer, white faced and shaking. Daisy reached out for the girl's cold hand. "Are you okay?"

Jenna shook her head and swallowed. "What exactly just happened?"

To the surprise of Spencer, it was Min who answered. "The marvel of modern science," he lied smoothly. "Seems almost like magic." He lifted an eyebrow at Spencer and Daisy. "You see, Jenna, the undercarriage of the bus is embedded with multiple gravitational field deflector arrays. When necessary, the driver can send out a signal to polarize the . . ."

Gratefully, Spencer and Daisy slipped away as Min continued his elaborate scientific explanation. Spencer hoped it was a sound theory, since Min would most likely have to repeat it to all the students in the runaway bus.

Meredith intercepted Spencer and Daisy, a concerned look on her face. "This isn't the end of the road for you." The lunch lady put a hand on Spencer's shoulder. "Walter's on his way to get you," Meredith said.

"How does he know where we are?" Daisy asked, glancing at the mountain scenery.

"We were supposed to rendezvous with him in a town called Boulder." Meredith pulled a cell phone from her pocket. "But when I saw that we weren't going to make it, I phoned in and told him where we had . . . landed." She pointed across the meadow. "The road's not far. He should be here any moment."

"What about the rest of you?" Spencer looked over to where the Academy rejects stood in shivering groups, trying to make sense of what had just happened.

Meredith glanced at the bus. "It'll take me some time to put the spare tires on the bus and get her back on the road. I'll form a contact list for all of the students. I might be able to drop off the ones that live close. I'll contact the rest of the parents and let them know where to pick up their children."

"Those are going to be some unhappy parents," Daisy said.

"I suppose so," answered Meredith. "But the alternative was Toxite-saturated children." She lifted her hands like she was balancing the options. "I think I can deal with unhappy parents."

Spencer and Daisy nodded.

Meredith looked back toward the students. "Perhaps

you two should head over to the road. Slip away before anyone asks more questions."

Spencer hesitated. Shouldn't he at least explain something to Min? And couldn't he say good-bye to Jenna? What if he never saw her again?

But Daisy quickly thanked Meredith, took Spencer by the arm, and headed toward the road. They skirted around the trees so the recruits wouldn't see them. Soon they stood side by side at the edge of the dirt road, watching both directions for Walter's familiar van.

"Why do you think Walter's coming?" Daisy asked.

Spencer had a hopeful idea, but he voiced another. "Probably just taking us somewhere safe. He must have found out that the Academy is run by the BEM."

"Or maybe he found out what's wrong with you," said Daisy. "You know, your fainting problem."

Or, Spencer thought, *maybe he's discovered something about my dad*.

No sooner had the hopeful thought taken root in his mind than a brown van appeared down the road, kicking up a wake of autumn leaves. Spencer felt the anxiety build as the van drew up and came to a stop in front of them.

Penny leapt out of the passenger seat, red hair shimmering in the sunlight. Her usual letter jacket was flung over one shoulder so the gymnastics patch hung upside down. She went to the back of the large van and opened the rear doors. "Jump in," Penny said.

Spencer and Daisy climbed into the back of the

cluttered, strange-smelling van. Walter looked over his shoulder from the driver's seat and greeted them.

"Where are we going?" Daisy asked as the van rolled away.

"Somewhere we can talk," said Walter. "Penny and I have learned a lot in the last week."

"About what?" Spencer probed.

"About New Forest Academy." Walter looked at Spencer through the rearview mirror. "About *you*."

CHAPTER 42

"WHY'S THIS SO IMPORTANT?"

They bounced off the dirt road and into the residential neighborhood. Walter merged onto a freeway, heading in what seemed like the direction of home. Penny passed some food to the kids as they drove: apples, granola bars, and some salty potato chips. Spencer was glad to have something to snack on. It kept his mouth from asking questions—questions that Walter refused to answer until they got safely away.

Spencer was looking for a place to dispose of his apple core when he saw a familiar object nestled on one of the van's dusty shelves.

His apple core forgotten, Spencer reached forward, gently touching the papery material. It was the Vortex vacuum bag. In the side of the bag he saw the tear. It was only a small hole, torn by a sharp pencil in Welcher Elementary

School. It seemed so long ago that he had ripped the Vortex and unleashed the overcharged magic.

Last time he had seen the bag, he'd been overwhelmed by grief at Marv's loss. But something was different this time. Marv was still alive in there. And from what they'd heard from that brief recording on Penny's phone, the big janitor might be bowling!

Spencer leaned closer to the shelf. There was a stack of papers under the vacuum bag. They looked like pages torn from a notebook. Nothing out of the ordinary, but the heading on the first page, scrawled in Walter's steady hand, instantly caught Spencer's attention.

OPERATION VORTEX

Spencer slid the vacuum bag aside to see the full page. There was a list in the top corner—an assortment of ingredients. Some items had been crossed out, others circled.

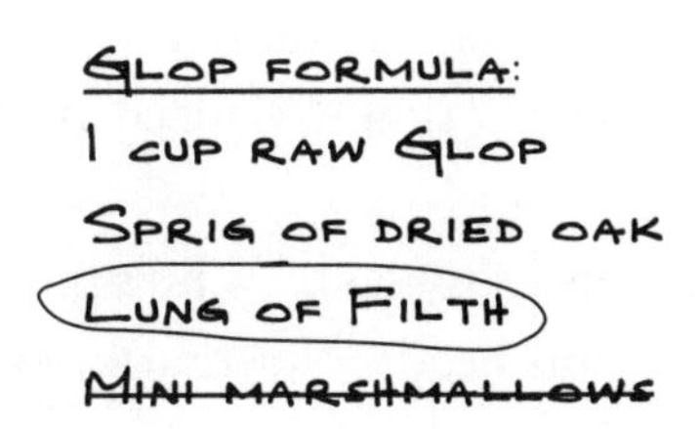

And the list went on, but Spencer didn't read it all. He pulled aside the paper to look at the next one. The second page was covered with a pencil sketch diagram. The black-and-white artwork depicted a small motor with a handle. Extending from the motor was a long plastic tube.

Spencer instantly recognized it. He'd seen plenty of neighbors using such a device, especially this time of year when the trees dropped their leaves. The sketch was labeled.

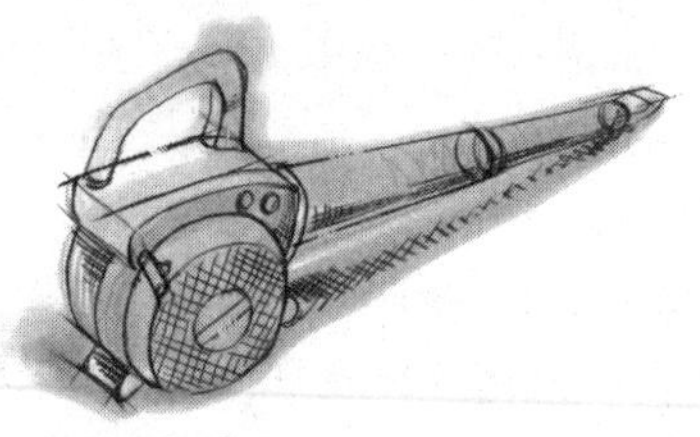

OPERATION VORTEX: LEAF BLOWER

This was Walter's plan to rescue Marv! It seemed perfectly logical. If the Vortex had strong suction power, pulling everything inward, then they would need something with the opposite power in order to reverse the effect. Walter was going to Glopify a leaf blower and blast his way into the Vortex!

"Operation Vortex," Spencer said, his hand resting on the shelf with the papers. He wanted to see Walter's reaction, but the old warlock simply glanced at him in the rearview mirror.

"Wait a minute," Daisy said. "Who's having surgery?"

Spencer shook his head. "Not that kind of operation." He grabbed the papers from the van shelf. "Operation Vortex. It's a plan. It's Walter's plan to get Marv out of the vacuum bag! It totally makes sense. He's going to Glopify a leaf blower and—"

"Slow down, Spencer." There was an edge to Walter's voice that cut off Spencer's excitement about rescuing

Marv. "Operation Vortex isn't a plan. It's only a hypothesis—a theory. And even if I get a leaf blower Glopified and running, there's still no way of knowing what effect it will have against the Vortex."

Spencer clutched the papers between both hands. He stared at the hand-drawn diagram of the leaf blower. "How long till we can try?" he asked. "How long till you have this thing Glopified?"

Walter sighed. "A couple of months at best."

"Months?" The plan on the papers looked close to completion. Spencer was expecting days, maybe weeks. But *months?* "Marv's alive in there," he said. "We've got to save him!"

"Save him?" Daisy said. "I thought he was bowling!"

"We don't know that," Spencer said. "That's just what we heard on the recording. Anything could have happened since then!"

"You're right!" Daisy agreed. "I bet he finished his game by now. Do you think he used bumpers? I'm no good without bumpers."

Walter pulled off the freeway and parked the van at a truck stop. He turned around to face Spencer and Daisy. "I know it seems important, but Operation Vortex is going to have to wait. For right now, we have other things to discuss. Things that cannot wait."

Spencer swallowed his questions about the leaf blower as Penny opened the vehicle's back door. Soon, all four of them were headed toward a picnic bench at the edge of the parking lot. The bench was dappled in late afternoon shadow from a tall evergreen tree. Spencer sat down and shivered, though he wasn't sure if it was from the cold or from his anxiety over hearing Walter's report. Daisy zipped her coat up to her neck.

"First off," Walter said, removing his cap, "my apologies. New Forest Academy was nothing but a trap." Walter shook his head. "Penny and I were already on our way when I got your e-mail. We'd heard the news about Roger Munroe, but we were too far out to help, so I sent Meredith. It took her a day to work into the kitchen. By then, that BEM janitor already had you."

"What really happened to Roger?" Daisy asked.

Walter grimaced. "The Bureau . . . disposed of him. Since the BEM founded the Academy, it was a simple effort to get rid of Roger and hire Slick just in time for your arrival."

"But I don't get it," said Spencer. "If the Academy is run by the BEM, why would they have hired a Rebel Janitor in the first place?"

"They were using our resources against us," said Penny. "Hiring Roger to clean the Academy accomplished two things. First, it got Roger away from helping other Rebel schools. And second, it made us think the Academy was part of the Underground. We never suspected that fighting Toxites in New Forest Academy was exactly what the BEM wanted."

Penny shook her head. "It took the news of Roger's death for us to realize that the Academy and the BEM were united. Now the Bureau's motives are finally beginning to make sense. The BEM is letting all the other schools in the nation suffer from Toxites while they raise up a clean Academy full of handpicked students."

"But why?" Daisy asked.

"In order to understand the BEM's motives, you have to think long-term," Walter said. "Imagine life in thirty or forty years. All schools will have crumbled. The next generation of American citizens won't even know simple math or science. The only people who will be capable of doing anything intellectual will be the Academy students. They will become the next doctors, scientists, and politicians. The BEM is handpicking them to suit their needs. And who knows what other devious lessons they will teach at the Academy?"

"Long-term," Penny said, leaning forward, "we're looking at the BEM taking over the entire nation."

"It won't work," Spencer said. "Even if they did take over, the country would just be full of uneducated people. They couldn't get anything done."

"But maybe that's exactly what the BEM wants," Walter said. "It's a plan as old as the devil. Uneducated people are easier to control. The uneducated simply believe what they are told, since they don't know anything else. The history of the world shows many sad examples of an elite upper class ruling the uneducated masses."

It was hard to digest. The janitors were trying to take over the nation. No one would ever expect it!

"So, what's your plan?" Spencer asked. "Are we going to infest the Academy with Toxites?" He remembered Slick dumping an Agitation Bucket on the front steps of that public school. It would feel good to return that gesture at the Academy.

But Walter shook his head. "We'll continue fighting Toxites, just as we have been."

"But we have to stop the Academy!" Spencer said. He thought of Dez and the ruthless brown team becoming the only educated people in America. Now that Spencer understood the BEM's motives, he was desperate to take action. "We have to bring them down!"

"Then what?" Walter said. "Then no one would be educated." He sighed deeply. "If we focus on bringing *down* the Academy, it will destroy us all. We must do everything to save education, not destroy it. We must focus on bringing *up* the Rebel forces."

"How?" Spencer asked.

Penny leaned forward. "We might have a secret weapon to help predict the BEM's moves."

"What is it?" Daisy asked.

Walter turned to Spencer. "How long has it been since you've cut your hair?"

The question was so far off topic that Spencer couldn't even think of an answer.

"Spencer's hair is the secret weapon?" said Daisy.

Penny couldn't suppress a grin. "No," she said. "But we need to know how long since he's cut it."

Realizing that they were serious about the question, Spencer thought back . . . and back. "I don't remember," he said. "Probably two months, maybe more." He ran a hand through his hair, surprised that it was still so short.

"And your fingernails?" Walter asked. "How long since you've trimmed them?"

Spencer looked defensively at his nails. He always kept them short and clean, just as they were now. But Spencer couldn't remember the last time he'd used nail clippers.

"Not for a long time," he mumbled. Before Penny and Walter could ask any more uncomfortable questions about his hygiene, Spencer cut in. "Why's this so important?"

"You're not growing, Spencer."

"What do you mean, I'm not growing?" He jumped up from the picnic bench.

"You've been suspended in time," Walter said. "Your body has stopped growing. It's too early to judge by height, but your hair and fingernails are the final clue we were looking for. Your body's being preserved in its current state."

"What?" Spencer looked around for someone to explain the joke. Penny and Walter looked deadly serious. Daisy was staring dumbfounded. "For how long?" His voice was tightening.

"Forever."

CHAPTER 43

"JUST LIKE ME."

Spencer took a step back. Hot tears were springing to his eyes, so he turned away. Penny called after him, but he ducked out of sight behind the warlock van. He expected the others to appear around the vehicle's bumper at any moment to see his tears.

Why? Why wasn't he going to grow anymore? He wanted it to be a lie, but Walter always told the truth. There was no mistaking the honest look in the warlock's eyes.

He was an ageless boy. A boy forever. Spencer tried to fathom it. He thought of time rushing on without him. He thought of little Max growing up, growing taller. His youngest brother would start a family, have children—*grandchildren!*—and Spencer would see it all through his twelve-year-old eyes. It felt as though Walter's statement had stripped away any hope for a normal future.

Spencer leaned heavily against the cold van, realizing that the others weren't coming after him. They were giving him a moment of contemplation. Walter must have known Spencer would come back on his own. He had to go back if he wanted an explanation of the warlock's ridiculous report.

Spencer took a deep breath, wiping tears from his cheeks. If he was going to be a kid forever, he might as well get over childish crying. He stepped around the van and strode toward his friends, determined to face the news like a hero.

Walter went straight into business, as though Spencer had never left. "This is going to take a bit of explaining," he said. "Did Marv ever tell you about the Aurans?"

Spencer shook his head, still too numb to respond verbally.

Walter rubbed his bald head and continued. "Remember that special dumpster behind Welcher Elementary where we put all the maxed-out Glopified supplies?"

This time, Spencer and Daisy nodded. Marv had taught them that Glopified equipment lost its power after killing fifty Toxites. All Toxite-fighting schools had a special receptacle where they could put used brooms and mops to dispose of them safely.

"When that dumpster fills up," Walter said, "someone has to come along and pick it up. There are thirteen people who serve that purpose. We call them Aurans. They were enlisted by the Founding Witches in the early 1700s."

"What?" Daisy stopped the conversation. "They must be super old!"

"Yes," answered Walter. "The Aurans are hundreds of years old. But their bodies are young, preserved in a perpetual state of childhood."

Spencer swallowed against the lump in his throat. Wasn't that what Walter had just said about him?

"The Aurans pick up the maxed-out Glopified supplies from the schools and take them to a secret landfill. Only the Aurans have the power to extract raw Glop from the cleaning supplies. Most of the raw Glop is destroyed in their facilities, but a small portion is delivered back to the three warlocks so we can use it to Glopify new supplies."

Walter stood up and headed over to the van. Spencer, Daisy, and Penny followed. Walter opened the rear door, crawled inside, and returned with a coffee can. Spencer peered over the lip of the can and saw a grayish mud, gurgling and bubbling like it was alive. It smelled of sulfur and a myriad of unidentifiable scents that caused Spencer to pull back, crinkling his nose.

"About a month ago, this batch of raw Glop was delivered to me by one of the Aurans." Walter set the coffee can back inside the van and closed the door. "So how do you think that Auran knew exactly where to find me?"

Daisy had a perplexed look on her face, but the answer was clear to Spencer. "The Aurans can see the warlocks," he said. "They can see through your eyes and they know exactly where you are." Spencer paused. "Just like me."

Walter wore a grave expression. It was as though Spencer's comment sealed the warlock's deepest suspicions.

"How did this happen to me?" Spencer asked.

Walter took a deep breath. "From the moment you moved to Welcher, Marv and I were watching you. With all the strange things the BEM had been doing, we didn't think it was a coincidence that the son of Alan Zumbro came to our school. We knew we had to keep an eye on you, but we had to keep the School Board safe also, remember? So we decided to put both our eggs in one basket where we could watch them together.

"Marv turned the School Board into a desk and we gave it to you. We could have kept it down in the janitor's closet, but that was the most likely place to get raided by the BEM. We thought the School Board would be safer and less conspicuous if it was out in the open, an everyday part of the school—your desk. What we didn't know was that you would end up saving the School Board and becoming the first child warlock by pounding the nail into the Board."

"But I'm not a warlock," Spencer said. "I gave that power back to you."

"Yes," Walter said. "But nothing changes the fact that, for several hours, you were cloaked in the protective Aura."

Spencer remembered being surrounded by that golden glow. It was a defense feature set into the School Board by the Founding Witches. While Spencer was cloaked in the Aura, no one could stop him from setting up a magical domain.

"The Aura had never before descended upon a child," Walter said. "I thought nothing of it at first. But when you told me of your strange visions last week, I immediately became concerned. Penny and I set off to find an answer. I didn't think it was possible for another child to become an Auran so many years after the original thirteen."

"But Spencer did it?" Daisy asked.

"There is one way to find out for sure," Walter said. "The Aurans use bronze objects to locate the three warlocks. Something about the metal makes a conduit for their visions."

"But I don't even have anything made of bronze," Spencer said.

"Think back to the times it happened," Walter said. "In the principal's office, for example. Did you touch something that could have been bronze?"

"No," Spencer said. "I was just trying to pick up some papers . . ." He suddenly remembered the elephant paperweight. Could it have been bronze?

"But what about when I shook Penny's hand?" asked Spencer. He was desperate to prove this theory wrong.

Penny held up her hand and pointed to a ring on her finger. "I wasn't sure what kind of metal it was at first, so Walter took it in to a jeweler to ask." She nodded. "Bronze."

And the fancy doorknob on New Forest Academy's library must have also been bronze . . .

Walter reached into the cargo pocket of his pants and withdrew Ninfa, his bronze warlock hammer.

"Take hold of this." Walter extended the handle of the hammer. "This is pure bronze. There shouldn't be a better conduit."

Spencer's mind was swimming. He'd never gone into these visions knowingly. They were disorienting and uncomfortable. It was one thing to stumble into them, but Spencer didn't know if he had the courage to willingly grasp the hammer.

"A true Auran should have the ability to see all three warlocks," Walter said.

"I can't hold on that long," said Spencer. "I'll pass out again."

"You must try, Spencer." Walter was serious. "If you succeed, this moment could provide the greatest advantage that the Rebels have had since the BEM defected."

"What do you mean?" There was a bitter taste in Spencer's mouth.

"The identity of the warlocks has always been kept secret, known only to those in the innermost circle of the Bureau," Walter explained. "When I discovered one of the warlocks, it didn't take me long to steal Ninfa and replace him. But in so doing, I revealed myself as the new warlock. The BEM has held that information over the Rebels since day one. If you truly have the power of the Aurans, Spencer, you will be able to level the playing field. You will be able to uncover the identity of the other two warlocks and tell us where they're hiding."

"What if I can't?" Spencer said. "What if I can only see through you?" But Spencer knew that wasn't true. He'd already had visions through more eyes than Walter's.

"Penny, Daisy," said Walter, "give him some support from behind." They moved around Spencer and took him by the arms. Walter stared at the boy with intense eyes.

"Once you grab on, I'm going to hold your hand around the hammer so you don't slip off, okay?"

Spencer nodded, and a shiver ran down his spine. He reached out a hand and wrapped his fingers around the bronze handle of Ninfa.

CHAPTER 44

"WE HAVE TO TEST HIM."

It started as pricks of bright light, like stars that outshone the sun. In less than a heartbeat, the brilliance had escalated to an intolerable level. Spencer closed his eyes as the familiar harsh whiteness clawed its way into his vision.

He was standing in the parking lot of a truck stop, nineteen miles northeast of Boulder, Colorado, staring at . . . himself! The experience was so disorienting that Spencer almost couldn't make sense of it. Then he remembered—he was seeing the scene through Walter Jamison's eyes.

"Hold him!" Walter said, wrapping his hand over Spencer's to keep it in contact with the hammer. Spencer saw himself go limp. Daisy and Penny supported him under the arms.

"Is he all right?" Daisy asked.

Penny reached up and pressed a hand to Spencer's neck.

"I'll watch his pulse," she said. "First sign of trouble and we let him go."

"We have to test him," Spencer said. But it wasn't Spencer speaking, it was Walter. "We have to know if he's capable of finding the other warlocks."

Ahh! It was so confusing. Spencer felt his mind stretching to its limit. Couldn't they just take his hand off the hammer and let him relax? But Walter was determined to push Spencer to the brink of his newfound power.

Spencer tried to relax his brain and focus on the bronze. If the metal was the conduit for these visions, then it must hold the key to seeing the other warlocks.

It began again, pinpoints of light that rushed together into a mass of whiteness. Then it faded and Spencer found himself in Washington, D.C. The time zone difference meant that night had already dropped around the government building, leaving dark windows.

He was in that office again, the one with the neutral paint job and the framed crest of the BEM hanging on the wall. A woman stood in front of him, wearing dirty janitor coveralls.

His hands pounded on the glass countertop of the desk and the woman flinched. "The whole operation was a failure, in my opinion!" The man's voice was deep and laced with anger. "If the kid really doesn't know anything about the package, then they should have disposed of him!"

"Yes, sir," the woman said.

"And tell those blundering idiots at the Academy that if

they're not man enough to do the job, then I'll do it myself . . . the *Clean* way."

"Yes, sir." The woman started to back out of the room.

"One more thing," the man said. But Spencer couldn't keep the focus. Inadvertently, his mind had returned to the bronze hammer in his real hand. It seemed like the only thing rooting him to reality, but the shift of attention caused the scene to dissolve into blinding brilliance. He had one more stop to make.

This time he was standing in a dim, multilevel parking garage, 117 feet below ground. It was quiet and secure, surrounded on all sides by thick concrete. The only sounds came from a humming fluorescent bulb overhead and the click of the man's hard shoes as Spencer sensed himself walking forward.

A large object came into view, tucked against the back wall of the underground garage. As the man strode forward, Spencer saw it clearly. It was a metal dumpster with a line of silvery duct tape around the black lid!

The man approached the dumpster, grasped the edge of the tape, and jerked it violently away. He pushed up the dumpster's black lid and a bit of fluorescent light found its way inside, illuminating the face of a man.

It was the dumpster prisoner.

He crouched in the darkness, looking thin and frail. Snarly brown hair fell to his shoulders and a thick beard and mustache concealed his face. But two blue eyes peered up through the hair in defiance.

Then the warlock, with a shred of duct tape still stuck

to his hand, shouted a single angry sentence. His voice carried the hint of a Spanish accent, and Spencer knew exactly who it was. But the shock didn't come from knowing that Director Carlos Garcia was the third warlock. The shock came from what he said to the dumpster prisoner.

"Your son has ruined everything!"

CHAPTER 45

"YOU'RE SURE ABOUT THIS?"

Spencer opened his eyes—his real eyes. He looked all around, testing to make sure that he had total control over his body. Walter stood in front of him, Ninfa in hand. Daisy and Penny still held him under the arms. Long shadows, cast from skeletal leafless trees, slanted across the truck stop parking lot.

"We have to go back!" Spencer blurted.

"Back where?" Walter asked, forcing eye contact with the boy.

"New Forest Academy," Spencer said. "There's a parking garage, bottom level, 117 feet below the main building." He knew the location without the slightest doubt. "My dad's down there!"

The last sentence was hard to get out. He finally knew where his dad was! Not dead, as he had so often feared, but trapped in a Glopified dumpster sealed with indestructible, fingerprint-sensitive duct tape.

"He's been there all week!" Spencer said. "My dad is the dumpster prisoner!"

It was difficult to believe that Spencer had carried on an entire conversation with him in the parking lot that first night. Why hadn't his dad told him who he was? Why hadn't Spencer recognized that voice? The memory of their brief and ominous meeting was maddening.

"But I thought they moved the dumpster prisoner," Daisy said.

"They moved him into the parking garage beneath campus." Spencer gritted his teeth in regret. "I should have stayed and watched instead of running back to the dorm." The clues were falling into place. "A truck picked up the dumpster, and I thought they were taking him far away. But do you remember how the gate mysteriously opened that night while we were climbing over it? They must have opened it to let the truck and dumpster inside."

"But how did they get it so far underground?" Daisy asked.

Spencer already had the answer. "When we first got to the Academy, there was a deep construction pit that Director Garcia told us led into the underground garage. They filled in the pit the very next day, once the dumpster prisoner—*Dad*—was lowered down!"

"You're sure about this?" Walter cut in. "The Aurans only have the ability to see the three warlocks. How could you have seen your father?"

"I saw him through the eyes of Director Garcia," Spencer said. "Garcia is a warlock!"

"And the other one?" Penny asked.

"Someone in Washington . . . I didn't learn his name."

"That's the BEM headquarters," Penny said.

Walter nodded. "They've divided their power. One warlock to rule over the BEM janitors, the other to govern New Forest Academy."

"We have to go back," Spencer said.

"Yes," Walter answered. "I will begin assembling a team. We'll have to be heavily armed. We should be able to mount a raid in a couple of days."

A couple of days? Spencer felt his excitement rush away, and an old feeling returned—that familiar feeling of despair that threatened to overtake him whenever he thought about his dad.

"No, Uncle." All eyes turned to Penny. "We have to go *now*."

Walter shook his head. "It's too dangerous for the children. We'll drop them off and return with a team of experienced janitors—"

"They," Penny pointed at Spencer and Daisy, "are experienced janitors. *And* they know their way around New Forest Academy's campus." Penny turned to Spencer. "Do you know any way we could get into the underground garage?"

Spencer thought for a moment. Besides the construction pit, which was now filled in, Spencer had never seen a way for a car to drive underneath the school. But maybe the garage wasn't really meant for cars. Maybe it was just a hidden space for the Academy to store important things like the dumpster prisoner. Like the secret tunnel that connected the rec center to Slick's main office. Spencer tried to remember if he had seen any other secretive passageways. Then it hit him.

"There's a wooden pallet in Slick's janitorial office. It lowered into the ground like a kind of elevator."

Penny looked at Walter. "These two know what they're doing, Uncle. If they guide us into the Academy tonight, it will be a quick job. In and out."

"We can't wait a few days," Daisy said. "What if they move the dumpster again?"

It was three against one. Walter shifted uneasily for a moment, but Penny's arguments were infallible. At last, the warlock turned to Spencer. "Do *not* mention this to your mother."

Spencer grinned. If they succeeded in rescuing his dad, Spencer wagered his mom would be so happy she'd never even ask how they had done it.

"I need to meet up with Meredith," Walter said. "Hopefully she's not far out of town yet. I'm going to give her the hammer and nail, just in case we don't . . ." the warlock janitor trailed off. Pulling a cell phone from his pocket, he strode away from the others.

"You heard my uncle," Penny said. "We'll have to be heavily armed to break into New Forest Academy." She waved the two kids toward the van. "Let me show you what Uncle Walter's been working on lately."

Penny reached into the back of the vehicle and pulled out a thick canvas tool belt. There was a large buckle on the front and many clips, pouches, and straps along the sides.

"Janitors use tool belts any time they have a major project in the school, so Walter figured it would be safe enough to experiment with one. Good idea, too. I'm sure you two have noticed by now that it gets pretty cumbersome carrying all that Glopified gear everywhere you go."

Daisy and Spencer nodded. It was hard to hold more than two objects, especially while trying to use them.

"This should fix the problem," Penny said. She held up the belt and pointed to the pouches on one side. "These are quick-access pouches. Great for storing vac dust or chalkboard erasers. The pouches are actually a lot bigger than they look. You'll be surprised what will fit into them, as long as it's small enough to go through the opening. Spill-proof, too. Nothing comes out unless you pull it out."

Penny pointed to some metal tool clips on the belt. "On the other side you've got these U clips. You can put anything with a handle into these clips and the belt will hold it tight. But it's even cooler than that."

Penny held up a finger to pause. She reached into the back of the van and grabbed a pushbroom with a long handle. Penny snapped the handle into one of the U-shaped clips, like a type of holster. As soon as the U clip gripped the wooden handle, the whole bottom half of the pushbroom disappeared. Only a few inches of the handle were visible above the metal clip. For emphasis, Penny ran her hand below the belt. Where the rest of the pushbroom should have been hanging, nothing was tangible.

"So the whole belt is Glopified?" Daisy asked.

"Yup," Penny said. "Practically weightless, too."

"That's awesome," said Daisy. "Why hasn't Walter passed these out to the Rebels?"

Penny glanced over to where the warlock stood, talking on his phone. "Well . . ." She scratched her head. "This isn't actually the final product." She pointed at two more belts in the back of the van. "These are just his early attempts. Uncle Walter has been working on the Glop formula for quite a while." She strapped the tool belt around her thin waist. "These are the closest he's gotten, but there are still a few hiccups he's trying to work out."

"Like what?" asked Spencer.

"Sometimes the supplies get a little stuck. Let's see . . ." She reached across with her right hand and grasped the handle of the pushbroom. As she drew it from the tool belt like a sword, the weapon snapped out of the U clip and the whole thing suddenly became visible. "Oh, good. Worked that time." She leaned the pushbroom against the van. "Sometimes you really have to tug."

"That's not so bad," Daisy said.

"Well, that's not actually the only problem . . ." Penny hesitated. "Sometimes the supplies actually backfire when you unclip them. But that's about it." Penny unbuckled the tool belt and put it back into the van by the other two. "I think we should take the belts. But I can tell you right now, Uncle Walter's not going to like that idea."

"Actually," Walter said, coming up behind his niece as she reached in the van, "I think we might as well wear them." Penny raised her eyebrows, so Walter explained. "We can charge in there with just a mop in each hand. Or we can take some backup supplies in the belt. In either case, we still have a mop in each hand, even if the belt malfunctions." Walter smiled. "Don't look so surprised, Penny. We're going to need everything we've got to break into the Academy. Four against . . . how many?"

"We can take 'em." Penny picked up the pushbroom that had been leaning against the van. "Let's lock and load."

CHAPTER 46

"I WROTE YOU A NOTE."

They were an odd sight, leaning against the bumper of a brown janitorial van at the truck stop: one aged man, two kids, and a young woman, each loaded with cleaning supplies, their cheeks rosy from the chill of late autumn. Spencer, Daisy, and Penny wore the packed canvas janitorial belts around their waists. Since there were only three belts, Walter had agreed to go without.

Penny wore a hooded sweatshirt and carried two short-handled mops over her shoulders. To Daisy's enjoyment, Penny had warmed up in the parking lot with a few back handsprings and round offs.

Walter wore his baseball cap even though the sun was far enough down that he didn't need it to block the light. He twisted the old bronze nail between his fingers, having pulled it from the janitorial van a few minutes earlier. In his other hand, he held Ninfa loosely. It was too risky to leave the bronze objects in the van while they entered New Forest Academy. If the nail and hammer were stolen, the entire Rebel Underground would collapse in no time.

Spencer felt a twinge of anxiety as the yellow school bus pulled into the truck stop. Once Walter handed the hammer and nail to Meredith, they would be on their way up the canyon to embark on a task that Spencer had dreamed about countless times. They were going to find his dad.

Walter stood up as the big bus stopped, hissing loudly. The door squeaked open and Meredith descended the steps. The lunch lady and the janitor came face-to-face in the parking lot, and Spencer watched Walter hand over the bronze objects, somewhat ceremoniously. They retreated out of earshot as Walter gave Meredith the necessary instructions on what to do if he didn't return.

Spencer tried to glimpse some of the Academy rejects through the dim bus windows. Daisy muttered something about how weird they must look in full janitorial battle gear. But Spencer kept looking, hopeful to catch the eye of Min or Jenna.

Suddenly, Min appeared in the doorway of the bus. He stepped down and approached Spencer and Daisy, the usual businesslike expression on his face.

"I assume that your attempt to sneak away from Meredith's bus means you have plans to return to New Forest Academy," the Asian boy said.

Spencer and Daisy looked at each other. There was no use hiding it. "We have to go back," Spencer said.

Suddenly, Jenna emerged from the big bus. She jogged across the parking lot, not stopping until she stood awkwardly close to Spencer. In her hand was a piece of paper, folded into a small triangle. She took a deep breath. "I wrote you a note." She stuffed the folded paper into Spencer's hand. He began to unfold it, but she stopped him.

"Don't read it till I'm gone," Jenna said. She took an awkward step back, gave Spencer one final smile, and took off running toward the bus.

Daisy sighed. "Isn't she pretty? Did you know that Jenna takes like an hour every morning just to do her hair?" Daisy shrugged. "I don't want to gossip, but I heard she's trying to impress somebody. And it's not me or Min. Or Dez."

Spencer rolled his eyes, but it couldn't prevent his face from heating up. Daisy was always a little late to pick up on social clues. Spencer shoved the note into his pocket and turned to Min, half expecting the Asian boy to explain the science behind blushing.

"Why are you going back?" Min asked.

"They've got my dad," Spencer said. "He's being held in a dumpster, somewhere below campus. We have to rescue him before it's too late."

"We stand ready to assist you," Min said. "That bus is full of thirty able-bodied, bright-minded students. Let us go back with you."

"No." Spencer shook his head. "It's too dangerous. They can't get involved."

Min raised an eyebrow. "We just flew over the trees in a school bus. That sounds 'involved' to me. I attempted to justify what happened, but their suspicions are aroused. They know it was more than science. They want answers. We trust you, and we're willing to help."

Spencer hesitated. He'd just risked all to rescue these students. Taking them back to the Academy was out of the question. But Min was right. The students deserved answers. And if they were willing to help . . .

"Detention," Spencer said.

"Detention?" Min repeated.

Spencer nodded. "If they want to help, tell everyone to go back to their schools and get detention with the janitors."

"A strange request . . ." Min started, but Spencer wasn't finished. Using everyone to raid the Academy was too dangerous, but if these students got involved at their own schools across a range of different states, maybe they could make a difference.

"You need to find out which side your janitor is fighting for—Rebel or BEM," Spencer explained. "If he's a Rebel, then team up with him. Learn what you can. But if he's with the BEM . . ." Spencer grimaced. "Watch him closely; sabotage his work. And tell all the recruits to report to me with any suspicious activity. SpenceZ@wahoo.com."

Spencer checked over his shoulder. Walter's conversation with Meredith was ending. The lunch lady headed toward the school bus, pocketing the hammer and nail. Walter didn't know that Spencer had just organized a nationwide network of student spies. He would tell the old janitor later, once they were safely away from New Forest Academy.

"Can I count on you to explain this to the others?" Spencer glanced at the bus. "And remember, it's got to be kept top secret."

"Of course," Min said. "We'll get detention in as many schools as we can. We'll be your eyes and ears against the BEM. The Organization of Janitor Monitors."

Meredith honked the bus horn, anxious to get on the road. But Min didn't go running yet. "I have only one question." He knit his eyebrows together in thought. "How exactly does one go about getting detention with the janitors?" Min, who had probably never broken a serious rule in his life, was stumped.

"Make a mess," Spencer said. A faint smile flicked across his face as he remembered throwing cans of root beer across the Welcher Elementary cafeteria at the ice cream social. "Make an epic mess."

CHAPTER 47

"IT COULD TURN THE TIDES IN THIS WAR."

The brown janitorial van snaked up the canyon road toward New Forest Academy. Walter had been over the plan twice, and now silence reigned in the vehicle. Spencer and Daisy crouched in the back of the van. Penny drove and Walter sat shotgun, anxiously gripping the handle of a toilet plunger. The warlock's face looked weary as twilight shadows flickered through the window.

They were almost there.

The plan was simple but effective. Walter would get inside the campus and create a disturbance and a distraction. The others would slip quietly through the gate, enter the main building, and descend into the parking garage. Penny felt confident that they could conquer whatever dangers awaited them in the dark underground.

But Spencer knew it wouldn't work.

The whole plan could go like clockwork, but there was one fatal flaw. They would never be able to rescue Alan Zumbro unless they convinced Director Garcia to peel away the Glopified duct tape sealing the dumpster. It was an oversight that Spencer didn't want to mention. Walter was already reluctant to storm the Academy. If Spencer explained the weak link in their plan, Walter might abort the whole mission.

No. It was better to get inside and see what might happen. If nothing else, Spencer could just talk to his dad again and promise to rescue him.

The van took a sharp corner, items shifting and skidding around the kids in the back. Spencer looked once more at the Vortex on the shelf. He now knew why Walter hadn't discussed the details of rescuing Marv. The old warlock didn't want to give Spencer false hope. What they were doing was so dangerous—if Walter didn't survive, there would be no Operation Vortex.

"This is it," Spencer said. "The parking lot is just over the next rise."

Penny pulled the van to the edge of the road.

"Ready?" Walter looked back at the two kids. He tried to give a confident smile, but Spencer could tell he was nervous. The warlock turned to his niece. "Remember, you're not waiting for me. As soon as you rescue Alan, get back to the van and go."

"Wait a minute," Spencer said. "We're not leaving without you."

"Look," Walter explained. "By the time you guys get

out, I expect to be long gone. Once you're inside the campus, I plan to lead as many of those Academy goons into the woods as I can."

"But where will you go?" Daisy asked.

"I'll work my way through the forest and cut toward Denver. It will probably take me a couple of days on foot, with the use of a broom. I have a Rebel friend there. He'll pick me up. The BEM will be searching for me. It should give you the chance to get Alan safely away."

Walter must have noticed Spencer staring out the window, his face somber. Would the warlock be all right? Walter was the most wanted Rebel Janitor. If they captured him, the BEM would be that much closer to reclaiming the bronze hammer and nail.

"Hey." Walter reached back to reassure Spencer, but the boy was too far away. "I'll be fine. This is important, Spencer, and not just because it's your dad. Alan has been kept alive and imprisoned by the BEM for two years. He's obviously valuable to them. If we can rescue your dad, he might have information to help the Rebels. It could turn the tides in this war."

Penny shut off the van and Walter stepped out, shouldering his backpack. With a broom in one hand and a toilet plunger in the other, Walter didn't look much like a man who was about to go risk his life to create a distraction.

"I guess this is good-bye," Walter said as Spencer approached him. "At least for a few days." He gave a few practice swings with the plunger. "I think I can manage to wreak some havoc with this." The warlock nodded to Spencer. "Let's go save your dad!"

Without waiting for a reply, Walter ran up the hill and lifted off the ground with his broom. Spencer stayed on the roadside, watching him rise and then descend until he was out of sight.

"All right," Penny said. "Let's get this van somewhere safe and hidden." She reached down to the U clips on her loaded janitorial belt. The tops of several wooden handles were visible, but everything below the belt was invisible and intangible. Penny grabbed one of the handles and pulled. A toilet plunger shimmered into sight.

Sticking the rubber cup to the side of the van, she easily picked it up and walked off the road, holding the large vehicle in front of her as if it were no heavier than a handbag. Daisy guided her, searching for a good hiding place in the trees.

Spencer stood alone on the side of the road. The mountain felt calm and deceptively peaceful. The coo of an owl seemed to bid farewell to the last glimmer of daylight.

Spencer suddenly remembered the note Jenna had pressed into his hand. The thought occurred to him that now might be his last chance to read it.

Digging in his pocket, Spencer pulled out the folded paper. He smoothed the page in his hands and squinted to read the few sentences in the fading light.

Spencer—I'm so glad we were on the blue team 2gether! It was gr8 meeting U! This was a super crazy week. I still don't really get what happened. But I felt like I could trust U no matter what. Next time we meet, I hope U will trust me.

U R different than other boyz. Good different. Stay that way.

Your friend,

Jenna

P.S. I got your address from the bus driver lady. I'll write U!

P.P.S. Don't forget me!

Spencer was glad he was alone so that no one saw his face turn red. He folded the letter along the same creases and slipped the note back into his pocket.

Why was Spencer different from other boys? Was it the fact that he could see and kill Toxites? Or did it have something to do with how he was stuck in this twelve-year-old body forever, a kind of janitorial Peter Pan . . .

Spencer sighed. Jenna was nice, but there was no time to fully digest what she'd meant by giving him that note. The mission ahead would need to occupy all his thoughts and energy.

Penny and Daisy returned from the trees. The plunger disappeared back into Penny's belt as they stepped onto the roadside.

A shattering crash cut through the cold night and drifted over the hill to resonate in Spencer's ears. The abrupt sound was the first in a chain of destructive noises.

"Well," Penny said. "That's our cue."

CHAPTER 48

"WHO'S GOING TO LEAD?"

The three figures crested the hill, and New Forest Academy's parking lot came into view. The scene looked like an automobile dump. Cars were strewn and scattered, undoubtedly the work of Walter's Glopified toilet plunger. The operating booth was smashed, and a large SUV had been thrown through the gate.

More sounds of destruction echoed from the other side of the brick wall, assuring Spencer that Walter had made it onto campus. The warlock's shoot-'em-up arrival had drawn every available person after him, leaving the wrecked parking lot empty.

They were halfway across the lot when Penny paused, scanning for danger. Daisy reached for a broom on her tool belt, but Penny said no.

"We go on foot," she whispered, setting off toward the crumpled gate.

Their feet crunched on shards of glass. An overturned sedan creaked. A small oil fire burned under a broken truck.

Spencer felt the tension of the moment as they stealthily raced toward the gate. Daisy kept checking over her shoulder, a subconscious motion that rattled Spencer's nerves.

They reached the gate, and Penny crouched behind the overturned SUV. "Once we get through, we shouldn't stop till we reach the underground garage," she said. "Time for you to make good on your knowledge of campus. I'll bring up the rear. Who's going to lead?"

Spencer shifted under Daisy's expectant stare. "Fine." He took a deep breath, cinched the tool belt around his waist, and nodded. "Let's go."

Spencer leaned around the mangled vehicle. The metal gate was warped and bent away from the brick wall, leaving a tight space to squeeze through. He ducked under the coils of sharp barbed wire. Pressing against the brick, he managed to slide past. Spencer waited just long enough to make sure that the others didn't get snagged before he took off running.

Spencer's legs pumped, trying to outrun his shadow from the overhead spotlights. Bathed in light, the three figures were completely visible. Spencer silently hoped that Walter's distraction was big enough to keep Academy eyes away from the gate.

They dropped into the shadows one by one, Spencer

leading Daisy and Penny along the campus's perimeter. The brick wall rose at their side, increasing the darkness and their feeling of claustrophobia.

The main building was at the center of campus, but Spencer didn't want to rush straight in from the gate. If they skirted around, it might be safer to approach from the side.

They glimpsed the rec center. Was it only a few hours ago that Spencer had led the recruits in a wild escape? So much had happened since then. He'd learned about his dad and about himself. He'd learned the depth of Director Garcia's involvement with the BEM. As one of the warlocks, Garcia was bound to be carrying his bronze hammer. Furthermore, one of the New Forest Academy buildings had to be the warlock's magical domain, set with a bronze nail in the wall.

Thinking of Director Garcia was only a reminder that their attempt to rescue Alan Zumbro could not succeed. The director was the only one with the power to open the duct tape on the dumpster prison. As much as Spencer wanted to shove that thought to the back of his mind, it kept resurfacing. It was a painful reminder that this risky rescue attempt was likely nothing more than a fool's errand.

Looking ahead, Spencer saw the illuminated porches of the student dorms. He thought of their old Glopified stash hidden underneath. Daisy had said she'd taken everything except for two items: a latex glove and the little spray bottle of ink remover. Hardly useful items for a mission like this.

They skirted around the art building and Spencer froze.

He lifted a hand to his head, where the craziest idea had just flickered to life.

"What's wrong?" Daisy whispered from behind. Spencer, so absorbed in this new thought, didn't even hear her.

"Come on," said Penny. "Keep going."

Spencer remained a statue, running through every aspect of his plan, checking for flaws that could be fatal. There were a lot of unknown variables, but it was better than nothing.

"Wait here," Spencer ordered his companions. "I'll be right back."

"Are we lost?" Daisy asked. But Spencer was already running for the dorms.

He slid under the dormitory porch like a baseball player stealing home. The cardboard box was still there, untouched. Spencer grabbed the glove and ink remover. He opened a pouch on the back of his tool belt and dropped the items in.

Checking that all was clear, Spencer scooted out from under the porch and made a mad dash back to where Penny and Daisy waited with puzzled expressions.

"No time to lose," he said, approaching the window of the art building and drawing a mop to break the glass.

Daisy came alongside him. "What are you doing?" she said, struggling to keep her voice low. "This isn't the right building!"

"There's something I have to do here," Spencer said.

The window exploded under his mop strings. Instinctively, all three of them ducked at the sound.

"Watch the door," Spencer said, unclipping a broom. "Make sure no one comes in. This should only take a second."

Spencer tapped his broom and drifted through the large window, leaving Penny and Daisy confused and annoyed.

"You better have a good reason for this!" Penny called.

And he certainly did.

CHAPTER 49

"YOU'RE NOT ONE OF US."

They were off and running again in less than five minutes. Spencer had what he needed in one of the belt's spill-proof pouches. He didn't bother explaining himself to Penny and Daisy. If his plan worked, there would be plenty of time to talk about it later. But if it didn't . . .

Spencer wouldn't allow himself to doubt. He had to keep his mind focused on the task ahead.

They were cutting through campus and had gotten almost to the main building when they stumbled into the first ambush. Six figures came out of the darkness, the whoosh of Glopified mop strings preceding them.

Daisy went down first, unable to get a weapon unclipped from her tool belt. Spencer reached for his pushbroom, but the handle was stuck in the malfunctioning belt. He pulled hard, but the enemy was closing in.

Two men raced toward Penny. Her twin mops were out in a flash and she lassoed an overhanging tree branch. The last few leaves clinging to the branch shook loose as Penny pulled herself straight up. She went into midair splits, dealing each man a deft kick to the face.

Spencer abandoned his pushbroom and grabbed the next available handle. As he drew it from the belt's U clip, a toilet plunger shimmered into view. But casting his eyes around, Spencer realized that there was nothing to plunge! He managed to get off one shot of vac dust before a BEM mop pulled him to the ground.

Penny swung forward, went into an acrobatic flip, and landed like a cat in the street. Her short-handled twin mops were ready to lash into action as the four remaining BEM workers turned for her.

Spencer twisted under the mop's restraint. If he could reach his tool belt there might be a way to get out of this. He could attack them from behind! But the surprise attack came before Spencer could even move his arms. A stocky figure jumped into view, bristly pushbroom springing into action, striking all four BEM workers before they could turn. With helpless cries, they drifted up into the night sky.

Daisy was already on her feet as Penny scanned for any other attackers. Spencer scrambled out of his mop strings and turned to their rescuer.

"Dez?"

"You chumps came back for me!" the bully said.

"Get out of here!" Spencer pointed his toilet plunger directly at Dez. "You're not one of us."

Dez blew a raspberry. "That's some way to say 'thank you.' If you didn't notice, I just saved your sorry little behinds." He put his pushbroom over his shoulder. "We should escape while there's still time," Dez said. "Everybody's on the other side of campus. Some crazy dude is making a racket over there."

"You had your chance to escape with us, Dez!" Spencer wouldn't lower the plunger. "We didn't come back for you. So get moving!"

"Are you nuts?" Dez said. "I'm not staying here! I want to go home with you guys."

"Well, you should have thought of that before you made a dirty deal with Slick behind our backs."

"Oh, come on!" Dez threw back his head. "That was nothing! Slick said he'd give me Toxite soap if I promised to stay at the Academy. I didn't think he'd hold me to it! Aren't promises made to be broken?" Dez rolled his eyes. "I'm sorry, okay? I shouldn't have made a deal with Slick. But don't . . . just don't leave me *here*."

Penny called softly from the street. "Better get a move on. We're about to have more company."

Spencer and Daisy stared hard at Dez, trying to read the bully's true intentions. He was obnoxious and selfish, yes. But did Dez really believe in the destructive ideals of New Forest Academy and the BEM? Dez was just a bully; a bully who belonged at home.

Finally, Spencer lowered the plunger. "One trick from you and it's over. Is that clear?"

"I don't even know any tricks," Dez said. "Unless you

count my armpit noises. 'Cause I can actually play 'The Star-Spangled Banner' with my armpit. But that's an okay trick, right?"

"Do you know anything by the Beatles?" Daisy asked.

"No!" Spencer raised the plunger again. "If you make any kind of noise at all, we'll leave you behind!" Without waiting to see the effect of his threat, Spencer turned and sprinted after Penny. Daisy and Dez followed, jogging the final distance to the main building.

The front door was open, and they entered the building unopposed. "This way to Slick's office," Spencer said, resuming his spot at the lead.

They turned corners cautiously, Glopified weapons at hand. But the building seemed deserted. Walter had effectively drawn the fight across campus.

The group paused at the top of the stairs that led into the janitorial closet.

"Let me clear the area," Penny whispered. Lifting her twin mops, she moved smoothly and silently down. The three kids scanned the hallways nervously until Penny called up. "Nobody here! Come on down!"

"There's the secret pallet," Spencer said when they reached the bottom of the stairs. He crossed the office, noticing the chair that he'd once occupied. The orange extension cord that Slick had used to grow the Filth was still on the floor.

Spencer jumped onto the pallet, calling the others over. Penny and Daisy joined him, and then, reluctantly, Dez.

A long chain dangled from the ceiling, anchoring into a

steel bolt in the center of the wooden pallet. Spencer took hold of the chain, gripping carefully so the links wouldn't pinch his skin. "I think Slick just gave this a pull," he said. Before anyone could speak, Spencer gave a sharp downward tug.

The wooden pallet dropped like a high-speed elevator, carrying Spencer, Dez, Daisy, and Penny into the waiting darkness of the underground parking garage.

CHAPTER 50

"YOU'LL THANK US LATER."

As the pallet dropped, the first thing they heard was Dez's voice. "Hey, wait a sec," the bully said. "Where are we going? I don't want to come down here! What are we doing? I thought we were trying to get *away* from the Academy!"

"Didn't I tell you not to make noise?" Spencer warned. The clank of the chain echoed in the dark concrete shaft as the wooden platform descended. Overhead, a new pallet slid down the links, sealing over the opening above and blocking all light.

The platform touched the ground, and Spencer instinctively reached for the many handles on his tool belt. A bit of fluorescent light filtered onto the wooden platform. Turning, Spencer saw a small archway cut out of the concrete.

They filed off the pallet one by one, stepping through the concrete doorway and into the dimly lit parking garage. The monotonous gray of the cement seemed to stretch on endlessly, like a man-made sea. The fluorescent bulbs gave the whole area an artificial feeling that caused Spencer's eyes to blur, making him wish for natural sunlight. Huge gray pillars supported the thick ceiling, titans of concrete holding the earth on their shoulders.

The silence and emptiness of the garage was maddening.

"Where's the dumpster?" Penny asked. Even at a whisper, the sound seemed to echo harshly off the walls and ceiling.

Spencer shook his head. "It's not here. We're not down far enough. There must be more levels under us."

"There's usually some car ramps in these things." Penny was scanning the walls, but there appeared to be no exit. "Not a very functional garage without ramps to get out."

"There!" Daisy pointed across the level. There was a metal grate set into the far wall. Even in the dreary light, they could see it was some kind of industrial elevator.

Without warning, Dez threw down his pushbroom and crumpled into a pitiful heap on the cold concrete floor. "It's no use," he said. "We'll never make it. What's the point anyway? I don't even want to try . . ." A shimmer rolled down his cheek. Was Dez . . . *crying?*

"Umm," Spencer said. "What's up with him?"

Dez let out a loud, resonant sigh.

Daisy shrugged. "Shh, shh." She patted him on the head like a dog. "Everything's okay."

"No," Penny said, glancing up. "It's not."

There was a loud rushing sound as huge leathery wings unfolded. A Rubbish dropped from its batlike perch on the ceiling. But this was unlike any Rubbish Spencer had ever seen.

It must have spent days plugged into the Glopified extension cords, because it had grown to an impossible size. Its black wings were the size of bedsheets, bits of dust flaking off as they gave a mighty flap.

The synthesized growth from the cords had caused the creature to evolve, developing new and terrifying features. Two red horns thrust up from the base of its skull. Its piercing eyes glowed pink, and a beak the length of Spencer's arm parted. The Rubbish gave a bloodcurdling call, its eight-inch talons flexed for an attack.

Penny's response was the fastest. One of her mops shot out, tangling the legs of the gigantic Toxite. But the creature was too strong. It jerked Penny off the ground, trailing her behind like the tail of a kite.

One monstrous Rubbish would have been plenty, but in the next moment, two more of equal size dropped from the ceiling, a glint of bloodlust in their eyes. They swooped forward in a rush of wings, weaving between the concrete pillars as they advanced toward their prey.

In the distance, lost in the darkness of the garage, Spencer could hear Penny locked in combat with the Rubbish that had carried her off. At least for the moment, the kids were on their own.

"Get up, Dez!" Spencer kicked the bully, trying to break through the symptoms of the Toxite breath.

Spencer was grateful it wasn't a giant Filth, or he would have been sleeping for sure. But Rubbish breath didn't have any effect on him or Daisy. Spencer had never known Dez to be affected by any of the Toxites, but apparently, these huge Rubbishes were too big even for a bully like Dez to resist.

"I don't feel like it." Dez slumped forward and covered his face with his hands. "I don't feel like anything."

"Oh, forget it," Spencer said, picking up Dez's fallen pushbroom.

The first Rubbish went into a dive, screeching some unearthly sound. Spencer crouched and thrust his weapon like a spear. The flat bristles of the pushbroom struck the Rubbish in the thick neck, cutting short its terrible cry. It floated backward in a flurry of wings that caused Spencer's hair to blow. Daisy threw a counterattack of vac dust, causing the Rubbish to spiral completely out of control.

The Glopified attacks, easily enough to kill an average Toxite, seemed only to enrage these overgrown beasts. The Rubbish quickly righted itself and joined its companion for a double attack.

Spencer and Daisy stood back-to-back. Daisy drew a plunger from her tool belt as the first creature landed sideways on the nearest pillar. Its oversized talons dug into the concrete, securing a good perch. The Rubbish bobbed its bald head and tensed its neck, making some horrid sound. It seemed to be choking, body convulsing as though it were trying to work something up from its stomach. A deep rumble issued from its black gut. Then the beak opened and a thick plume of dark dust breathed outward like dragon fire.

Spencer and Daisy stumbled backward, coughing and wiping the grit from their faces. The second Rubbish used its companion's distraction to fly into action. It burst through the cloud of Rubbish dust, drawing a wake of particles behind it. The creature's legs came forward as it descended on Spencer.

Daisy sidestepped the monster and stabbed with her plunger, the rubber end making good suction with the leathery wing. Daisy whirled around, dragging the huge Rubbish by the wing and flinging it into one of the concrete pillars. The damage to the pillar was devastating, but the Toxite hardly seemed affected. Flapping those giant wings, it took flight again, jerking the plunger out of Daisy's hand.

Talons closed only inches above Spencer's head as the other Toxite swept in. A deft blow from his pushbroom knocked the Rubbish off course. Cawing loudly, it circled a pillar and came in for a fresh attack.

But this time, it didn't go for Spencer or Daisy. The Rubbish was on a hungry course for Dez. The bully was lying facedown, wracked with careless disinterest—total apathy. Not even the danger of the moment could spur him into action.

With a hop, the Rubbish landed, its massive wings folding in. The monster shuddered and breathed out a stream of dust, black as soot. Dez disappeared in the cloud. The

Rubbish hopped forward, talons scraping on the concrete floor.

Spencer hurled his pushbroom like a javelin, knowing that a miss could prove fatal for Dez. The bristles struck the Rubbish, but the force was barely enough to knock it aside. The monster snatched the handle of the pushbroom in its beak and snapped it like a matchstick. The dark cloud of Rubbish breath settled around Dez. Through the haze, sickly pink eyes honed in on the prey once more.

Suddenly, from behind the Rubbish, twin mop strings lashed out, encircling the body and pinning the wings at the creature's side. The Rubbish hopped sideways, dragging Penny to her knees.

Thick dust began to billow from the mop string wounds. The Rubbish thrashed, but Penny's mops were secure. Spencer dug into one of his pouches and pulled out a fistful of vacuum dust. Jumping over Dez's prone form, he hurled the dust into the Rubbish's face. The added Glopification proved too much, and the giant winged beast exploded in a flash of light and a wisp of blackness.

"One down," Penny said, pulling back her mop strings. But the other Rubbishes were winging through the pillars toward them, enraged by their companion's death.

"We've got to get Dez out of here," Spencer said.

Daisy ran to the bully's side. "I'll get him over to that elevator." She reached to her tool belt and paused. "But I need a plunger."

As the two Rubbishes swooped in from opposite sides, Penny flicked out both mops and ensnared the legs of the nearest creature. Leaning back, she swung the Toxite around, causing it to collide with the other in midair.

Spencer drew the toilet plunger from his belt and handed it to Daisy. Propping the bully partway, Spencer pulled up Dez's shirt to expose his big, flat stomach.

"No," Dez moaned. "This is stupid. I don't want to do it."

"Trust me," Daisy said. "You'll thank us later." She clamped the rubber cup of the plunger onto Dez's stomach and glanced at the long distance to the elevator. Then Daisy turned to Spencer. "Cover me."

Daisy lifted Dez easily. She held him upright, the bully dangling awkwardly at her side. Then she took off running across the parking level.

Instantly, one of the Rubbishes flew over Spencer's head in pursuit. There was no time to draw a weapon. He leapt up, catching one of the legs. The Toxite shifted under the added weight and clipped a wing on one of the pillars. Spencer and the Rubbish tumbled to the ground, racing to see who could recover first.

The second Rubbish was screaming toward Penny. She stood between two pillars, watching Daisy's run but leaving her back exposed to the advancing monster. In the last moment, she saw it sweeping in.

The Toxite spewed a stream of dust to confuse its prey, but Penny's mops were already in action. She lassoed the opposing pillars at her sides and, using the spring from the mops, leapt above the cloud of Rubbish breath. The

monster dove beneath her and Penny let go of the mops, falling heavily onto the creature's back.

The Rubbish went into a tight roll, cutting between pillars and trying desperately to shake Penny from its back. But Penny held tightly to the creature's red horns. Her knees dug into the scruff of the Toxite's side while one hand reached to her belt and drew a plunger. Stabbing downward, she struck the Rubbish on the top of its head. She pushed with all her strength as smoky black dust began venting from the dissolving Toxite.

The creature had just opened its beak to shriek in pain when it exploded, sending Penny tumbling to the hard concrete.

Spencer backed up against the pillar, digging into his belt pouch for more vac dust. Without looking, he realized that he'd reached into the wrong pouch. Spencer's hand closed around a rectangular object.

Just then, the Rubbish hopped around the pillar to attack. Its neck convulsed and the beak opened wide, working up the power to release a plume of blackness into the boy's face. Pulling the chalkboard eraser from his pouch, Spencer hurled the bomb into the Toxite's open beak. The eraser lodged in the Rubbish's throat and detonated. The huge beak opened and closed silently, wisps of white chalk leaking out the sides.

Spencer backed away as the Toxite began to twitch. It flopped onto its side, writhing. Leathery wings folded and unfolded, unable to take flight. Then the Rubbish dissolved from the inside until all that was left was a ghostly cloud of Glopified chalk dust curling toward the ceiling.

With the final Rubbish destroyed, Dez's senses started to return.

"Hey!" he said, bouncing at Daisy's side. He glanced down at the toilet plunger stuck to his stomach. "What the . . . ? Put me down! What are you trying to do?"

Daisy reached the elevator and set Dez on his feet. With a twist of the handle, the toilet plunger popped off his belly, leaving a large round welt. Dez instantly pulled his shirt down.

"I don't think you want to mess with this!" Dez pointed to his stomach like it was a weapon of mass destruction.

"Relax," said Daisy. "I just saved your life."

Spencer and Penny arrived, covered in dust and breathing heavily from their run across the garage.

The elevator wasn't much more than a big metal cage set into a concrete shaft. "Freight elevator," Penny said. Reaching her fingers through the links, she heaved, sliding the metal grate upward like a castle portcullis.

The four of them stepped into the elevator. Penny let go of the grate and it slammed down. Immediately, the elevator began to descend, exposed concrete walls flickering past.

"That wasn't so bad. Just a few relocated Toxites." Penny forced a smile. "Who's ready for level two?"

CHAPTER 51

"THINK YOU'RE BAD?"

The elevator came to rest. Through the metal grate that served as a door, Spencer and the others could see the vast expanse of the underground parking garage. It looked calm and monotonous, but after the first level, Spencer was expecting the worst.

"Ready?" Penny asked. She grasped the metal grate and attempted to lift it like before. But even when the three kids joined her, the grate wouldn't budge.

"Rusted shut," Dez said.

"There's no way," Spencer said. "We just barely opened it."

"Do you even know what rust is?" Daisy asked.

"Hey!" Penny interrupted. She stood in the back corner of the elevator, her hands around a thick chain like the one from the pallet. "This should do it." She heaved on the chain and the grate lifted an inch. Hand over hand, Penny hoisted until the kids were able to duck under and exit the elevator.

"What now?" Spencer said, seeing the obvious problem. Penny, holding tight to the chain, couldn't let go or the grate would close.

"I've just got to be quick," she said. Penny released the chain and dove for the exit, but the grate slammed shut with alarming speed, trapping her inside the freight elevator. Returning to the chain, Penny pulled again, but this time nothing happened.

Penny breathed a sigh of annoyance. "Chain won't work." She drew her twin mops from her tool belt and flicked the strings at the elevator grate. But even the Glopified mops couldn't bend the metal.

"Look," said Dez. "There's another elevator over there!" He pointed across the dim garage.

Daisy was checking her tool belt when Spencer suddenly collapsed into a slumbering heap on the cold ground.

Penny stopped struggling against the elevator. She pressed her face to the grate, peering across the parking garage. "They're coming," she whispered.

Dez suddenly gave a high-pitched scream. Daisy whirled around to see three gigantic Filths scuttling forward, their sharp claws clicking on the hard cement. In the dim light, Daisy could see their dilated pupils and long, gnashing teeth. As a long-term result of the extension cords, the Filths had expanded to the size of grizzly bears. They were covered in deadly sharp quills as thick as pencils.

"Dez!" Penny shouted from the caged elevator. "Take Spencer's tool belt!"

The bully blundered, riddled with shock at the size of the Filths. It took him a second, but Penny's instructions sank in.

Dez rolled Spencer over and unclipped the belt buckle. Twisting sideways, Dez wrapped the belt around his own middle, sliding the buckle to allow for more stomach.

One of the Filths turned aside, and Daisy got a glimpse of the mutations that had resulted from the Toxite's evolution. A thick tail dropped down behind the monster, wagging back and forth. Attached to the end of the tail was a ball, rock hard and heavy. To make things worse, this bludgeoning tail weapon was studded with thick, barbed spikes.

"We've got to lead them away from Spencer!" Daisy shouted. She took off running directly toward the huge beasts, drawing a pushbroom from her belt.

Dez hesitated for only a moment before his sense of boyish pride kicked him into action. He couldn't let a girl do all the fighting!

Daisy shoved her weapon into one of the Filths, pushbroom scraping past the thick quills and striking it on the flank. The beast lost balance, rose a few feet, and came crashing down on its back with a squeal. It rolled over, sharp teeth gnashing and stringy saliva dangling from its jowls.

Dez's mop strings twisted forward. They slashed across a Filth's face, wrapping around the wide skull. The dangerous tail whipped around, severing the Glopified mop strings and forcing Dez back. The overgrown beast grunted, a deep-throated, guttural sound. Wicked cuts from the strings crisscrossed the Filth's face. But the wounds, instead of oozing blood, flaked away like crumbling dirt.

The third Filth paused in the darkness between two pillars. A single ray of fluorescent light fell on its face, causing the blue eyes to glint like those of a feral beast on the roadside. It arched its back and began to quiver violently, every muscle flexed.

Daisy saw the odd behavior, saw pressure building under the Filth's long quills. "Get down!" she shouted, diving behind a pillar.

Dez dropped to the ground as the Filth blasted its quills into the air. They fell like a thick volley of arrows, clattering off Daisy's pillar and narrowly missing Dez's body. This new defense was another deadly evolution brought on by the Glopified extension cords.

The Filth was hideous as it turned toward Dez. The creature's patchy fur was pocked with exit holes where the quills had been. It looked much thinner without its bristling spikes. But already, a new array of needles was rising out of the gray flesh with a sickening tearing sound.

As the Toxite turned, Dez reached out and grabbed one of the discarded quills. It was over a foot long and surprisingly lightweight. The tip was as sharp as a giant needle. He gripped the quill in his hand like a dagger.

There was no telling if the tactic would work, but as the Filth advanced, Dez rolled underneath the monster. Gagging at the putrid stench of the wild beast, he stabbed the long quill into the soft underbelly of the Toxite. Dust spewed from the wound, falling thickly onto Dez's face and arms. The Filth groaned as the boy pulled himself away.

The injured Toxite looked confused. Stabbed with its own weapon, the beast had felt its magic turned on itself. Dez staggered to his feet, cast the mop, and let the strings add to the pain. The Filth reared back on its hind legs, thumped its spiked tail against the ground, and exploded in a shower of gray dust.

Penny shouted something from the elevator. Her message resounded off the naked concrete walls, echoing again and again until the words became muddled and the meaning was lost.

Behind a pillar, Daisy thrust the handle of her pushbroom into a Filth's face. There was an audible *pop* as the eye erupted into a fountain of sludge. The creature reeled away, chattering. Before it could recover, Daisy raised her weapon with both hands above her head and brought it down. The well-placed blow to the Filth's neck was fatal. In a moment, all that was left was a scattering of dust.

Spencer tried to open his eyes. Daisy was patting his cheek and calling his name. But she felt so far away. He was sleeping comfortably. Why bother getting up?

Daisy checked over her shoulder. Dez was taking on the last Filth with a flurry of insults.

"Bring it on, beastie! You're nothing but a dust-munching pack rat! I've seen baby hamsters that looked meaner than you!"

The Toxite couldn't possibly understand Dez's lingo, and Daisy wished he would fight more and talk less. But the bully's distraction should buy her time to get Spencer across the level to the next elevator.

Daisy unclipped a broom from her belt. Taking Spencer by the arm, she slid the broom under him. She held on to the back of his coat and gripped the handle. Then, giving one last forlorn look to where Penny remained trapped in the elevator, Daisy kicked the broom bristles. The action sent her and Spencer skimming along the floor of the garage.

"Hey!" Dez called as they slid past. "Why doesn't Spencer have to get plunged?"

A second kick to the bristles pushed them out of harm's way. The broom clattered against the far wall, toppling both kids onto the ground. Daisy let go of the slumbering Spencer and stood up. Her knuckles were bloody and bruised from bumping along the cement floor. She looked back at Dez in time to see the final injured Filth go into a defensive, quivering hunch.

"Think you're bad?" Dez insulted the creature. "I totally kicked your spiky butt! You're just an overgrown, blubber-bloated, bucktooth chipmunk! With bad breath!"

"Look out!" Daisy shouted. But it was too late.

As Dez leapt forward to deal the injured Toxite a deathblow, the creature's quills released with an angry hiss. The projectiles pierced the air, shattering an overhead lightbulb in a burst of sparks. Dez screamed and fell to the ground out of sight behind the monstrous Filth.

Daisy sprinted away from the elevator, stripping a mop from her belt. As soon as she was in range, the strings leapt out, wrapping around the quill-less Filth and squeezing the life out of it.

The Filth was gone. Dust drifted to the ground like dirty snowfall. Daisy dropped the mop and fell to her knees at Dez's side.

The big kid was groaning, face ashen and teeth clenched. He was curled in a ball, both hands gripping his leg. Daisy covered her mouth when she saw the wound. Like a giant needle, the long quill had made a gristly stitch through the outside of Dez's leg, just above the knee. His hands were covered in dark red. Dez clutched desperately at the spot, as if hoping that the pain would go away.

"No, no, no," Daisy muttered. Tears welled in her eyes as she watched the veins bulge on Dez's face. He grunted and pitched, desperate for help.

Spencer appeared behind Daisy, still rubbing sleep from his eyes. He yawned. "Sorry, guys. I must have fallen . . ." He saw the gory quill in Dez's leg. "Whoa!"

"What do we do?" Daisy asked.

Spencer glanced at the distant elevator where Penny was trapped. "We can't go back," he said. "Let's just get him to the next elevator. The faster we get through this, the sooner we might find a way out."

Daisy nodded, sniffing back the tears. "Should I plunge him again?"

Spencer carefully reached around Dez and unclipped the tool belt. Daisy took the plunger and suctioned the cup onto Dez's stomach again.

"No!" Dez said. "Let me walk! I can . . . aghhh!"

Daisy carefully hoisted the bully. Walking as smoothly as she could, Daisy carried him toward the next elevator. Spencer clipped on the tool belt, cinching the straps around his own waist.

Spencer reached into the back pouch of his belt to make sure he still had what he needed from the art building. "Hang in there, Dez."

A moment later, the three kids were inside another cage elevator, plummeting to the next level of the parking garage nightmare.

CHAPTER 52

"LOOK AT THIS COOL THING!"

Hold the chain, Dez," Spencer said when the elevator stopped. The bully was sitting in the corner, still grabbing his leg with bloodied hands.

"You can't . . . can't leave me here!" Dez shouted.

"You won't be able to keep up," Spencer said. "It'll kill you."

The bully shook his head, teeth still clenched. "You . . . chumps!"

"We'll be back," Daisy said. "We won't leave without you or Penny."

Wordlessly, Dez lifted his red hands and grasped the chain. He pulled twice, just enough for Spencer and Daisy to crawl out onto the next level. Then Dez released the chain and the metal grate slammed.

"Okay," Spencer said, scanning the parking level. "I

don't see the dumpster here, either. Must not be to the bottom yet."

Daisy unclipped her pushbroom, nervously awaiting an ambush. Spencer started forward, a plunger in his grip.

"We've seen Rubbishes and Filths," Spencer said. "So we have to assume that this level has Grimes. You know what that means? You've got to focus harder than ever." Spencer looked back at Daisy. She had stopped to examine a concrete pillar.

"Look at this cool thing!" Daisy had a huge smile on her face.

"Daisy!" Spencer hissed. "There's nothing special about that!"

"Are you sure? I think it's kinda cute . . ."

The most enormous Grime dropped from the ceiling and landed with a squelching sound ten feet in front of Spencer. It was larger than any alligator he had ever seen at the zoo. Its black eyes were the size of softballs.

The creature's skin was stretched so tightly that it appeared almost transparent. The long body was coated in a slimy film that shimmered with iridescence in the artificial light of the garage. A hideous forked tongue darted out of the wide mouth, feeling the ground and flicking back to moisten its large eyes.

Spencer made one last hopeful glance toward Daisy. She had dropped her pushbroom and was now hugging the pillar, a contented expression on her face.

Spencer took a deep breath. He was on his own for this level.

The Grime was holding still, sizing up the boy as if trying to decide whether to eat him in one or two bites. As the creature stared, Spencer noticed that its throat had begun to balloon outward like a croaking toad. The Grime swiveled its head, and Spencer saw that the extension-cord evolution had caused two pale sacks to develop behind the Grime's neck. The sacks glowed with a frightening greenish hue.

The Grime made a gurgling noise, its bloated throat stretching tighter. Suddenly, the sacks behind the neck emptied, the glowing greenish sludge emptying into the Toxite's throat.

Spencer drew his broom as the Grime's throat contracted, spewing a chug of venomous green slime into the air. Spencer slammed the broom bristles against the ground and shot over the deadly projectile. The slime splashed below him, sizzling and smoking as it hit the concrete.

Spencer's hasty launch sent him soaring directly over the Toxite. Fighting against the sickening odor of the Grime's venom, Spencer reached down with his plunger and suctioned onto the Toxite's yellow back. With a gurgling cry, the creature was peeled away from the ground and flung backward. Its gelatinous body skidded along the concrete as it twisted to get its feet down again.

Spencer landed carefully a few yards away. He was planning his next attack when he saw a flicker of movement snaking around a nearby pillar. Another Grime leapt, sticky fingers adhering to Spencer's shirt. The Grime tossed Spencer through the air, his broom flying out of his hand in the process.

The boy tumbled to the ground, tearing his pants at the knees. Before Spencer knew what was happening, a third massive Grime dropped to the floor, its long tongue lashing around Spencer's ankle. He didn't have time to panic about the gigantic germs that were surely climbing up his leg. The Grime was sucking him hungrily toward its dark open maw! Judging by its size, it wouldn't be hard for the Toxite to swallow Spencer whole.

"Daisy!" Spencer screamed. But she was too distracted, playing some kind of hand-slapping rhyme game with the concrete pillar.

Scrambling at his belt, Spencer drew a mop. He cast the Glopified strings into the Grime's open mouth. The mop wound around the base of the long tongue, and Spencer pulled for all he was worth.

With a disgusting snap, the tongue broke off. The Grime skittered backward, croaking painfully and leaving a line of pale goo on the cement.

Spencer sprang to his feet, shaking off the severed tongue that still clung to his ankle. The injured Grime backed against the wall. It started trembling violently, its throat beginning to expand and contract. The venomous pouches on the Grime's neck pulsed with an eerie light.

This time, instead of waiting for the Toxite to vomit the poisonous sludge, Spencer raced directly toward it, leading one of the other Grimes in pursuit. He plunged his hand into his belt's spill-proof pouch and pinched out a heavy dose of vac dust.

The creature ahead was filling its throat. Only feet away,

Spencer could smell the acrid stench of the poison. Spencer reached over his shoulder and hurled the vacuum dust, not at the venom-filled Grime, but at the pursuing monster close behind him. The Toxite went down under the suction, plowing into the first Grime. The Toxite's throat deflated, and glowing acid spewed everywhere, searing and burning both Grimes.

The attack proved too much for the tongueless Grime. Accidentally ingesting its own acid, the creature shuddered uncontrollably and disintegrated into a puddle of slime.

The other Toxite rolled out of the vac dust. It reared on its hind legs, hissing like a cobra. Burn marks smoldered across its shoulder and head. One of the venom sacks had burst, and glowing ooze smeared down its side. The creature sprang from its upright position, but Spencer was already sprinting away.

The Grime moved skillfully and silently. Gravity seemed no hindrance to its reptilian movements. Bulbous fingertips gripped wall and pillar, ceiling and floor, as it slithered after the boy.

Spencer intentionally collided with Daisy, knocking her away from the pillar of her obsession.

"What are you doing?" she yelled. Her eyes narrowed to angry slits. "Can't you see? I'm busy!"

Spencer pointed toward the advancing Grime. "Someone's trying to steal your pillar!" Spencer cried.

"What?" Daisy made her hands into fists. "Who?"

The injured Grime leapt onto the pillar and Spencer pointed. "Him!"

Daisy whirled on the Grime, tossing a fistful of vac dust into its face. Retrieving her fallen pushbroom, she sprang into action, enraged that someone would try to steal her precious piece of cement.

Turning Daisy's distraction against the Grime was a smooth tactic, but there was no telling how long she would stay vengeful before some new distraction claimed her. For now, she was wreaking savage retribution, Grime slime oozing from her victim.

Spencer turned around once, scanning the garage for the third and final Grime. It had fled the action early on. Where was the monster? Unable to see it, he ran to Daisy's aid, arriving in time to join her for the killing blow. Yellow slime spattered everywhere. The air was ripe with a pungent odor, but Daisy didn't seem to notice. Immediately, she turned her face upward to the nearest fluorescent bulb.

"Hello, bright light!"

So much for that . . .

The third Grime sprang from behind, silent as a shadow. It tackled into Spencer and sent him head over heels on the hard floor. Groaning against the pain, Spencer rolled onto his back just as the Grime lowered a huge hand onto his chest. Those wide fingertips, sticky with acid, burned against his coat to leave searing welts on his skin. He tried to jerk free, but the huge monster pinned him like a prize specimen in a bug collection.

Spencer reached for the Glopified weapons at his side, but all he felt were empty U clips. The Grime's tongue flicked out, the forked tip dancing on Spencer's face and neck. In desperation, he shoved his hand into the spill-proof pouch of vac dust and scooped up as much as he could hold.

Then came the panic. His hand was stuck! The malfunctioning belt did not want to let go of the vacuum dust. The Grime withdrew its tongue, opened its mouth, and reached its slimy head downward. Spencer saw the Toxite's wet black gums, nubs of jagged teeth poking through like broken glass. Its breath smelled fetid and rotten, the stench of a hundred carcasses.

Spencer pulled on his fistful of vac dust, screaming with urgency!

Just as the creature's dark mouth began to close around Spencer's head, his hand yanked free. But the belt had chosen this crucial moment to malfunction yet again. As soon as the dust cleared the pouch, it backfired. Spencer felt the suction pull at his tool belt as the vac dust dropped back into the pouch, the magic causing a chain reaction with the remaining dust.

Spencer grabbed his belt, feeling like it might fly off at any second. He didn't realize exactly when it happened, but suddenly, the Grime was gone.

The suction in the belt pouch subsided and Spencer jumped up, bracing himself for a fresh attack.

Daisy blinked and squinted against the light she had been staring at. "I named him Louis," she said.

"Huh?" Spencer asked.

"Louis the Lightbulb." Daisy wrinkled her forehead.

"That was really weird." She turned to Spencer. "Are you all right?"

He nodded. "Not really sure what just happened. I was about to get Grimed and my tool belt backfired. I don't know where the last Toxite went." Then it clicked. "Oh, no . . ." Spencer looked down at his spill-proof pouch of vac dust. "I think it went into my belt."

"But how's that possible?" Daisy asked. "Wasn't it huge?"

"Penny said these pouches are bigger than they seem. Besides, you know how Grimes can compress themselves into tiny spaces."

"What are you going to do about it?"

Spencer poked a finger into the pouch opening. He quickly pulled away when he felt something cold and slimy. "It's a spill-proof pouch. Penny said nothing would come out unless I pulled it out."

"Seriously?" Daisy said. "You're just going to leave it in there?"

"What else can I do? The minute I free it, you and Louis the Lightbulb will leave me to fight the Grime on my own. Besides, we've got to keep going. Dez needs help." Spencer looked back toward the black space where the bully was trapped.

They reached the next elevator, lifted the metal grate, and slipped inside. As in the previous elevators, they immediately plummeted into darkness.

Spencer reached down to his tool belt. The U clips were empty and his vac dust was spent, replaced by a deadly

Toxite. If the dumpster wasn't on the next level, Spencer didn't know if they would survive.

He touched the pouch on the back of his belt. All his hopes were riding there. And still, Spencer could think of a hundred ways this could go wrong.

CHAPTER 53

"YOU CANNOT WIN THIS."

The elevator stopped. Like the last three levels, this one looked dim and uninviting. Spencer and Daisy stood silently, staring through the metal grate.

It was there.

The dumpster prison sat on the far side of the large garage, butted against the concrete wall. Spencer and Daisy didn't need to discuss strategy or shout warnings. This was it. This was what they had come for.

Alan Zumbro was a hundred yards away.

Daisy pulled the chain, lifting the metal grate. Spencer stepped out alone, the grate shutting firmly behind him. Daisy might have told him to be careful, but Spencer was so absorbed by the sight of the dumpster that he heard nothing.

Spencer walked forward, struggling to keep his

breathing steady. It was a déjà vu moment with the soft hum of the fluorescent light and the pad of his shoes on the concrete. He'd walked this distance before, through the eyes of Director Carlos Garcia.

He approached unopposed. Details of the dumpster came into view: the ridges on the black plastic lid, a scratch down one side, the line of silvery duct tape that kept the dumpster closed.

When he was only feet away, Spencer became aware of a figure standing beside a nearby pillar. The man stepped out of the shadows, and Spencer wasn't surprised to see Director Garcia.

"I've been waiting for you." His familiar voice carried that hint of a Spanish accent. "As soon as Walter Jamison breached the gate, I knew you would be coming." Garcia did not seem the slightest bit flustered or anxious. He was frightfully composed and collected.

Spencer froze. His dad was almost within reach. He was probably hearing every word of this conversation.

"Frankly," Garcia said, "I'm surprised you survived Slick's watchdogs. He's been growing those Toxites for weeks. He assured me they would be sufficient to stop an army of janitors."

Garcia strode forward, hard shoes clicking on the concrete. "You can't win this, Spencer. And I don't want to hurt you. I'm going to give you a chance to go. Just turn around and go home."

Spencer said nothing but stared unblinking at the dumpster, noting the slightly curled edge of the duct tape.

"I have orders," Garcia said. "Orders to kill you on sight. My superior would not give you this chance to flee."

Spencer's brow furrowed. Superior? Garcia was a warlock, top of the command chain. Who would be giving him orders?

"I'm not a fighter," the director said. "I'm not a villain. If only you understood what was at stake here. New Forest Academy must rise. And I will do anything to ensure that it does."

Without a word, Spencer stepped forward and seized the edge of the tape. He pulled, but it was hopelessly sealed.

"You cannot win this," Garcia repeated, shaking his head. He held out his hand and wiggled the fingers arrogantly. "Only *one* hand can open that dumpster."

As Garcia spoke, Spencer slipped his right hand into the back pouch of his tool belt. This was the moment. He pushed aside any doubts about his plan and slipped into the glove. Drawing his hand out of the pouch, Spencer grabbed the curled edge of the duct tape and stripped it away from the dumpster lid.

"NO!" Garcia cursed. His eyes bulged in sheer disbelief.

Spencer held out his hand. "Looks like I caught you red-handed."

Spencer wiggled his fingers. His face registering his shock, Director Garcia saw that his own red, inky fingerprints had somehow been copied from Daisy Gates's sloppy art project and pasted onto the fingers of a latex glove.

Director Garcia, white-faced and trembling, ran toward Spencer. He seized the boy by the throat, but the latex glove made it impossible for him to get a grip. Spencer slipped away and reached back to the dumpster, using the finger-printed glove to peel up another strip of tape. Garcia lunged for the lid of the Glopified dumpster, but Spencer threw it open.

Alan Zumbro rose up, tangled hair and beard shadowing whatever fatherly features Spencer might have recognized. Director Garcia swung a fist, but Alan grabbed his hand and dragged him closer. Garcia's face slammed against the side of the metal dumpster with shocking force. Blood streamed from his nose.

Alan dropped the injured director to the concrete floor of the parking garage. Lifting himself along the dumpster's rim, Alan swung a leg over the side and lowered himself down.

Spencer watched in wonder. The dumpster prisoner—his father!

Alan looked so frail. His arms were so thin, his shirt tattered. But as the light glinted across his blue eyes, Spencer saw strength from deep within. Strength and determination to stay alive for countless months in such a horrid prison.

Alan took the moaning director by the collar of his shirt. Garcia's eyes rolled back, still stunned from the pain. Spencer couldn't stand to watch as Alan hefted Director Garcia violently against the side of the dumpster. Reaching inside Garcia's sport coat, Alan withdrew a bronze hammer. Director Garcia cried out and reached for it, but Alan tossed the hammer aside. It clattered on the concrete floor, filling the garage with a harsh metallic ringing.

Garcia was muttering something in Spanish. It sounded penitent, prayerful, laced with desperation.

Alan narrowed his eyes to bitter slits. "Get used to the dark!"

In a moment of absolute vengeance, Alan gave a mighty cry. With strength beyond his frail form, he heaved Director Garcia over the rim of the dumpster prison.

The force of impact caused the lid to swing shut. Before Garcia could utter a single cry, Spencer stepped forward, seized the duct tape, and used the red fingerprinted glove to seal the dumpster prison.

CHAPTER 54

"IS IT GONNA HURT?"

Spencer turned to his father, eyes shimmering in the dim light. For a moment, he saw through the filthy beard, and the face took Spencer far away from the cold, gray garage. He was a ten-year-old boy again, riding his bike around the block with his dad . . .

"Hey, kiddo," Alan said. The corners of his unkempt mustache turned up in a smile. He held out his arms.

"Dad," whispered Spencer. He stepped into his father's open arms, feeling a tight lump of emotion in his throat.

"Have to admit," Alan said, "didn't think it would be you that rescued me." Alan patted his son on the back, then held him away to look into his eyes. "How'd you get through the tape?"

Spencer held up the glove. "I used some Glopified ink

remover to copy Garcia's fingerprints and paste them onto this glove."

Alan grinned and shook his head in amazement. "Unbelievable." He held Spencer by the shoulders, sizing him up. "It's been a long time, son. I can't believe how you've changed . . . look how much you've grown!"

Funny that his father should mention the one aspect of Spencer's life that would never change again.

"You've got a lot to explain, Spence."

Spencer nodded, wiping tears from his cheeks. "So do you," he said. The grim realization of their location settled in again.

Alan took one last glance at the dumpster prison. Garcia was quiet inside, probably trying to sort out what had just happened. Alan stooped and picked up the bronze hammer he'd stolen from the director's coat.

It looked similar to Ninfa, but it was shorter and the edges seemed rounder. This would be a double strike to the BEM. Spencer would escape New Forest Academy with Alan Zumbro *and* Garcia's warlock hammer.

Alan faced his son. "I don't know how long it's been since I've been able to run." Alan tucked the bronze hammer into the threadbare pocket of his pants.

"We'll probably be doing plenty of that," said Spencer.

Together, they set off across the parking level at a steady jog. When they reached the elevator, Daisy was waiting, her face pressed nervously against the metal grate.

"You got him!" she said. Daisy tried to lift the grate, but it still wouldn't budge.

"Here," Alan said. He was looking at something on the wall next to the elevator. "Some kind of safety switch." He clicked it over, and the grate lifted under Daisy's strain.

"Must lock down the whole system so the grates only lift once," Spencer said.

"Makes sense," said Alan. "That would control how many people can get down here."

The elevator trundled upward, bearing Spencer, Alan, and Daisy to the previous level. In a moment, they were racing across the parking garage. Spencer noticed the tracks of goo and venomous slime from the dead Grimes.

"Hey," Dez grunted when they reached his elevator. Spencer slid the grate open and everyone stepped inside. The bully looked up at Alan. "Where'd you find the caveman?"

Dez looked pale and weary. His hair was matted on his forehead and his shirt was soaked with sweat. Red streaks marred anything that Dez had touched with his hands.

"What happened?" Alan dropped to his knees at Dez's side.

"Filth got him," said Daisy.

Alan inspected the wound and grimaced. "That must have been the world's biggest Filth. We need to remove the quill."

"No!" Dez grunted. "Is it gonna hurt?"

"Have you ever had a shot from a nurse?" Alan asked. Dez nodded. "Did it hurt when she pulled the needle out?"

"No," Dez muttered, a hint of his old toughness back in his voice.

"This is going to feel kind of like that," Alan said, grabbing the bloodstained quill. "Except this is going to hurt a lot."

Before Dez could react, Alan jerked the quill out of the boy's leg with a swift motion. Dez moaned and gasped. He said a couple of bad words through clenched teeth. Blood started gushing freely from the wound.

"I need some cloth for a bandage," Alan said, pressing on the wound.

Immediately, Daisy and Spencer produced their team handkerchiefs. Alan didn't hide his surprise. "Not only did I get rescued by some twelve-year-old kids . . ." Alan accepted the handkerchiefs, "but they brought first-aid kits."

Alan folded one handkerchief into an absorbent triangle and pressed it over the stitch holes above Dez's knee. He tied the other handkerchief securely around the boy's leg. "Keep the pressure on it," Alan instructed. Dez nodded and pressed with both hands.

The elevator had arrived at the next level. Daisy opened the grate. Spencer and Alan helped Dez to his feet, and they hobbled out.

It was slow going with Dez. The injured boy let off a steady stream of complaints. When they passed the spot on the level where Dez had been injured, Spencer couldn't look down. The pile of Filth dust had soaked up the blood, making a disgusting crimson mash.

Daisy pushed up the next grate. "Welcome back, Mr. Zumbro," said Penny. She smiled and nodded respectfully. There was a look of awe in her eyes, and Spencer remembered what Walter had said about Alan turning the tides for the Rebels. It was hard to believe. His dad was practically a hero!

"This is the last level," Daisy said as the elevator stopped. Penny and Alan took Dez under the arms and helped him hobble forward. They all crossed the garage, climbed through the concrete archway, and settled onto the wooden pallet.

"The last chain," Spencer muttered, giving it a jerk. Far overhead, he heard the gears kick in. The chain went taut, and instantly the wooden platform shifted as they started to rise into the blackness. Spencer couldn't help but duck as they neared the top, fearing for a moment that they would all be crushed against the pallet above. But at the last moment, the overhead pallet lifted out of the way.

They stumbled off the platform and into the janitorial closet. Alan braced Dez against some low shelves while they scavenged around Slick's office for any fresh Glopified supplies. Penny made sure that everyone had a broom, since their escape route would most likely take them over the brick wall.

Alan took the warlock hammer from his pocket and readjusted it so it wouldn't fall during a long run.

"Hey, hey!" Penny said when she saw it. "Look what you got!"

"No sense in leaving it in the hands of an enemy." Alan grinned.

They moved up the stairs, down the hallway, and into the chill night. It was nerve-wracking to wait for Dez. Penny and Alan helped him along, but they seemed to move like tar. This was the crucial escape! They should be running!

They crossed the street over to the sidewalk in front of the rec center. Spencer and Daisy moved ahead of the others, scanning the shadows for a BEM ambush.

"Wait!" Dez gasped. The procession came to a reluctant halt. "The nail," he said. "Garcia's bronze nail!"

"Forget it," Penny said. "We don't know where it is. Let's just get out of here while we can."

"I know where . . ." Dez pointed a finger toward the rec center. "Boys' locker room . . . Slick showed me. Part of the deal."

"Why didn't you tell us sooner?" Spencer asked.

"I didn't . . . aghhh!" Dez gripped his leg. "I didn't think of it till now."

"Spencer and I will go in," Alan said. "The rest of you stay here." Spencer felt an immediate swell of pride that his dad had chosen him.

"Hidden . . ." Dez said. "I have to show you."

"I think we should keep going," said Daisy. "Forget the nail."

The group exchanged glances, their frosty breath billowing in the light of the streetlamp.

"We might not get another chance like this," Penny finally said. "We've already got the hammer. If we can take the nail, then the Rebels could have *two* warlocks." She gestured toward the building. "You three go in. We'll stay here and watch the entrance."

"Come on." Alan took Dez by the arm. The opportunity

was too good to pass up. Spencer took Dez's other arm as Penny and Daisy lingered on the rec center steps.

Spencer and his dad guided Dez down the hallway and around a corner. Their breathing was ragged and their eyes scanned the dim halls, but the building was empty.

Alan opened the door to the locker room and slipped inside, leaving Spencer and Dez in the hallway. A moment later, he reappeared. "Coast is clear," Alan whispered. He took Dez by the arm again, and the three figures moved into the shadowy locker room.

"Over there." Dez hobbled down an aisle of tall lockers. Alan drew the bronze hammer from his pocket. They'd need to use it to remove the nail.

Bracing himself against the wall, Dez bent over. "Here." He held out his hand, beckoning for the hammer. For a brief second, Spencer saw a greedy look consume Dez's eye, but before Spencer could say anything, Alan handed it over.

That was the first sign that something bad was about to happen.

Dez snatched the bronze hammer, pulled back his arm, and hurled the object through the air, high over their heads. Spencer flinched against the loud sound it would make when the hammer hit the floor, but the sound never came.

Turning, Spencer saw Slick standing in the doorway, the bronze warlock hammer in his hand.

"Nice toss, Dez."

CHAPTER 55

"DON'T ANSWER, SON."

Before anyone could move, more than a dozen armed BEM workers stepped out of the tall lockers, completely blocking the way out.

In utter shock, Spencer turned to Dez. The big kid slid down against the wall. Sitting painfully, he pressed on the blood-soaked handkerchiefs.

"Sorry," Dez muttered. "Tried to tell you. It was part of the deal."

Any hope that Spencer had held for Dez shattered into countless pieces. He was more than just a bully. Dez was a filthy traitor!

Two of the BEM workers pushed past Alan and Spencer until they reached Dez. Taking him under the arms, they picked him up and carried him to the doorway. He groaned and complained.

Just as he passed out of sight, Dez made eye contact with Spencer. It was hard to see through his anger, but Spencer thought there might have been a glimmer of regret. But no matter what he'd seen in the bully's eyes, it was too late now.

The deal was done.

Slick passed the bronze hammer to another worker, giving her instructions to take it somewhere safe. Then he casually strode toward the cornered Rebels.

"Father and son," the Academy janitor said. "What a happy little family reunion! Maybe now you can put your heads together and tell me just what exactly was in that package?"

"Don't answer, son," Alan said. He put a comforting hand on Spencer's shoulder.

But Spencer couldn't have answered, not even to save their lives. Spencer glared at Slick, with his oily hair and dirty glasses. The janitor was wicked—a brutal henchman in the BEM's ruthless plan to overgrow Toxites and turn kids' brains to mush.

Spencer's hand dropped to his tool belt. Maybe it was time for Slick to experience the terror of his own creations.

Spencer reached into the pouch where he'd once kept vacuum dust. Now his hand closed around something cold and slimy. Jerking it out by the tail, Spencer flung the gigantic Grime directly at Slick.

The janitor shrieked and lifted his hands. Several of the other BEM workers tried to strike, but the creature's momentum was too great. The long tongue lashed out, coiling tightly around Slick's neck. The dark mouth opened, drawing him in like a toad catching a fly in slow motion.

The Grime didn't bite or chew. It took Slick whole. Its long, yellow body shuddered, neck expanding to accommodate the meal. Slick thrashed, and Spencer could see him punching and kicking all the way down.

Then the creature convulsed once, seeming to gag on something. The tongue flicked out as the Grime regurgitated one of the janitor's steel-toed boots. The gooey mess landed with a thud on the floor of the locker room.

The scene was horrifying. The other BEM workers fell back, crowding at the doorway. Only a delicate thread of loyalty kept them from deserting. The Toxite's throat expanded, filling with greenish slime. Then the giant Grime spewed a stream of viscous poison toward the doorway.

Without another moment's hesitation, the BEM workers ran, their thundering footfalls and cries of alarm fading down the hallway. They didn't want to find out who would be the Toxite's next meal.

The huge Grime sprang onto the bank of metal lockers, forked tongue dancing out again. Alan drew back defensively. But Spencer had a theory.

Spencer had returned the relocated Toxite to its desirable habitat. It had taken a moment for the monster to realize it—a fatal moment for Slick. But now that the Grime was inside New Forest Academy, it clung calmly to the lockers and enjoyed the residual student brain waves.

Spencer gave a huge sigh of relief. The Grime's head swiveled around. Suddenly noticing the father and son against the back wall, it gave a frightened swish of its broad tail and scuttled out the door to hide.

Alan looked at his son. The man's mouth opened and closed a few times, unable to find words. He pointed at Spencer's belt pouch, then gestured to the lockers where the Grime had been. When Alan spoke at last, he couldn't complete his sentence. "That thing was . . ."

"I know." Spencer wiped his hand against his jeans. "Slimy."

"Huge!" Alan squinted at his son's tool belt. "What else have you got in there?"

Spencer scanned the locker room. "We've got to get out of here, Dad." Alan nodded in agreement. "But what about the bronze hammer?" It was hard to leave empty-handed, especially since they had been so close to stealing the warlock tool. Slick had passed the hammer off to another BEM worker, but maybe it was still nearby.

Alan shook his head. "Forget it. The hammer's long gone by now." He ran a hand through his beard. "Just like we should be."

Alan steered his son out of the locker room and into the empty hallway. A moment later, they burst out the door and onto the rec center steps.

"You guys all right?" Penny asked. "A dozen BEM workers just came out the front door with their tails between their legs. I was ready to fight, but they weren't interested in sticking around. What happened in there?"

"Trap," said Alan.

Daisy looked from Spencer to his dad. "Where's Dez?"

For the second time, Spencer had to break the news. "Dez isn't coming."

Noise drifted through one of the rec center windows. Penny lifted her double mops defensively. "Let's move."

Without Dez, the group ran swiftly across the lawn. The campus was silent. That meant that either Walter had succeeded in escaping into the forest . . . or he had been captured. Spencer wanted to find him—rescue him if necessary. But meeting up with Walter wasn't part of the plan. The warlock was on his own.

The group sprinted down the road, the broken gate coming into view. One by one, they tapped their brooms and floated over the brick wall and the wreckage of the outer parking lot.

New Forest Academy was finally behind them. They raced down the road, the mountain surroundings still and peaceful. Their heavy breaths came out in frosty, moonlit plumes. The calmness of the night offset Spencer's thumping heart as he ran through the cold air, side by side . . . with his dad!

They paused anxiously at the side of the road as Penny ran into the trees to plunge the janitorial van from its hiding spot.

Spencer's mind didn't stop. It rolled over and over, imagining the joyous expressions his family would make when he walked into the house with his dad. It was a moment he had dreamed about so often. It was finally real!

"Son." Alan's voice cut through his thoughts. Spencer turned to face his father, standing beside him. Alan tried to tuck a strand of gnarled hair behind his ear, but it fell to shadow his face once more.

"They questioned you," Alan said. "Didn't they?"

Spencer nodded.

"What did you tell them about the package I sent?"

"Nothing, Dad." Spencer felt a twinge of worry. "Everyone keeps talking about it, but . . ." He swallowed. "I never got a package from you."

Alan closed his eyes and ran a hand through his long beard. "Everything I worked for . . ." He muttered the words like a eulogy.

"What was in the package, Dad?" Did he dare ask that question?

"I don't know." Alan opened his eyes. "I never looked. If I had opened the package, the BEM would have pried the information out of me. I couldn't take the risk, so I sent it to you without looking inside."

Daisy shook her head in disbelief. "So, the BEM locked you up for something you didn't know anything about?"

Spencer looked at his father, eyes silently begging for an explanation. Penny suddenly emerged from the trees, the large van dangling weightlessly from the toilet plunger in her hands. She trudged up the slope and set the van onto the road.

"Come on," Penny interrupted. "We're not out of the woods yet." The escapees quickly piled into the van, the cranking engine cutting through the darkness.

At last they were away, Penny driving them swiftly down the canyon. "Anyone behind us?" she asked.

"Nobody," Daisy said, glancing out the back window. "I think we're all safe."

Penny exhaled a sigh of relief. "We're not *all* safe."

"Walter," Spencer whispered.

He wondered again about the warlock janitor. Walter had sacrificed himself as a distraction. How long until they heard from him? What if Walter didn't make it away? Would they ever know what happened?

"I need you to find him, Spencer," Penny said, glancing in the rearview mirror. "Make sure he got out."

Spencer's heartbeat heightened and he glanced around the van for an excuse. "But I can't . . . I don't know . . ." He saw his dad, a puzzled look on his shadowy face.

"Here." Penny slipped a ring from her finger and reached to the backseat. "It's bronze. And it worked before."

"Bronze?" Alan muttered.

Spencer took a deep breath. He felt Daisy steady his shoulders, preparing for a blackout. Penny dropped the ring into Spencer's palm. His fingers closed around it, and the van exploded into a vision of white.

CHAPTER 56

"IT'S TIME."

The first vision took him back to New Forest Academy's underground parking garage. It lasted only a moment through the eyes of Director Garcia. The warlock was silent in the chill darkness of the dumpster prison. Spencer was suddenly overcome by a wave of horrible claustrophobia. For a moment he almost lost track of his true location. Was he inside the dumpster prison, pressing hopelessly against the Glopified lid? Or was he in the back of Walter's janitorial van, speeding away from New Forest Academy?

The claustrophobic feeling lasted only until Spencer realized that this was merely a vision. He forced himself to focus on the bronze ring in his hand, using it as an anchor to reality. But as the panicked feeling of confinement faded, Spencer considered the countless months his father had been prisoner. It wrenched at his heart, knowing what the BEM had done to Alan—the way they had mistreated him!

With his focus directed away from Garcia and the dumpster, the scene filtered into brightness. When the light dimmed, Spencer found himself running through dense foliage, his footfalls crunching on fallen leaves. He could see a puff of white vapor billowing from his mouth with every gasp of breath. Spencer's Auran sense kicked in and he immediately knew that this was Walter cutting through the forest, one and a half miles southeast of New Forest Academy's campus.

Walter slowed to a halt, and Spencer felt him lean against a tree. Glancing back through the trees, the old warlock squinted. Shouts cut through the forest, angry Academy teachers and BEM workers following Walter's trail. The warlock janitor dropped to a crouch behind a bush, and the first woman passed him unnoticing. A man came into view, paused, and then darted off through the trees.

Walter let out the breath he'd been holding. Lifting himself from the bush, he cut up the hill, backtracking toward the Academy. The enemy was still after him, but at least for the moment, Walter Jamison was free.

A blinding whiteness pierced the forest. For a moment, Spencer wondered if the sun was rising. But it was much too soon for dawn, and the light spread until it claimed his whole spectrum of sight.

"They've escaped, sir." Spencer heard the speaker's voice before his sight returned. As the scene came into focus, he found himself in that familiar D.C. office, facing a janitor in tan coveralls. "No word from Slick yet, but reports from the Academy are coming in on every phone line downstairs."

Spencer felt himself lean across the table. His voice was low, an attempt to suppress his obvious anger. "What about Garcia?"

The janitor shook his head, indicating that the Academy director was still unaccounted for.

The speaker inhaled sharply and righted himself. Spencer knew he was tall by the way the other janitor cowered.

"It's time," he said. The tone was unwavering and authoritative. Spencer felt the big man move around the glass-topped desk and head for the door. He didn't rush, but his gait seemed measured and unstoppable.

"What word should I send to the Academy, sir?" asked the janitor. "Our men are tracking the warlock Jamison into the forest. Should they kill or capture?"

The big man stopped by the door. "Fah, Jamison! A perfect decoy! Those Academy fools played right into Jamison's hands. It's not the warlock they should be tracking."

"I'll tell them to pull back, to follow the others . . ."

Spencer felt the tall warlock shake his head. "No more mistakes. I'll deal with Zumbro." His strong hand pulled open the door. "Ready the helicopter. We fly to Salem tonight."

The other janitor's face paled and he swallowed hard. "Not to the Academy?"

"Not yet," the big man said. "Garcia has failed me. He will expect punishment. But I am still in need of his services. We will rescue Garcia from this miserable failure. Let him think he has escaped my wrath."

Spencer's vision began to fade into bleary light. He tried to hold on to the scene as the warlock's final phrase left his lips.

"No one escapes the wrath of Mr. Clean."

ACKNOWLEDGMENTS

There are countless people to thank for helping this series take off. The ranks of Rebel Janitors are growing, so keep spreading the word!

Thanks to you, reader, for picking up this sequel. Thanks for meeting me at book signings and school assemblies. Your enthusiasm for the story inspires me. I hope you've had fun reading this, and I can promise lots of exciting surprises for the rest of the series.

Thanks to all the librarians, teachers, and bookstore associates who have helped share the story. I've been able to meet some of you and I appreciate your dedication to learning and literature.

I can't say thanks enough to the amazing team at Shadow Mountain. You have honestly made my dreams come true. Thanks to Chris Schoebinger for making this all happen. To Heidi Taylor for helping me every step of the way. To Emily Watts for changing all my "affects" to "effects." To Lois Blackburn and Roberta Stout for the intense amount of effort you put into my book tours and events.

Brandon Dorman, you did it again! Your fantastic cover art and illustrations are truly captivating. I know many readers who picked up the book off the shelf solely because of the artwork.

Thanks to my agent, Rubin Pfeffer, whose coaching keeps me motivated and encouraged. You are a great friend and mentor. I look forward to many more years.

Thanks to Lance, for our numerous discussions over fine cuisine.

To the McDonalds (my in-laws, not fast food). Thanks for your interest in me and everything I do.

I think I have the most supportive family ever! Thanks to Mom and Dad, Jess and Dave, Laura and Martin, Molly and Mike, and C and Hil. Thanks to my nieces and nephews, who are current (and future) fans of the books: Anna, Maren, Kira, Sadie, Quinn, Max, Mae, Grey, and Ruby.

Last, but not least: Thanks, Connie. Your support and love overwhelm me. Thank you for letting me chase my dreams.

READING GUIDE

1. Spencer acts impulsively when he pulls the fire alarm at Welcher Elementary. When have you done something impulsive? How did it turn out?

2. Spencer uses jump ropes, a toilet plunger, and a broom to fly the family car away from Hillside Estates. How would you escape from the BEM if they surrounded your house?

3. Walter tells Spencer and Daisy not to go anywhere alone at New Forest Academy. When have you been in situations where there is safety in numbers?

4. Spencer didn't recognize his dad's voice when he talked to him in the dumpster. Is there someone you care about that you haven't heard from in a long time?

5. Glopified duct tape is fingerprint sensitive and indestructible. What would you do with a roll of tape like that?

6. Slick pays each member of the brown team fifty dollars to stay quiet while he attacks Spencer. What could you buy with fifty dollars? What would you do if someone offered you money to do something wrong?

7. Meredith uses mashed potatoes to pass messages to Spencer. What food would you use to hide a message? Who would the message be for? What would it say?

8. Spencer's Auran powers make it possible for him to

see through the eyes of the warlocks. Whose eyes would you like to see through? Why?

9. Grimes cause distraction, Rubbishes cause apathy, and Filths cause sleepiness. Which Toxite would affect you the most?

10. In the end, Dez betrays the Rebels by staying at New Forest Academy. When have you felt betrayed or tricked? What did you do about it?

11. As an Auran, Spencer will no longer age. What's the benefit of staying young? How would you feel if you stayed young while your friends and family got older? Why?

11. Director Garcia thinks New Forest Academy is superior to all other schools. What are three great things about your school?

Enjoy this sneak peek of *Janitors 3, Curse of the Broomstaff,*
coming Fall 2013!

TYLER WHITESIDES

JANITORS

CURSE OF THE BROOMSTAFF

Visit www.tylerwhitesides.com

CHAPTER 1

"THE CLEAN WAY."

Mrs. Natcher's chalk squeaked against the board, and Spencer shuddered at the sound. The teacher stepped away from the chalkboard so the students could see what she'd drawn. It was another story problem. And this time there was a pie chart to go with it.

Why did Mrs. Natcher have to ruin pie by turning it into a math problem?

Spencer sighed and picked up his pencil. He finished the problem quickly and still had time to double-check his work.

Class was different without Dez. Spencer found that it was much easier to finish his assignments without the bully's grubby hands poking him. Dez's absence, under any other conditions, would have been a great relief. But Spencer was troubled.

Three months had passed without any word from Dez. Under Slick's persuasion, the bully had stayed at New Forest Academy. But Slick was long gone, eaten by his own overgrown Grime. So what was keeping Dez from coming home? Had the bully given in to the BEM? Was he truly one of them now?

Glancing around the classroom, Spencer saw that he was practically the first student finished with the pie chart problem. Daisy sat a few desks away, her nose an inch off the math notebook as she scribbled out numbers.

Spencer sighed as he thought through the rest of his day. It was Max's fourth birthday. Spencer's mom would be busy planning a party for his little brother. They'd have cake. But Max would probably slobber when he blew out the candles, getting his germs all over, so Spencer probably wouldn't eat any.

Life had actually become quite boring lately. If it weren't for his bronze visions, Spencer would feel completely left out of what the Rebel Underground was doing. Ever since Walter had escaped through the woods around New Forest Academy, Spencer liked to check on the old warlock. Just to make sure everything was all right.

Spencer's hand drifted to his left pocket. He knew he shouldn't do it. Not during class. But a quick checkup wouldn't take long. Spencer could be back before Mrs. Natcher sliced the pie chart.

Spencer plunged his hand into his pocket, his fingers slowly lowering to the object concealed there. It was an old high school swimming medal that his sister had bought at a yard sale. It wasn't gold or silver. It was third place—bronze.

Spencer's hand closed around the cold medallion. He tried to keep a casual gaze forward, but almost immediately, Mrs. Natcher and the chalkboard were blurred away in a blizzard of white. It spread, consuming his entire vision, until it fell away, point by blinding point.

He stood in a parking lot only fifty-two miles west of Welcher Elementary. Spencer tried to remain calm. His power was still new and, in many ways, uncontrollable. Even though he'd been able to increase the length of his warlock visions, Spencer still didn't know who he would be spying on at any given time. He had hoped for a glimpse of Walter, but the man in the parking lot was too broad and tall.

Spencer knew at once who it was.

The man was Mr. Clean, the president of the BEM and the most mysterious of the three warlocks. The name was clearly an alias, which prevented Walter from discovering his true identity or anything about Mr. Clean's past.

Spencer had seen through Mr. Clean's eyes a number of times. The warlock was usually at his BEM office in Washington, DC, causing everyone nearby to cower in fear. But not this time. What was Mr. Clean doing in Idaho, standing in the parking lot of a prison?

The sun was brilliant, sparkling on the mounds of snow at the edge of the parking lot. The warlock looked down, his breath billowing in the frosty February morning. He was wearing a long white lab coat, but as his gloved hand moved the lapel aside, Spencer saw that something was attached to his belt.

It was a large black battery pack with a dial in the center. Plugged into one end was a thick orange extension cord. Mr. Clean's eyes followed the trailing cord, and as he looked over his shoulder, Spencer gasped.

Not three feet behind the warlock crouched a gigantic Filth. The rodent's face was downturned, its hideous buck-teeth jutting crookedly from a slobbering mouth. It was purring softly, a deep-throated, phlegmy sound that caused the deadly sharp quills on its back to rise and fall.

The other end of the cord was nestled into the monster's dingy fur, plugging into the gray flesh near the spine. The Filth's eyes were half closed and the beast pulsated lazily as energy flowed through the extension cord and into the creature's body.

The warlock did not seem the least bit terrified that an overgrown Toxite was breathing down his neck in the open parking lot. In fact, the broad man reached out a gloved hand and stroked the creature's muzzle.

Then, with a blur of movement, the man leapt into the air, his white lab coat swinging wide. To Spencer's surprise, the warlock landed atop the huge Filth, straddling it like a warhorse. The Filth made no reaction, completely contented, apparently due to the energy coming through the cord.

The warlock adjusted his weight, and Spencer noticed that there was a floor mat draped across the Filth's back like some kind of primitive saddle. The man's hand dropped to the battery pack at his waist. As soon as he twisted the dial, the Filth roared to life.

The huge creature leapt forward, bounding across the parking lot with a snarl. When it reached the doors of the prison, the Toxite lowered its broad head. Spencer flinched at the sound as both doors were ripped open, the Toxite and rider tumbling into the reception area. The Filth stomped its clawed feet, shaking broken glass from its fur as the alarm blared.

There was a uniformed woman behind the reception desk. She sprang from her seat, fumbling to draw her gun. The warlock and his beast paused in the center of the room, reveling in the chaos they had just created.

In seconds, the reception area was swarming with armed guards. But Spencer couldn't understand what was happening. The guards raced past the warlock, inspecting the walls and shattered doors. Of course they wouldn't be able to see the huge Toxite, but had Mr. Clean somehow made himself invisible as well?

"Was it a bomb?" asked the uniformed woman.

The warlock drew a deep breath. "No," Mr. Clean said aloud. Every guard turned, pistols aimed randomly across the room. "It was a phantom."

Then, with terrifying speed, both gloved hands plunged into his lab coat. Two plastic spray bottles flashed from concealment. He took aim and pulled the triggers.

It was over in a moment. A drip of green solution glistened on the nozzle of each spray bottle, and an emerald mist hung in the room. The guards collapsed into a heap on the hard floor, their guns slipping from limp hands.

Spencer felt a stab of fear pass through him. He was aware of himself, sitting stock straight in his school desk, hand gripping the bronze medallion so tightly that the edge dug into his palm. He wanted to let go, to end the vision on his terms. But the fallen security guards, the green spray, the warlock atop that fearsome creature . . .

Mr. Clean twisted his head from side to side in satisfaction, his neck popping from the motion. The reception area was littered with bodies—all of them trained security guards, but none of them a match for the warlock in the white coat.

The big man touched the dial on his belt, and the Filth moved away from the wreckage. They walked down the hallway, the warlock holding his spray bottles like dual pistols in his gloved hands.

In a moment, Mr. Clean had found the cell he was looking for. He twisted the dial and dismounted the giant Filth in the middle of the hall, keeping the extension cord stretched between them. Peering through the bars, Spencer saw the limited contents of the cell. Curled upon the bed was a figure in an orange jumpsuit.

"Knock, knock," the warlock whispered through the bars.

The startled prisoner leapt from the bed, tripped in surprise, and came to rest on her knees not three feet away. Her thin face upturned, she stared through the bars.

It was Leslie Sharmelle!

Spencer's breath caught when he recognized her. *Leslie Sharmelle!* She was a BEM worker who had substituted for Mrs. Natcher at the beginning of the year. Leslie was the one who had teamed up with Garth Hadley to get Spencer involved with the BEM. She had survived the Vortex, but the classroom had collapsed on her. Walter had framed her for the accident, and once she was released from the hospital she had gone to jail.

Now she knelt before the mysterious warlock. And with fear and respect in her eyes, she muttered his name.

"Mr. Clean."

"Aren't you going to invite me in?"

Leslie swallowed hard. "You . . . you have the key?"

"Why would I need a key," Mr. Clean asked, "when I have this?"

His fingers turned the dial on the battery pack, and the Filth bellowed. Leslie jumped away from the bars, but it was too late. The creature had already caught sight of her.

Mr. Clean stepped aside as the Filth sprang at the cell bars. Its jaws snapped through the metal. Clawed toes scraped, bending and twisting the bars aside. In less than a heartbeat, the Filth was inside the cell.

In panicked shock, Leslie collapsed against the back wall, shielding her face as fragments of metal fell around her. Her hands reached out and she screamed as the slavering jowls of the beast opened to destroy her.

But the Filth did not bite. It bowed its head in relaxation as a surge of electricity flowed down the Glopified extension cord. Mr. Clean stepped through the twisted bars and approached the cowering woman.

"I see you've met the Bureau's newest weapon," the warlock said, one hand scratching the creature behind the ears "An Extension Filth."

Leslie did not move from her place against the wall, the Filth's face inches from hers. Mr. Clean reached out for her. Leslie put her thin hand into his, carefully sliding away from the huge Filth as he hoisted her up.

The warlock drew a strip of gray cloth from his white lab coat. "Do you know what this is?" he asked. "It is the cuff of a shirtsleeve, ripped from the arm of a very elusive man." He held up the scrap. "But I'm about to make sure that he never escapes again."

Mr. Clean paused. For a moment, Spencer was afraid that the man had somehow detected his spying eyes. Then the warlock continued, his voice metered and steady. "You're going to bring me Alan Zumbro—dead or alive."

Spencer almost lost contact, his hand slipping on the bronze medal in his pocket. He forced himself to linger in the vision a moment longer, to face Mr. Clean's terrible pronouncement.

Leslie wrinkled her forehead. "I thought Alan was—"

"The Rebels rescued him," the warlock cut her off. "But he doesn't have the package. He's out there now, looking for it."

"Where?" Leslie asked.

Mr. Clean approached the Extension Filth. He adjusted the dial on the battery pack just enough to cause the creature's head to perk up. Then he lowered the scrap of cloth to the beast's nose.

The Toxite inhaled sharply, its slit nostrils opening wide to take in the scent. Then the warlock dropped his hand lower. The Filth's coarse tongue emerged and the razor teeth snapped together, Mr. Clean barely pulling away his hand in time. The creature chewed noisily on the scrap of cloth and then swallowed.

"All is ready now," said the warlock. "The Extension Filth has been baited."

"So your beast will lead me to Alan?"

Mr. Clean laughed. "It's not *my* beast." He unclipped the belt and battery pack. "It's *yours*." He held the items out. "On its own, an Extension Toxite is reckless. Plug it in, wear the battery pack, and you have the power to control it. Saddle up, Leslie. Become a Plugger."

With shaking hands, Leslie Sharmelle accepted the pack. She turned to the huge Filth, and Spencer could see her reluctance to climb onto its back.

"I have a gang of Pluggers waiting to meet you at the edge of town," Mr. Clean said. "They will teach you to control your beast and prepare you for the manhunt."

The big warlock stepped away, passing through the wrecked bars. "I'm trusting you to prove yourself," he said. "To do better than your previous assignment." Mr. Clean turned away from the cell. "If you fail me again, Leslie, there will be no forgiveness. I'll have no choice but to deal with you . . . the *Clean* way."

PHOTO BY MEGAN KNORPP

ABOUT THE AUTHOR

TYLER WHITESIDES worked as a janitor at a middle school to put himself through college. It was there that he discovered the many secrets and mysteries that can be hidden in a dusty school. Tyler graduated from Utah State University with a degree in music. He enjoys spending time in the mountains, cooking on the barbecue, and vacuuming. Tyler lives in Logan, Utah, with his wife, Connie, a third-grade teacher. He is the author of the Janitors series (*Janitors*, *Secrets of New Forest Academy*, and the forthcoming *Curse of the Broomstaff*).